WHAT THE READERS SAY ABOUT NORA ROBERTS!

"I just love your books. You make the characters…so believable, and their stories so interesting…. I love it when you do a series of books because when you get to love a family (in a book) you hate to see the story end."

H. Davis
New Hampshire

"Too many authors who cross over into the hardcovers tend to leave…a lot of devoted readers behind…. Ms. Roberts hasn't done that and I, for one, appreciate this thoughtfulness…she has no equal when it comes to writing the romantic novel with a great deal of suspense thrown in for added enjoyment. Thank you Nora Roberts for every moment of enjoyment and happiness."

E. B. Dulitz and D. Dulitz
Louisiana

"I'm going in for back surgery. So I saw your book… thought I'd save it for the hospital…. I was going to be strong…. Ah! We make promises, but we are weak. I thought I'd just take a look to see what it was about. I finished it last night…. Nora, you are the best…I love your books."

C. A. Telesco
New York

"Truly, I do look forward with pleasure to reading your books…. Thank you again for sharing your considerable talents in character and plot development. You stand apart in a field crowded with contenders."

Marcia E. Roan
Indiana

Also available from Silhouette Books by

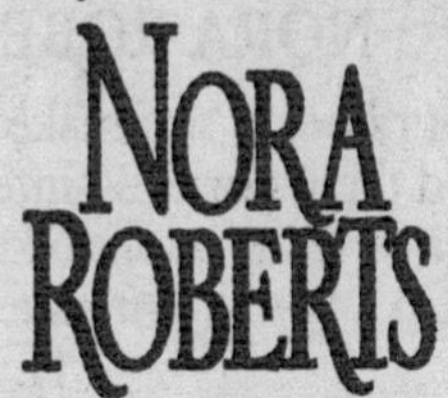

WAITING FOR NICK
Silhouette Special Edition #1088

THE STANISLASKI SISTERS
Silhouette Books

HIDDEN STAR
Silhouette Intimate Moments #811

Coming soon

December 1997
CAPTIVE STAR
Silhouette Intimate Moments #823

January 1998
THE CALHOUN WOMEN—Catherine and Amanda
Silhouette Books

February 1998
SECRET STAR
Silhouette Intimate Moments #835

March 1998
THE CALHOUN WOMEN—Lilah and Suzanna
Silhouette Books

Be sure to look for more Nora Roberts titles in your local stores, or contact our Silhouette Reader Service Center,
U.S.A.: 3010 Walden Avenue P.O. Box 1325, Buffalo, NY 14269
Canada: P.O. Box 609, Fort Erie, Ontario L2A 5X3

NORA ROBERTS

THE MACGREGOR BRIDES

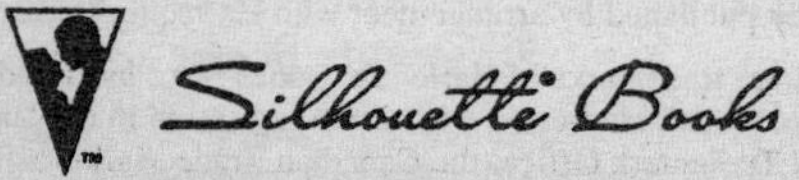

Published by Silhouette Books
America's Publisher of Contemporary Romance

For Candy Lee of the sparkling intellect, tireless energy and marvelous laugh

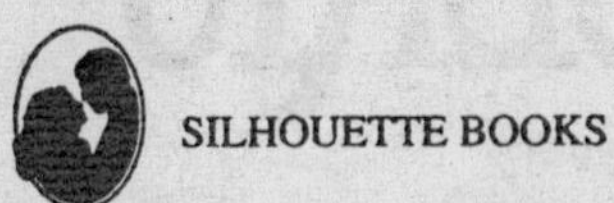

THE MACGREGOR BRIDES

ISBN 0-373-48350-3

This edition published by arrangement with Harlequin Books S.A.

Printed in U.S.A.

CONTENTS

THE MacGREGORS

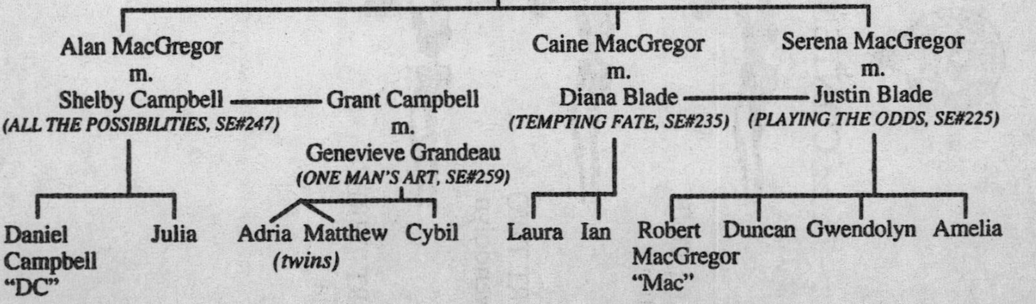

More *MacGregors* to come in fall 1998!

From the Private Memoirs
of
Daniel Duncan MacGregor

When a man reaches ninety years of living, he is tempted to look back on his life, to evaluate, to consider his triumphs and his mistakes. Often he might think, "What if I had done this instead of that?" or "If only I had that to do over."

Well, I don't have time for that kind of nonsense.

I look forward, have always done so. I'm a Scotsman who has lived most of his long life away from the land of his birth. America is my home. I have made my family and raised my children here. I have watched my grandchildren grow. For nearly sixty years I have loved one woman, lived with her, admired her, worked with her. And worked around her, when there wasn't any other way.

My Anna is all that is precious to me. Between us—well, we've had a hell of a time.

I'm a rich man. Oh, not just in dollars and possessions and property, but in family. Family comes first. That's something else that always was and always will be part of my life. My Anna and I made three children between us. Two sons and a daughter. My pride in them is nearly as great as my love.

I have to admit, though, that it was necessary, at one time, to nudge these three strong individuals along, to remind them of their duty to the MacGregor name, to the MacGregor line. I regret to say that my children were a bit slow in this area, and their mother worried.

So, with a little help, they married well. By well, I mean they found the mate of their heart, and those unions gave Anna and me two more daughters and another fine son to dote on. Good stock, strong blood to match a MacGregor.

Now I have eleven grandchildren—three of them honorary MacGregors, though they be Campbells by name. Campbells, God help us, but good children they are despite it. They all have been the joy of our later years, Anna's and mine, as we watched them grow from babes to adults.

Like their parents, they're slow to do their duty, to understand the richness of marriage and family. It worries their grandmother day and night. I'm not a man to stand by and watch my wife fret, no indeed, I am not. I've considered this carefully.

My three oldest granddaughters are of marriageable age. They are strong, intelligent and beautiful women. They're making their way in this world well, on their own. Such things—so Anna has taught me—are as important for a woman as for a man. With Laura, Gwendolyn and Julia I have a lawyer, a doctor and a businesswoman on my hands. Bright and lovely, are my girls, so the men I'll pick for them to build their lives with must be rare men indeed. I'll not have them settle for less than that.

I've got my eye on a fine trio of lads. All come from good, strong stock. Handsome lads, too. Ah, won't they make lovely couples and give me pretty babes?

One at a time is the plan. It's best in such matters to give each one my full skill and attention.

So I'm starting with Laura, she's the eldest after all. If I don't have young Laura smelling orange blossoms by Christmas, my name isn't Daniel MacGregor.

Once she's settled down, I have just the boy in mind for my darling Gwen. Julia might be the toughest nut of the three, but I'm working on that.

Just a little push is all I'll give them. I'm not a meddler, after all, just a concerned grandfather in the winter of his life—and I intend for it to be a very long winter. I'm going to watch my great-grandchildren grow.

And how the devil am I to do that if these girls don't marry and get me babies, I ask you? Hah. Well, we're going to see to that—so Anna won't fret, of course.

Part One

Laura

Chapter 1

It took six rings of the phone to reach a corner of her sleeping brain. By the eighth, she managed to slide a hand out from under the blankets. She smacked the alarm clock first and slammed the cheery face of Kermit the Frog to the floor. It was the third dead Kermit that year.

Her long, unadorned fingers patted along the glossy surface of the walnut nightstand, finally gripped the receiver and pulled it under the covers with her.

"'Lo."

"It rang ten times."

With the blankets over her head, Laura MacGregor winced at the booming accusation, then yawned. "Did?"

"Ten times. One more ring and I'd have been calling 911. I was seeing you lying in a pool of blood."

"Bed," she managed, and snuggled into the pillow. "Sleeping. Good night."

"It's nearly eight o'clock."

"When?"

"In the morning." He'd identified the voice now, knew which one of his granddaughters was burrowed in bed at what Daniel MacGregor considered the middle of the day. "A fine, bright September morning. You should be up enjoying it, little girl, instead of sleeping it away."

"Why?"

He huffed. "Life's passing you by, Laura. Your grandmother's worried about you. Why, she was just saying last night how she could barely get a moment's peace of mind, worrying about her oldest granddaughter."

Anna had said nothing of the kind, but the ploy of using his wife to finagle his family into doing what he wanted them to do was an old habit. The MacGregor appreciated traditions.

"'S fine. Everything. Dandy. Sleeping now, Grandpa."

"Well, get up. You haven't visited your grandmother for weeks. She's pining. Just because you think you're a grown-up woman of twenty-four doesn't mean you should forget your dear old granny."

He winced at that a bit himself and glanced toward the door to make certain it was firmly shut. If Anna heard him refer to her as a dear old granny, she'd scalp him.

"Come up for the weekend," he demanded. "Bring your cousins."

"Got a brief to read," she muttered, and started drifting off again. "But soon."

"Make it sooner. We're not going to live forever, you know."

"Yes, you are."

"Ha. I've sent you a present. It'll be there this morning. So get yourself out of bed and prettied up. Wear a dress."

"Okay, sure. Thanks, Grandpa. Bye."

Laura dumped the receiver on the floor, burrowed under the pillow and slid blissfully back into sleep.

Twenty minutes later she was rudely awakened with a shake and a curse. "Damn it, Laura, you did it again."

"What?" She shot up in bed, dark eyes wide and glazed, black hair tangled. "What?"

"Left the phone off the hook." Julia MacGregor fisted her hands on her hips and smoldered. "I was expecting a call."

"I, ah..." Her mind was an unfocused blur. Laura shoved her hands through her sleep-tousled hair, as if to clear it. Mornings were just not her time of day. "I think Grandpa called. Maybe. I can't remember."

"I didn't hear the phone." Julia shrugged. "I guess I was in the shower. Gwen's already left for the hospital. What did Grandpa want?" When Laura continued to look blank, Julia laughed and sat on the edge of the bed. "Probably just the usual. 'Your grandmother's worried about you.'"

"I seem to remember something about that." Smiling a little, Laura plopped back onto the pillows. "If you'd have gotten out of the shower faster, you'd have caught the call. Then Grandma would have been worried about you."

"She was worried about me last week." Julia checked her antique marcasite watch. "I've got to run look at this property in Brookline."

"Another one? Didn't you just buy another house last month?"

"It was two months ago, and it's nearly ready to turn over." Julia shook back her curling mane of flame-colored hair. "Time for a new project."

"Whatever works for you. My big plan was to sleep until noon, then spend the rest of the afternoon on a brief." Laura rolled her shoulders. "Fat chance around here."

"You'll have the place to yourself for the next few hours. Gwen has a double shift at the hospital, and I don't expect to be back until five."

"It's not my night to cook."

"I'll pick something up."

"Pizza," Laura said immediately. "Double cheese and black olives."

"It's never too early for you to think about dinner." Julia rose, smoothed down the moss-green jacket she wore over pleated trousers. "See you tonight," she called on her way out. "And don't leave the phone off the hook."

Laura studied the ceiling, contemplating the sunlight, and considered pulling the covers back over her head. She could sleep another hour. Dropping off at will or whim had never been a problem for her, and the skill had served her well in law school.

But the idea of pizza had stirred her appetite. When there was a choice between sleep and food, Laura faced her biggest dilemma. Laura tossed the covers back as food won the battle. She wore a simple white athletic T-shirt and silk boxer shorts in electric blue.

She'd lived with her two female cousins all through college and now for two years in the house in Boston's Back Bay. The thought of grabbing a robe never occurred to her. The attractive little town house—one of Julia's recent renovations, and their newest home—was decorated with an eclectic mix of their three tastes. Gwen's love of antiques vied with Julia's appreciation for modern art and Laura's own attraction to kitsch.

She jogged downstairs, trailing her fingers over the satin finish of the oak railing, glanced briefly through the etched-glass window in the front door to see that it was indeed a brilliantly sunny fall morning, then swung down the hall toward the kitchen.

Though each of the cousins had a fine mind, conscientiously applied to their individual areas of expertise, none of them was especially gifted in that particular room. Still, they'd made it homey, with soft yellow paint setting off the deep blue counters and glass-fronted cabinets.

Laura had always been grateful that the three of them had melded so well. Gwen and Julia were her closest friends, as well as her cousins. Along with the rest of the MacGregor brood, as Laura thought of them, the extended kin of Daniel and Anna were a close-knit, if diverse, family.

She glanced at the sapphire-blue cat clock on the wall, its eyes diamond-bright, its tail swinging rhythmically. She thought of her parents and wondered if they were enjoying their much-deserved holiday in the West Indies. Undoubtedly they were. Caine and

Diana MacGregor were a solid unit, she mused. Husband and wife, parents, law partners. Twenty-five years of marriage, the raising of two children and the building of one of the most respected law practices in Boston hadn't dimmed their devotion.

She couldn't conceive of the amount of effort it took to make it all work. Much easier, she decided, to concentrate on one thing at a time. For her, for now, that was law. Correction, she thought, and grinned at the refrigerator. For right now, that was breakfast.

She snagged the Walkman lying on the counter and slipped on the headphones. A little music with the morning meal, she decided, and cued up the tape.

Royce Cameron parked his Jeep behind a spiffy little classic Spitfire convertible in flaming red. The kind of car and color, he mused, that screamed out, *Officer, another speeding ticket here, please!* He shook his head at it, then shifted his gaze to study the house.

It was a beaut. That was to be expected in this ritzy area of the Back Bay—and given the lineage of the owners. Boston was the Red Sox and Paul Revere. And Boston was the MacGregors.

But he wasn't thinking of money or class as he studied the house. His cool blue eyes scanned windows and doors. A lot of glass, he mused, while the crisp autumn breeze ruffled his thick, mink-colored hair. A lot of glass meant a lot of access. He started down the flagstone walk, with its brilliant edgings of fall blooms, then cut across the neat sloping lawn to consider the atrium doors that opened onto a small patio.

He tested them, found them locked. Though one good kick, he thought, one good yank, and he'd be inside. His eyes stayed cool, his mouth hardened in a face full of planes and angles. It was a face the woman he nearly married had once called criminal. He hadn't asked her what she meant by that as they'd been well into their skid by then, and he just hadn't wanted to know.

It could be cold, that face, and was now, as he calculated access into the lovely old house, which undoubtedly was packed with the antiques and jewelry rich women of a certain class enjoyed. His eyes were a pale, chilly blue that could warm and deepen unexpectedly. His mouth was a firm line that could curve into charm or straighten to ice. A small scar marred his strong chin, the result of abrupt contact with a diamond pinkie ring that had ridden on a curled fist. He skimmed just under six feet, with the body of a boxer, or a brawler.

He'd been both.

Now, as the freshening breeze whipped the wave of his collar-length hair into disarray, he decided he could be inside with pitifully little effort in under thirty seconds.

Even if he didn't have a key to the front door.

He walked back around, gave a quick, loud series of buzzes on the doorbell while he gazed through the fancy glass of the entryway. Looked pretty, he thought, with the etching of flowers on frosted glass. And was about as secure as tinfoil.

He buzzed one more time, then took the key out of his pocket, slid it into the lock and let himself in.

It smelled female. That was his first thought as he stepped into the foyer onto polished parquet. Citrus, oils, flowers and the lingering whiff of a nicely seductive perfume in the air. The staircase was a fluid sweep to his right, the front parlor a welcoming opening to his left.

Tidy as a nunnery, he thought, with the sensual scent of a first-class bordello. Women, to Royce's mind, were an amazement.

It was pretty much as he'd imagined. The beautiful old furniture, the soft colors, the expensive dust-catchers. And, he thought, noting the glitter of earrings on a small round table, the pricey baubles one of them left sitting around.

He slid a mini tape recorder out of the back pocket of his jeans and began to make notes as he wandered through.

The large canvas splashed with wild colors that hung over the cherrywood mantel caught his eye. It should have been jarring, that bold scream of brilliance and shape in so quiet a room. Instead, he found it compelling, a celebration of passion and life.

He'd just noted the signature in the corner—D. C. MacGregor—and deduced that the painting was the work of one of the many MacGregor cousins when he heard the singing.

No, it couldn't, in all honesty, be called singing, he decided, turning the recorder off and slipping it into his pocket as he stepped back into the hall. Screaming, howling, perhaps caterwauling, he reflected, were better terms for such a vocal massacre of one of Whitney Houston's anthems to love.

But it meant that he wasn't alone in the house after all. He headed down the hallway toward the noise, and as he stepped through the doorway into a sunny kitchen, his face split with a grin of pure male appreciation.

She was a long one, he thought, and most of it was leg. The smooth, golden length of them more than made up, in his estimation, for the complete lack of vocal talent. And the way she was bending over, head in the fridge, hips bumping, grinding, circling, presented such an entertaining show, no man alive or dead would have complained that she sang off-key.

Her hair was black as midnight, straight as rain, and tumbled to a waist that just begged to be spanned by a man's two hands.

And she was wearing some of the sexiest underwear it had ever been his pleasure to observe. If the face lived up to the body, it was really going to brighten his morning.

"Excuse me." His brow lifted when, instead of jolting or squealing as he'd expected—even hoped—she continued to dig into the fridge and sing. "Okay, not that I'm not enjoying the performance, but you might want to take five on it."

Her hips did a quick, enthusiastic twitch that had him whistling through his teeth. Then she reached for a note that should have cracked crystal and turned with a chicken leg in one hand and a soft-drink can in the other.

She didn't jolt, but she did scream. Royce held up a hand, palm out, and began to explain himself. With the music still blaring through her headset, all Laura saw was a strange man with windblown hair, faded jeans and a face that held enough wickedness to fuel a dozen devils.

Aiming for his head, she winged the soda. He nipped it one-handed, an inch before it smacked between his eyes. But she'd already whirled to the counter. When she sprang back, she had a carving knife gripped in her hand and a look in her eyes that warned him she wouldn't think twice about gutting him with it.

"Take it easy." He held up both hands, kept his voice mild.

"Don't move. Don't even breathe," she said loudly as she inched along the counter toward the phone. "You take one step forward or back and I'll cut your heart out."

He figured he could disarm her in about twenty seconds, but one of them—most likely him—would need some stitches afterward. "I'm not moving. Look, you didn't answer when I knocked. I'm just here to..." It was then that he got past looking at the face and saw the headphones. "Well, that explains it." Very slowly, he tapped a finger to his ear, ran it over his head to the other and said, with exaggerated enunciation, "Take off the headphones."

She'd just become aware of the music over the blood that was roaring in her head and ripped them off. "I said don't move. I'm calling the cops."

"Okay." Royce tried an easy smile. "But you're going to look pretty stupid, since I'm just doing my job. Cameron Security? You didn't answer when I knocked. I guess Whitney was singing too loud." He kept his eyes on hers. "I'm just going to get out my ID."

"Two fingers," she ordered. "And move slow."

That was his intention. Those big, dark eyes of hers held more temper and violence than fear. A woman who could face a strange man down alone, kitchen knife in hand, without trembling wasn't a woman to challenge. "I had a nine-o'clock to assess the house and discuss systems."

She flicked her gaze down to the identification he held up. "An appointment with whom?"

"Laura MacGregor."

She closed her free hand around the phone. "I'm Laura MacGregor, pal, and I didn't make an appointment with you."

"Mr. MacGregor arranged the appointment."

She hesitated. "Which Mr. MacGregor?"

Royce smiled again. "*The* MacGregor. Daniel MacGregor. I was to meet his granddaughter Laura at nine, and design and install the best security system known to man in order to protect his girls." The smile flashed charmingly. "Your grandmother worries."

Laura took her hand from the phone, but didn't put down the knife. It was precisely the kind of thing her grandfather would do, and exactly what he'd say. "When did he hire you?"

"Last week. I had to go up to that fortress of his in Hyannis Port so he could check me out face-to-face. Hell of a place. Hell of a man. We had a Scotch and a cigar after we did the deal."

"Really?" She arched a brow. "And what did my grandmother have to say about that?"

"About the deal?"

"About the cigars."

"She wasn't there when we closed the deal. And since he locked the door of his office before he got the cigars out of a hollowed-out copy of *War and Peace,* I have to conclude she doesn't approve of cigars."

Laura let out a long breath, set the knife back in the wooden knife block. "Okay, Mr. Cameron, you pass."

"He said you'd be expecting me. I take it you weren't."

"No, I wasn't. He called this morning, said something about a present he was sending. I think." She shrugged, her hair flowing with the movement, picked up the drumstick she'd dropped and dumped it in the wastecan. "How did you get in?"

"He gave me a key." Royce dug it out of his pocket, and put it into the hand Laura held out. "I did ring the bell. Several times."

"Uh-huh."

Royce glanced down at the soft-drink can. "You've got a good arm, Ms. MacGregor." He shifted his gaze back to her face. Cheekbones that could cut glass, he thought, a mouth fashioned for wild sex, and eyes the color of sinful dark chocolate. "And possibly the most incredible face I've ever seen."

She didn't like the way he was looking at it, savoring it, she thought, with a stare that was arrogant, rude and unnerving. "You have good reflexes, Mr. Cameron. Or you'd be lying on my kitchen floor with a concussion right now."

"Might have been worth it," he said with a grin

that tried to be disarming, but was just wicked, and offered her back the soft drink.

"I'll get dressed, then we can discuss security systems."

"You don't have to change on my account."

She angled her head and gave him a look that encompassed him from his overly appreciative expression to his don't-mess-with-me stance. "Yes, I do. Because if you keep looking at me that way for another ten seconds, you will have a concussion. I won't be long."

She sailed by him. Royce turned as she passed so that he could enjoy watching her walk away on those endless, fascinating legs. And he whistled through his teeth again.

One way or the other, he thought with a long appreciative sigh, Laura MacGregor was a knockout.

Chapter 2

In the law offices of MacGregor and MacGregor, Laura sat at a long oak table, surrounded by books. She'd buried herself in the library all morning, determined to find an additional precedent for the brief she was refining on her latest assignment.

When her parents returned the following week, she'd have it perfected. Her mother was trying the case of Massachusetts v. Holloway, and Laura was doing research on it for her, but she'd developed an emotional attachment to this particular case.

If she handled the paperwork, the legwork, the hours of research, she might earn a seat beside her mother in the courtroom. And maybe, just maybe, she'd be allowed to question a witness.

She wanted the intensity of the courtroom, the drama of judge and jury. She understood the value of research, the necessity of planning every move and every eventuality of a trial case. She'd read and study until her eyes crossed, but by God, she was going to earn her stripes. And eventually, her own caseload.

Amanda Holloway had killed her husband. There was no question about the deed. But guilt, by law, was another matter. She'd been battered emotionally and physically for five miserable years. Five years of broken bones and a broken spirit, Laura thought. It was easy to say she should have walked out—she should have run, and never looked back. In fact, Laura sometimes caught herself thinking just that. But Amanda Holloway hadn't walked and she hadn't run. In the end, she had snapped.

One night during the heat of high summer, after another beating, another rape, she had taken her husband's service revolver and emptied the clip into him while he slept.

The pity of it, Laura thought coolly, was that she'd waited more than an hour after the rape. An hour equaled premeditation. The fact that John Holloway had been a cop with a file full of commendations also didn't help matters.

Some might think that justice had been done that night, but the law trod a colder line. And Laura was determined to use the law to keep Amanda Holloway out of prison.

Royce really enjoyed watching her. Just now, she didn't resemble the woman who'd sung in her underwear, or the coolly polite one who'd worn a simple sweater and discussed alarm systems with him. She'd tamed that waterfall of dark hair into a complicated braid that lay down the center of her back. She had simple gold drops at her ears and a slim gold watch on her wrist, along with the wink and flash of a diamond tennis bracelet.

Her white silk blouse was very tailored, and a navy blazer hung over the back of her chair. The room smelled of leather, polished wood, and woman.

Just now, he thought, Laura MacGregor looked classy, expensive and utterly unapproachable. Unapproachable, Royce mused, unless a man had seen her hips wiggling about in a pair of silk boxers.

He leaned on the doorjamb. ''You look like a lawyer.''

Her head shot up. He admired the speed with which she recovered. Surprise was no more than a flash in those dark chocolate eyes before they cooled. ''I passed the bar last summer. I am a lawyer. Do you need one?''

''Not at the moment, but I'll keep you in mind.'' The fact was, he'd kept her in mind for the better part of a week.

Windswept hair, that intriguing little scar, those damn-the-devil eyes combined to make him a man a woman couldn't help wondering about. Since she didn't want to wonder, she wanted him gone. ''The offices are basically closed until the end of the month.''

''So the receptionist told me downstairs. But I'm not here to hire you or your parents.'' He walked in—his movements making her think of a cat poised to spring—and edged a hip on the table.

''Why are you here?''

''I had a job to look over in the neighborhood. I

thought I'd let you know we'll start installing your system Saturday morning."

"That's fine. I'm sure my grandfather will be pleased."

"He's got the right idea, protecting what matters to him. He's proud of you and your cousins. It shines right out of him when he talks about you."

Laura's eyes softened, and her body lost its defensively rigid posture. "He's the most wonderful man in the world. And one of the most exasperating. If he could, he'd tuck all of us into his castle in Hyannis."

"Boston can be a dangerous city for a pretty young girl," Royce said, in a deep burr that mimicked Daniel and made Laura's lips twitch.

"Not bad. A little more volume and you'd have almost nailed him."

"And he's right, it can be. You're three single women living in a big house filled with expensive things, easily fenced merchandise. One of you is the daughter of a former U.S. president, and all of you granddaughters of one of the richest men in the country. And you're beautiful. All of that makes you potential targets."

"We're not fools, Mr. Cameron."

"Royce."

"We're not fools," she repeated. "We don't walk into dark alleys, open the door to strangers or pick up men in bars."

"Well, Slim, that's commendable."

Her shoulders were tightening again. "My grandfather is overreacting, but if installing a complicated security system eases his mind, then that's what we'll do."

"But you don't think you need security."

"I think my cousins and I are perfectly safe in our own home."

"Do you consider having a man walk into your kitchen while you're dancing in your underwear safe?"

"You had a key—and I wasn't in my underwear."

"I'd have been inside as easily without the key as with it. And what was it, if it wasn't your underwear?"

"Pajamas," she snapped.

"Oh, well, then, that's different." Royce grinned down at her, enjoying the sizzle of temper in her dark eyes.

"Look, you install the damn system, we'll use the damn system. Now I've got—" She strained backward when he leaned down. "What are you doing?"

He drew in a slow breath. "Just getting the full impact. I like your perfume." And his eyes gleamed with amusement. "You're awfully jumpy all of a sudden."

"I don't like being crowded."

"Okay." He eased back, just a subtle movement of that compact body that didn't give her quite the distance she would have liked. "How long are you going to be at this?" he asked, waving a hand at the stack of law books.

"Until it's finished."

"Why don't I come back, around seven? We could get some dinner."

"No." She said it firmly, and shifted in her chair to give an open book her attention.

"Are you involved?"

"Obviously."

"I don't mean with work, Slim. I mean with a man."

"That's none of your business."

"Could be. I like the way you look, the way you smell. I like the way you talk, the way you move. It would be interesting to find out if I like the way you...think," he ended, as her narrowed eyes lifted and fixed on him.

"Do you want to know what I'm thinking right now?"

He smiled, then grinned, then roared with laughter. "No. If you change your mind about the meal, you've got my number."

"Oh yeah, I've certainly got your number."

He chuckled, started to rise, then saw the label on the folder nearly buried under a stack of books. "Holloway," he murmured, then looked back at Laura. "The homicide?"

"Yes."

"I knew John Holloway."

"Did you?" She'd liked his laugh, nearly been charmed enough by it to reconsider dinner. Now both her voice and her eyes went frosty. "Do you number many spousal abusers among your friends?"

"I didn't say we were friends, I said I knew him. He used to be a cop. So did I."

This time, when he started to straighten, she put a hand over his. Her eyes were focused on his face now, calculating, considering. "Did you work with him?"

"No. We worked out of the same precinct for a few months a while back. I was transferred. He was a good cop."

"He was..." She shut her eyes. "Oh, that's typical. He kicked his wife around for years, but he was a good cop. Wear the blue and stick together."

"I'm not a cop anymore," Royce noted mildly. "And I didn't know much about him off the job. He did the work, he made the collars, he closed the cases. I wasn't interested in his personal life."

"I'm very interested in his personal life." She'd watched his face while he spoke. He didn't give away much, Laura mused, but she'd go with her hunches. "You didn't like him, did you?"

"No."

"Why not?"

"Just personal taste. He made me think of a loaded gun with a broken safety. Sooner or later, it goes off."

"You'd still have contacts on the force, know people who knew him. Cops hate talking to lawyers, but—"

"Maybe because lawyers put scum back on the street before cops can clean up the stain."

She took a steadying breath. "Amanda Holloway isn't scum. She simply had the bad judgment to marry scum."

"That may be, but I can't help you." He rose, stepped back. "I'll be at the house between eight-thirty and nine on Saturday." He smiled again, a quick quirk of lips. "As much as I'd like to see them again, I wouldn't wear the pajamas. You'll distract my crew."

"So, what does he look like?"

In the mirror over the bathroom sink, Laura's gaze

shifted from the already dark lashes she was coating with mascara to her cousin's face. "Who?"

"This ex-cop security expert that Grandpa hired to keep us safe from Boston's nefarious criminal element." Gwen leaned over Laura's shoulder so that their heads were close.

No one would have taken them for cousins, much less—as they were connected on both the MacGregor and Blade branches of the family tree—cousins twice over. Gwen's hair was a shiny reddish-gold cap, short as a boy's, in contrast to Laura's sweep of raven tresses. Gwen had inherited her mother's coloring, the creamy skin, the eyes that edged from blue into lavender, the rich blond hair that hinted of red.

She had a small, almost delicate build, as well. A combination that gave the deceptive illusion of fragility. She could, when necessary, put in a double shift at the hospital, work out in the gym for an hour and still have fuel left over.

She was, Laura thought, beautiful, brilliant and bossy.

"Are you going to try to tell me you don't remember what he looks like?" Gwen prompted.

"Hmm? No, I remember. I was thinking of something else. He's attractive enough, I suppose."

"Details, Laura, the truth is in the details." Gwen arched a brow. "Cameron, right? A good Scottish name."

"That would please Grandpa."

"Definitely." Gwen ran her tongue around her teeth. "Is he married?"

"I wouldn't think so." Laura went back to the unnecessary mascara. ''He wasn't wearing a ring when he put the moves on me.''

''And he's what? About thirty?''

''Somewhere around, I'd guess.'' Her gaze shifted again. ''Hunting, are we?''

''No, collecting data. He's single, attractive, runs his own business, thirtyish and a Cameron. My assessment is that Grandpa picked him out for you.''

''We already know that.'' Laura set the mascara down and picked up her lipstick. ''Grandpa hired him to install a security system, which he'll be doing today.''

Gwen sighed, then rapped the top of Laura's head lightly with her knuckles. ''Hello? You're not usually so slow. I'm talking matrimony.''

''Matri—'' On a choked laugh, Laura set down the tube of lipstick. ''Not a chance.''

''Why not? Grandpa's been making noises for the past year about how not one of his grandchildren has the common sense, or the sense of duty, to settle down and raise a family.''

''And Grandma's pining for babies to bounce on her knee,'' Laura finished dryly. ''I'm telling you, there's no way he's fixed on Royce Cameron as a potential grandson. The man isn't the type an overprotective grandfather chooses.''

Gwen perched on the long rose-colored counter. ''Because?''

''There's something dangerous about him. You can see it in the eyes—something not quite tame.''

''Mmm. Sounding better and better.''

''For a lover, sure. I imagine he'd be amazing in bed.'' Laura smirked as she brushed back her hair. ''I doubt that's what the MacGregor would have in mind."

Idly, Gwen picked up the lipstick, swiveled the creamy red tube up and down. "On the contrary, I'd say it would be exactly what he'd have in mind. The boy has spirit," she continued, in a deep, exaggerated burr. "He's got fire in his blood. He'll breed strong sons and daughters."

"Ridiculous." But Laura experienced a sick sensation deep in her stomach. "That's absurd. He couldn't... He wouldn't."

"Could and would," Gwen disagreed succinctly. "And so far I'd say it's working."

"What do you mean, what are you talking about?"

"I mean it's Saturday morning." Gwen angled her wrist to check her watch. "Just eight o'clock on a Saturday morning, when you don't have to be anywhere. Not only are you up, but you're dressed. You're wearing mascara, which you don't even need, and lipstick, and—" she leaned forward and sniffed "—your best perfume."

"I'm only—"

"And she's got a new blouse lying out on her bed," Julia added as she stepped into the doorway and leaned against the jamb. "A red silk blouse."

"Aha, a red silk blouse for a Saturday morning at home." Gwen slid off the counter, patted Laura's shoulder. "My diagnosis, honey, is a strong case of physical attraction."

"I am not attracted to him. I'm just... I'm thinking of going shopping, that's all. Christmas shopping. So I'm up and dressed."

"You never shop on Saturday," Julia pointed out

ruthlessly. "You hate to shop, period, which I find very sad. And you never start your Christmas shopping until the middle of December."

"I'm making an exception." Annoyed, Laura maneuvered by them both and stomped toward her room.

The blouse lay on the bed like a bright red alarm. She hissed at it. Then, slamming her door, she decided to wear it anyway. She liked strong colors, she thought as she yanked it off the bed. She liked silk. Why shouldn't she wear the damn thing?

She muttered to herself as she buttoned it up. She was not attracted to Royce Cameron in the least. He was far from her type. The man was arrogant, rude and self-congratulatory. And, she reminded herself, he'd seen her at her most ridiculous.

And in the fourth place, she thought as she slipped on dark gray trousers, she wasn't looking for a relationship. Not that a man like Royce would be interested in something as civilized as a relationship, but for herself, she wanted a few more years of absolute freedom.

A man in general, and a mate in particular, could wait.

She heard the front door buzzer, sniffed. She took her time putting on her shoes. Then, to prove to herself that she didn't care how she looked to Royce or any other man that morning, deliberately turned away from the mirror before heading downstairs.

He was in the foyer. A scarred leather jacket, faded jeans, dark, tousled hair. He was talking to Julia and Gwen, and he laughed at something Julia said. Laura made it halfway down the stairs before he turned his head, before those oddly intense blue eyes, with their dark fringe of lashes, met hers. Before that slow, dangerous smile curved his mouth.

Before her heart gave one jerky kick that warned her she might be in trouble after all.

"Morning, Slim," he said, giving her a very slow once-over. "Nice shirt."

Chapter 3

Royce didn't pursue women. He particularly didn't pursue a woman who indicated a lack of interest—or one who was sending out mixed signals. When he met a woman who attracted him, he let her know it. Straight out, no games, no pretenses. He figured it was up to the woman in question to pick up the ball from there.

Since Laura MacGregor wasn't picking up the ball, hadn't even acknowledged that he'd tossed one in her direction, he should have shrugged it off, forgotten her and gone about his business.

But he wasn't having any luck in doing that.

It had been nearly three weeks since he first saw her, four days since he last saw her. And she was still on his mind. Not just the picture of her in that sexy little outfit she'd worn in the kitchen—though that image certainly popped into his mind with annoying regularity. It was her face that hounded him, he thought, the cold courage in it when she'd whipped up that knife and faced him down. It was the intelligence and determination in her eyes when she'd spoken of law and justice. It was the cocky smile curving that incredibly tempting mouth as she'd walked down the stairs the day he began the installation of her security system.

It was, he was forced to admit, the whole damn package.

In his small, crowded office off Boylston, he rubbed his tired eyes, ran his hands through hair badly in need of a trim. She was keeping him up at night, and it was ticking him off. What he needed to do was pull out his address book and find a companionable woman to spend an evening with. Someone uncomplicated and undemanding.

Why in the hell didn't he want someone uncomplicated and undemanding?

He'd be damned if he was going to pick up the phone and call Laura. He'd asked her out, she'd refused. He'd told her he'd be available if she changed her mind. She hadn't changed it. He hadn't made a fool of himself over a female since he was twelve and fell madly in love with his best friend's older sister, the sixteen-year-old goddess Marsha Bartlett. He'd mooned over her for two months, followed her around like a slavish puppy and suffered the taunts of the entire seventh grade of Saint Anne's Elementary.

Marsha Bartlett had never paid any attention to him, and had gone on to marry an oral surgeon. And Royce didn't moon after females anymore.

"Grow up, Cameron," he ordered himself, and

turned back to his computer screen to fiddle with the proposed security system on an office building in South Boston.

When the phone shrilled, he ignored it until the fourth ring. Swearing, he snatched it up. Obviously his secretary was off powdering her nose again.

"Cameron Security."

"And this would be Cameron himself?"

Royce recognized the voice. There was no mistaking that full-blooded Scot. "It would be, Mr. MacGregor."

"Good, just the man I'm after. You've seen to my granddaughters."

"The system's up and operative." And the bill, he thought—the hefty bill—was in the mail. "It's the best money can buy."

"I'm counting on that, boy. I want my wife's mind at rest. She frets."

"So you said."

"And you tested the system personally?"

"As you requested. Any attempt to break in or undermine the system sends an alarm straight to the nearest cop shop and my own personal beeper."

"Good, good. But those girls have to use it to be protected. They're young, you know, and busy with their interests. My wife's worried that they may be careless and forget to turn it on altogether."

"Mr. MacGregor, I can only guarantee the system if it's in use."

"Exactly, exactly. Why, I was telling Anna just this morning that you've done everything you could do. But she's got this in her mind now, and is worrying on it. I was thinking, just to soothe her, we could do a test. If you'd go by sometime—tonight's as good a time as any—and just see if you can get inside..."

"Hold it. Let me get this straight. You want me to break into your granddaughters' house?"

"Well, you see, if you manage to do it, then we'll know we need to adjust the matter a bit. And if you can't...well, then, I can ease my wife's mind. She's old," Daniel added in a low voice, keeping an eagle eye on the doorway. "I worry about her health. We're more than happy to pay you for your time and trouble."

"Do you know what the cage time is for nighttime breaking and entering, Mr. MacGregor?"

Daniel laughed heartily. Indeed, he'd picked a rare one for his Laura. "Now, Royce, as a former officer of the law, I'm sure you'd know that well enough. And you'd know how to be sure you weren't caught at it. I meant to tell you that I'm considering having a new security system installed here, at my home. It's a large house, and I'd want only the best. Cost would be no object."

Royce leaned back in his chair and stared, meditatively, at the ceiling. "Are you bribing me, Mr. MacGregor?"

"Indeed I am, Mr. Cameron. Are you an enterprising young man?"

"Indeed I am. And this is going to cost you."

"What's money compared to the peace of mind and safety of those we love?"

Royce tipped back in his chair, waited a beat. "I've met a lot of demons and clever people in my life, Mr. MacGregor. You could give lessons."

Daniel's roar of laughter had Royce's ears ringing.

"I like you, lad, damned if I don't. Camerons, strong stock. You get back to me when you've checked this matter out. And we'll arrange for a time for you to come up here and modernize my security."

It was going to earn him big bucks, Royce calculated the zeros as he slipped out of the moonlight and into the shadows of the grand old trees that guarded the house.

He stood studying the dark windows. It was easy enough for Royce to think like a thief. He'd handled countless burglaries during his years on the force. It was for that very reason that he'd decided to go into private security. Most people had no idea how vulnerable they were while they dreamed in their beds.

He approached the house as a thief would, using the trees and hedges for cover. The well-established grounds added to the ambience, and also blocked any nefarious enterprises from the view of neighbors and street traffic.

If he was a smart B-and-E man—and Royce had decided he would be—he'd have already taken the time to study the house, the accesses, the security. He'd have worn khaki work clothes, carried a clipboard and come in broad daylight. No one would have looked at him twice. But instead, here he was in the middle of the night, responding to the "request" of an overly canny, overly protective Scot.

He'd have known the alarm system was hot. Of course, if he had a solid knowledge of electronics—and Royce had decided to get into the spirit of the job and assume that he, as thief, had a degree in electronics. Amused at himself, he set to the task of undoing his own work.

Fifteen minutes later, he stepped back, scratched his chin. He was damn good, he decided. Not quite as good a thief as he was a security expert. The system was very close to foolproof, if he did say so himself. If he hadn't designed it personally, he would never be able to work his way through the backups and safety checks to override it.

Since he had designed it, he could have gotten in—if he'd wanted to get in—by working another ten minutes or so. But a thief would have to be very determined, very educated and very lucky to have gotten even this far. The MacGregor, he decided, could sleep easy.

Satisfied, he started to step back, when a light flashed on. Laura MacGregor stood in full view on the other side of the atrium door, dark hair down to her waist, a bright yellow T-shirt skimming her thighs and a Louisville Slugger gripped in her hands.

He watched her mouth fall open when she recognized him and her eyes catch fire.

"What the hell are you doing?"

Her voice was muffled by the glass, but he caught the drift. "Spot check," he said loudly back. "Customer's request."

"I didn't request any spot check."

"Your grandfather did."

He watched those furious eyes narrow, saw her hands shift their grip on the handle of the bat, as if she were going to swing away regardless. Then she spun around, giving him a blood-pumping view of leg, and snatched up the phone.

Royce scratched his chin again, his fingers brushing absently over the ridge of scar. If she was calling the cops, he was going to be in for a long night of explanations. He had enough friends on the force to cushion the worst of it—but he knew those same friends would toss him in a holding cell just for the amusement factor.

The fee for the spot check doubled.

Moments later, Laura slammed down the receiver. She strode to the control unit for the alarm system, punched in the code, then flipped the locks on the door.

"You're both idiots, you and my grandfather."

"You called the MacGregor."

"Of course I called him. Do you think I'm going to take your word when you're standing outside the door wearing breaking-and-entering black and carrying burglar's tools? I ought to bash you with this on principle," she added, before tipping the bat against the wall.

"Your restraint is appreciated." His grin flashed, humor sparking his eyes like summer lightning. "Look at it this way, your grandmother can now sleep peacefully at night."

"My grandmother always sleeps peacefully. It's him." Exasperated, she threw up her hands. The movement had the T-shirt sliding dangerously high. "The man stays up at night dreaming up ways to complicate all our lives. It's his one driving goal—to drive his family insane. At least I have the satisfaction of knowing his ears will be ringing for the rest of the night."

"Busted his chops, huh?" Smiling, Royce took advantage of the situation and moved closer. "If you'd been in bed like you were supposed to be, you'd never have known I was here. I'd have been gone in another two minutes." He reached out to toy with the ends of hair that draped to her elbows in a soft black curtain. "Why aren't you in bed?"

"I was hungry," she muttered.

"Me, too." He moved a little closer, deciding that fate had put the chair exactly there to prevent her from backing away. "Whatcha got?"

Her heart was thudding against her ribs now. She felt the winged side of the armchair press into her back. He looked more than dangerous at the moment. With his eyes hot, his smile wicked, he looked fatal. He looked...tempting. "Look, pal—"

"I keep walking in on you in your pajamas." He let his gaze wander down lazily before sliding it up again and placing his hands on the chair on either side of her. "Don't you think it's a little too much to expect me to keep walking away?"

Her skin tingled as little pulses of excitement danced over it. "I expect you to take no for an answer."

"Do you?" He leaned in, just a little—a brush of bodies, the feather of breath over her mouth. "I would have sworn you were expecting this."

He lowered his mouth toward hers, stopping an inch before contact. He saw her eyes darken, heard the long intake of breath, knew she held it. He waited, while his blood surged, waited until he knew they were both suffering.

"Kiss me back," he demanded, and crushed his mouth to hers.

She couldn't have stopped herself. In that long moment when their eyes held, desire had poured through her like heated wine. In the instant when their mouths met, need had slammed into her like a velvet fist. In the shuddering time the kiss deepened, pleasure streaked through her like light.

She moaned, wrapped her arms around him and met greed with greed.

This was no gentle exploration, no easy sampling. It was all heat and hunger, passion warring against passion, strength pitted against strength.

She was wild tastes and silken textures. She was arousing scents and soft sighs. Her mouth was pure sin, and was rapidly driving him beyond reason. His hands tangled in her hair, dragged her head back so that he could have more, still more, of that impatient, erotic mouth.

"Let me have you." He tore his lips from hers to race them over her jaw, down her throat.

"I..." Her head was spinning, her breath came in ragged gulps. "Wait. Just...wait."

"Why?"

"I need to think." She put her hands on his shoulders, straining back. "I wasn't thinking."

Blue eyes fixed on her chocolate brown ones, dark hair tousled on both of them, he skimmed his hands in one long stroke down her sides. "I can fix it so neither one of us is thinking again."

"I'm sure you could." She kept her grip firm, locked her arms to ensure some distance. But it wasn't nearly enough. "Back off a minute."

"It won't change anything. I'm still going to want you. You're still going to want me."

"Back off anyway."

It cost him, but he dropped his hands, stepped away. "Far enough? Or should I just back out the door so you can pretend this didn't happen?"

"I don't have to pretend anything." Laura's spine straightened. "If I hadn't wanted that to happen, it wouldn't have happened. I'm responsible for my own actions, Royce."

"Fair enough. Why aren't we rolling around on this fancy rug, finishing what we started?"

"That's blunt."

"That's honest."

"All right. We're not rolling around on the Aubusson because I don't have sex with men I barely know."

He nodded, tucked his hands into his pockets. It was lowering to realize they weren't entirely steady. "That's fair enough, too." His lips curved when he saw the surprise, then the speculation, flit over her face. "Didn't expect me to be reasonable, did you, Slim?"

"No, I didn't. Which just proves my point. I don't know you." She braced, but didn't evade when he stepped close again, when his hands slid up her arms to her shoulders, then back down to her wrists.

"Royce Cameron," he said quietly. "Thirty-one, single, ex-cop, currently self-employed. No criminal record. I had a couple of years of college, but it didn't suit me. I like big, stupid dogs, loud rock, Italian food and dangerous women."

Amusement darkened her eyes. "That's informative, but not entirely what I meant."

"I figure it's a start. Do you want to know more?"

She knew he had to feel the way her pulse was hammering under his fingers. "Apparently I do."

"Tomorrow night, seven-thirty. We'll try the Italian food."

"All right. We'll try the Italian food." She didn't move, kept her eyes on his when he leaned forward and caught her bottom lip between his teeth.

"I really like your mouth. I could spend hours on it."

She thought his grin flashed before he turned away, but her vision had blurred.

"Lock up, Slim, and reengage the system."

"Yeah." She took two slow breaths, in and out. It occurred to her that the system, so to speak, had already been breached.

Chapter 4

Gwen burst into the bathroom wearing underwear and full makeup. "I just ran my last pair of black panty hose. I'm a desperate woman."

"Mine'll bag on you," Laura called from the shower. "I'm four inches taller than you are."

"I said desperate. Julia doesn't have any dark hose. I don't have time to run out for any, and Greg will be here in fifteen minutes."

Laura poked her head out from behind the curtain. "A date with Dr. Smarm?"

"It's not a date." Snarling, Gwen snatched a pair of hose from the jungle of delicates hanging on the drying line. "It's a hospital function, and he's my escort."

"He's a creep."

"He's chief surgical resident."

"Chief creep," Laura corrected, and turned off the

shower. "And all he wants to do is add another notch in his scalpel."

"Then he's going to be bitterly disappointed." Gwen sat down on the toilet lid and began to pull on the hose.

"Why didn't you go with Jim Proctor? He's a nice enough guy."

"Engaged. Two weeks ago. Kindergarten teacher."

"Oh." Hooking a towel at her breasts, Laura stepped out. "Better to go alone than with Greg the Operator."

"Cocktails and dinner at Dr. and Mrs. Pritchet's. Mrs. Pritchet frowns on extra women at her table." Gwen stood, swore. "Damn it, these bag on me."

"I told you they would."

"Found a pair." Julia came in waving a package of hose like a flag. "These are why my drawer wouldn't close all the way. They were stuck behind it."

"Thank God." Gwen grabbed them and sat again to make the exchange.

"You're all dressed up," Laura commented, noting Julia's long velvet gown of deep green.

"Country-club deal. Peter."

"Ah, old reliable." Laura walked out into the bedroom to contemplate her own closet.

"Peter's all right, just a little too earnest." Julia wandered out, watched Laura debate between red silk or blue wool. "Now you seem to have the hot date of the evening."

"We're just going to hear some music."

"Dancing. Third date in two weeks." Julia wiggled her brows. "The red, definitely."

"It's a little..."

"It's a lot," Julia corrected. "A lot everything. His eyes'll pop out of his head and plop on his shoes."

Feeling stubborn, Laura pulled out the blue. "We're not really dating. We're just seeing each other."

Gwen stepped out. "Well, when you're tired of seeing him, can I have him?"

"Ha, ha."

"It is the third date," Julia pointed out. "First date is the test. Second is a review. But the third, well, that's the big one. That's when you move from dating to relationship."

"We don't have a relationship. I don't want a relationship."

"Can I have him?" Gwen asked again, then bubbled with laughter at Laura's seething look. "Come on, Laurie, what's wrong with being interested in a gorgeous, available, intriguing man? Count your blessings." Then she rolled her eyes as the buzzer sounded. "That's Greg. Jules, go entertain him for a minute, will you?"

"If he comes on to me again, I'm going to knock his caps loose."

"Five minutes," Gwen promised, rushing out. "Just hold him off for five minutes."

"I don't know why she doesn't knock his caps loose," Julia muttered, then, taking a deep breath, fixed a bright smile on her face and turned to Laura. "How's this?"

"Try to make it look less like a grimace."

"Can't. Wear the red," she ordered, then headed down to do her duty.

* * *

She wore the red. Laura told herself the outfit was simply more suited to an evening at a club. She hadn't worn it because it was sexy, or because the blend of Lycra turned the silk into a curve-clinging statement of female confidence. And she only wore the high, thin heels because the dress demanded them.

This third-date business was nonsense, she told herself as she hooked on thick gold hoops. Who was counting, after all? They were just seeing each other because they enjoyed each other's company, because they found a lot to talk about and they made each other laugh.

And when he kissed her, her brain exploded.

She pressed a hand to her jittery stomach. Okay, she admitted, yes, there was a strong physical attraction. But he hadn't pressured her to take it any farther than those brain-draining kisses.

Why the hell wasn't he pressuring her? It was driving her crazy the way he left her shuddering, all but gulping for air, and never attempted to lure her into bed. Not since that first time.

She was crazy, Laura admitted. Hadn't she told him she needed to get to know him? Wasn't he giving her the time and space to do just that? And she was sulking because he wasn't grabbing her by the hair and dragging her off to his cave.

Pitiful.

When the buzzer sounded, she shook her cloud of hair back. Just seeing each other, she repeated as she started downstairs. Just getting to know each other. Just two people enjoying each other's company for the evening. Steady now, she opened the door, smiled.

He looked good in black. The black jeans, jacket and shirt suited his dark-angel looks. "You're right on time," she told him. "I'll just get my—"

"Hold it." He'd grabbed her hands, his own sliding up to her wrists like cuffs. He indulged himself with a long look. The stoplight red fit like skin, riding high on smooth thighs, dipping low and straight over firm breasts. His lips curved slowly. "Excuse me a minute."

With one hard tug, he had her in his arms, and his mouth was branding her, devouring hers. She made a little sound of shock as the heat punched into her. Then she was free, breathless and teetering.

"What was that for?"

"To thank you for the dress you're almost wearing." His smile was quicker this time. It was impossible for him not to be pleased by that dazed look in her eyes. "You'll need a coat, Slim. It's cold outside."

The club was hot, and so was the music. Laura had regained her balance over a glass of white wine at the tiny corner table, with its single flickering candle. She hadn't thought him the type to sit and listen to blues.

But he was constantly surprising her.

"Why did you leave the force?" She hadn't realized the question was there until she asked it. "Is that too personal?"

"No. I figured out I wasn't a team player, that I was lousy at politics, and that I'd lost the passion you need to keep going out on the streets to do the job."

"What made you lose it?"

Light eyes under dark brows flicked over to hers, held. "Lawyers."

In automatic defensiveness, her chin angled. "Everyone's entitled to representation under the law."

"Yeah, that's the law." He picked up his club soda, rattled the ice in the glass. "But that's not justice. You've got a client right now who'd agree with me."

"Really? And who is that?"

"Amanda Holloway."

"I thought you didn't approve of what she'd done."

"It's not up to me to approve or disapprove. I wasn't inside her head that night. But to me, she's just one more example of a system that's defective."

"Her trial begins in ten days. You might be able to help."

"There's nothing I can tell you."

"It's obvious you didn't like him."

"I don't like the guy in the apartment across the hall from me. There's not a lot I can tell you about him, either. Your mother knows her job, Laura, or she wouldn't be where she is."

"I don't see how you can back away from everything you must believe in. You wouldn't have joined the force if you hadn't wanted to help."

"And a few years on it showed me I wasn't making much of a difference."

She heard something in his voice, just a hint of disappointment, of disillusionment. "But you wanted to."

"Yeah, I did. Now I'm making it my own way.

Without the politics and restrictions. And I'm better at electronics than I was at toeing the line."

"You just like being your own boss."

"Damn right I do."

"I can't blame you," she said with a sigh. "Working for my parents, well, it's a dream. They're wonderful. I don't think I'd have done well in a big firm, with all the agendas and carved-in-stone policies. In so many, it's all about billable hours and corporate or high-profile clients. MacGregor and MacGregor is about making a difference."

"I'm surprised they haven't been disbarred for a surplus of ethics."

Her eyes narrowed. "It's so easy—and so trite—to bash lawyers."

"Yeah." He grinned. "Why resist? I should tell you something else."

"What?"

"You're incredibly beautiful."

She eased back, angled her head. "You're trying to change the subject."

"And smart, too. If we sit here and talk about law, we're going to argue, because it's something we come to from different angles. Why waste the time?"

"I like to argue. That's why I'm a lawyer."

"I like to dance." He took her hand and stood up. "That's why we're here."

She stared at him. "You dance?"

"Well, I never achieved my lifelong dream of joining the Bolshoi," he said dryly as he led her toward the dance floor. "But I manage."

"You just look more like the type to go five rounds with the champ than to—" The words slid down her throat as he spun her out, then whirled her back until her body meshed intimately with his. "Oh, God."

"We'll box later."

The heels brought her face-level with him so that eyes and mouths lined up. He guided her over the floor with smooth, intricate steps. She didn't have to think to follow. Couldn't have thought, with the way her heart thudded, the way the sax wailed, the way his eyes stayed focused on hers.

"You're very good," she managed.

"Dancing is the second-best thing a man can do with a beautiful woman. Why not do it right?"

She had to moisten her lips. "You've had lessons."

"At my mother's insistence. Which is why I can also go five rounds with the champ. In my neighborhood, if a guy took dance lessons, he either got the stuffing beat out of him on a regular basis or he learned to use his fists."

"That's quite a combination. What neighborhood was that?"

"South Boston."

"Oh." Her head was swimming, her pulse pounding. "That's where you grew up then. Did your father—"

He dipped her, low and slow. "You talk too much," he murmured, and closed his mouth over hers as he brought her back up. And kept it there as he moved with her, as the music pumped over them, as her hand slid over his shoulder to cup the back of his neck.

She felt her stomach drop away, her knees turn to water, and murmured his name, twice, against his mouth.

"Do you know who I am?" He waited until her eyes fluttered open and met his. "Do you know who I am now, Laura?"

She knew what he was asking, and understood that every moment they spent together had been a dance with steps leading to this. "Yes, I suppose I do."

"Come home with me." He kissed her again, tracing her lips with his tongue until they trembled. "Come to bed with me."

She didn't care that the music had stopped, that the club was crowded. She poured herself into the kiss. "My house is closer."

"How do you know?"

"I looked up your address." She was smiling as she eased back. "Just in case. My cousins are out for the evening." She slid her hand down to his, linked fingers. "Come home with me."

"I thought you'd never ask."

He kissed her again when they stepped out into the chilly autumn evening. The instant they were in the car, they were diving for each other. "I didn't think I'd be in such a hurry." Gulping in air, she attacked his mouth again. "I'm in a hurry. Drive fast."

"Tell me what you've got on under that dress."

She laughed. "Perfume."

"I'll drive fast." He slammed the car in gear. "Strap in, and keep your hands to yourself. I want to live to make love with you."

She fumbled with her seat belt as he shot out into the street. She gripped her hands together in her lap. She wanted to use them on him, she realized. She wanted to use them to tear off his shirt, to touch, to take, to drive him crazy. She had no precedent for this wild animal lust snarling inside her.

"Tell me something else," she demanded. "Your family. Brothers, sisters."

"No, none." He accelerated, coolly threading through traffic and zipping through a yellow light.

"Your parents, do they still live in the old neighborhood?"

"My mother moved to Florida with her second husband. My father's dead."

"I'm sorry."

"Line of duty. That's the way he wanted it. Wouldn't you think these people would have something better to do than to be driving around tonight?"

She laughed, then pressed a hand to her racing heart. "God, I'm nervous. I never get nervous. I'm going to babble. I can feel it. You'd better talk to me or I'm going to babble."

"I could tell you what I'm going to do to you the minute I get you out of that dress."

"Royce. Drive faster."

He careened around the corner, headed up her street. And his beeper went off. Swearing viciously, Royce dug into his jacket pocket. "Read the code off for me, will you?"

"All right. It's…it's mine. Royce, it's my house."

His eyes hardened. He could already hear the alarm shrilling. He whipped the car to the curb two houses down from Laura's. "Stay here," he ordered. "Lock the doors."

"But you can't— The police will—"

"It's my system." He slammed out of the car and,

avoiding the light from the streetlamps, slipped into the dark.

It only took Laura ten seconds to decide to go after him. She cursed the ridiculously thin heels as she darted up the sidewalk. Even as she burst into the wash of light pouring out of her windows, she saw two figures grappling.

Without a second thought, she ran forward, her eyes darting right and left in search of a handy weapon. Terrified, inspired, she yanked off her shoe and dashed forward, leading with the ice-pick heel.

Then she saw the glint of bright gold hair in the light. Heard the curse and the grunt as Royce's fist plowed into a familiar face.

"Ian! Oh, my God! Ian, are you all right?" Dropping her shoe, she stumbled to where Royce's adversary was sprawled on the ground.

"God, what hit me, a rock?" Ian shook his head, tried to work his throbbing jaw. "What the hell is going on here?"

"Oh, honey, your lip's bleeding. I'm sorry. I'm so sorry." She bent forward and kissed him gently.

"I'm fine, thanks," Royce said from behind her. The whip of jealousy stung nearly as much as his abused knuckles. He frowned down as the couple on the ground glared at him. "I take it you two are acquainted."

"Of course we're acquainted." Laura stroked Ian's hair. "You just punched my brother."

"Hell of a punch, too." Ian lifted a hand, wiggled his jaw and decided it probably wasn't broken. "I didn't even see it coming. Of course, if I'd seen it, you wouldn't have landed it."

"Come on, let me help you inside. We'll put some ice on it."

"Stop fussing, Laura." Now that his ears had stopped ringing, Ian took a good look at the man who'd decked him. It soothed his ego a bit to see the tough, compact build and wide shoulders. At least he hadn't been taken down by a suit and tie, which would have been his sister's usual type. "Ian MacGregor," he said, and held up a hand.

"Royce Cameron." Royce gripped it, hauled Ian to his feet. "You caught another one," he said, and tapped a finger to the side of his eye.

"I thought so. I was a little off my stride. I mean, a guy goes to let himself into his sister's house, and all of a sudden alarms start screaming, lights flashing..."

"New security system," Royce told him. "I installed it a couple weeks ago."

"Yeah, well, it works." Ian's crooked grin offered a truce. "Want a beer?"

Royce judged his man and smiled. "Sure. Let me disengage this and call off the cops."

"I guess you changed the locks," Ian began conversationally as he trooped along with Royce.

Laura stood where she was, off balance on one skyscraper heel, her mouth hanging open. "If that isn't just typical," she muttered, and hunted up her other shoe. "Men bash each other in the face, then they're friends for life."

Chapter 5

"I don't suppose you'd like to tell me what you're doing breaking into my house at ten o'clock on a Saturday night?"

Ian held the cold bottle of beer against his bruised jaw and smiled at his sister. "I wouldn't have been breaking in if you'd told me you'd changed the locks."

"If you'd let someone know your plans—"

"I didn't have any plans. I just decided to swing by for the weekend." He grinned over at Royce. "Harvard Law, first year. A guy needs a little break."

"I imagine so." And as his own plans for the evening had taken an abrupt turn, Royce decided he had no choice but to take it philosophically. But he wished to God Laura would change out of that siren's dress and into something dull and baggy.

"Where are the cousins?"

"They're out."

"Got anything to eat around here?" He grinned at Laura, and the gleam in his eye told her he knew exactly what he'd interrupted. And that he wasn't the least bit sorry. "I'm starving."

"You want food, fix it yourself."

"She dotes on me," Ian told Royce as he rose to raid the refrigerator. "Want a sandwich?"

Royce exchanged one long look with Laura. "Why not?"

"You know, Laurie, I was going to go up and sponge off Grandpa, but I just had this urge to see you." He beamed at her as he began unloading cold cuts and condiments.

"Oh, let me do it, you're making a mess." She nudged him aside, then sighed when he slid an arm around her shoulders and kissed her cheek. "Go sit down and drink your beer."

He sat, lifted his long legs to prop his feet on the opposite chair. At twenty-two, with golden hair, a sharp-boned face offset by a poet's mouth, and eyes that were nearly violet, he was already doing his best to meet, and exceed, the reputation his father had left behind at Harvard Law. In his studies, and with the ladies.

"So, Royce, tell me, how are things in the security business?"

It wasn't a question, Royce understood. It was a statement. Ian MacGregor wasn't budging an inch, and had no intention of letting Royce get his hands on Laura until he was satisfied.

Fair enough, Royce decided.

Seeing they understood each other, Royce lifted his beer. "It's a living," he said.

For the next week, Laura buried sexual frustration in work. Ian had all but moved in, spending each evening, each night, in the Back Bay with her, then driving back to Cambridge in the morning to class.

He was, Laura thought, an unshakable, unmovable guard dog.

"He needs a damn leash," she muttered.

"Who does, honey?"

Laura looked up from her files. Her mother stood in the doorway, head cocked, brow lifted. Diana Blade MacGregor's hair was as dark as her daughter's, and was scooped up in a polished French twist as a concession to the court appearance she'd made that morning. Her eyes were dark and warm, her skin a dusky gold, thanks to her mix of Comanche blood. Her bronze-toned suit was tailored to set off her slim figure.

Perfect was the word that often came to Laura's mind when she thought of her mother. Absolutely perfect. But she wasn't in the mood for family loyalties at the moment.

"Your son. He's driving me insane."

"Ian?" Diana stepped into the room and fought to keep the twinkle out of her eyes. Ian had told her Laura was more than interested in a man. "What's he doing?"

"He's hovering. He's smothering me. He's got some weird notion he's protecting me. I don't want to be protected."

"I see." Diana perched on Laura's desk, smoothed

a hand over her daughter's hair. "Would this have anything to do with Royce Cameron?"

"It has to do with me not needing my little brother running interference with my social life." Then Laura blew out a breath. "And yes, it has something to do with Royce."

"I'd like to meet him. Your grandfather certainly thinks highly of him."

"Grandpa?" Confused, Laura flipped back her hair and frowned up at her mother. "He barely knows him. He hired Royce's company, that's all."

"You should know the MacGregor better than that." With a laugh, Diana shook her head. "Sweetheart, Daniel MacGregor wouldn't have put anyone in your path—particularly an attractive man—unless he knew all there was to know, and then some. According to him, Royce Cameron comes from strong stock."

"That's just his Scottish bias."

"And you're his eldest granddaughter." Diana's smile softened. "A delicate position your father and I put you in."

"I don't see what— Oh." She stood when she caught the movement in the doorway. "Royce."

"Sorry, your receptionist said you weren't busy, and to come up."

"That's all right, I..." She detested being flustered. Was uneasy acknowledging that he could fluster her simply by existing. "Mama, this is Royce Cameron."

"I'm so pleased to meet you." Diana rose from the desk to hold out a hand. She found herself being assessed by cool blue eyes.

"I'm sorry." Royce smiled at her. "I was just seeing what Laura's going to look like when she flowers. She's very fortunate in her heritage."

Smoothly done, Diana mused. "Thank you. My husband says that the Comanche wear their bones well. I'm sure you want to speak with Laura. I hope to see you again, Mr. Cameron. Laura, I'll have a word with Ian on that matter we were discussing."

"Thanks."

"Your mother is...impressive," Royce murmured when Diana slipped out and shut the door. Then he turned to Laura. "Comanche?"

"Yes, my mother's part Comanche." She rose slowly, almost in challenge. "So am I."

"I'd have to agree with your father. You wear your bones well." He stepped closer, moving around the desk until they were face-to-face. "Is your brother hiding in the storage closet?"

She had to chuckle. "Not at the moment."

"Well, then." Watching her, he slipped his arms around her waist and drew her slowly close, closer, saw her lashes flutter as he lowered his mouth to touch hers. "I've got to see you, Laura. Alone."

"I know. I want... It's just that everything's so complicated now, and... Kiss me again. Just kiss me again."

Not patient this time. Not gentle. She could taste the impatience, the frustrated desire that echoed inside her and the promise of heat and speed.

"I should have hit him harder." His hands slipped to her hips to bring her more intimately against him. "I'm going to go find him and hit him again."

"No." Laura tangled her fingers in his hair. "Let me do it."

"Tell your secretary you're going to lunch."

"It's ten in the morning."

"A really early lunch." Royce nipped her jaw, then went back to her mouth. "And it's going to last most of the day."

"I really can't." His lips trailed down her throat and made her skin sing. "I shouldn't." Then came back to hers and set her heart leaping. "Okay, just let me—"

"Laura, do you have the file on—" Caine MacGregor froze, the doorknob still in his hand. And stared narrowly at the man who was currently devouring his little girl. "Excuse me," he said, just coldly enough so that no one would suspect he meant it.

"Dad." Laura cleared her throat, wiggled free of Royce and cursed the flush that burned her cheeks. "I was— We were—"

"Were what, Laura?" Dismissing her, Caine measured the man. "And you would be…?"

"Royce Cameron." A well-toned wolf, was Royce's impression. He didn't think the gray at the temples of the bronze hair would affect the man's fangs whatsoever. "And I was kissing your daughter."

"I've eyes in my head, Cameron," Caine said, in a tone that would have made his own father swell with pride. "Security, right? Shouldn't you be making someone's business safe, instead of kissing my daughter in the middle of the morning?"

Royce tucked his thumbs in his front pockets. He hadn't gotten around to shaving yet, certainly hadn't intended to see Laura that morning. But he'd stepped out to do a few errands and found himself standing outside her office, he still wasn't quite sure how. He was wearing a leather jacket that had plenty of battle scars, and jeans that were worn white at the stress points and frayed at the cuffs.

He had a pretty fair idea what he looked like to a doting father at the moment. A rich, doting father who wore Savile Row as if he'd been born in it.

"I've just come back from Hyannis Port. I spent the last two days there designing and discussing an upgrade of a security system for your father's home."

Caine's eyes narrowed and flashed. "Is that so? Interfering old tyrant," he muttered, striking straight to the core of the matter. "In that case, I imagine you've got your work cut out for you. We wouldn't want to keep you from it."

"Dad." Appalled, Laura gaped at him. "There's no reason to be rude."

"Yes, there is," Royce said mildly. "You look just like your mother. He'd know there's every reason to be rude."

"Well said," Caine murmured.

"I'll be back." Royce strolled toward the door, pausing when he was toe-to-toe with Caine. "And I'm going to kiss your daughter again, Mr. MacGregor. You'll have to get used to it."

"If the two of you think you can stand there and discuss me as if I'm some sort of trophy—"

"We're done." Royce cut her off, flicking a glance over his shoulder before he walked out the door. "For the moment."

"Arrogant son of a bitch." Caine dug his hands into his own pockets and felt a smile twitch at his mouth. "I like him."

"Oh, do you?" Running on full steam, Laura stalked from around the desk and, when she was close enough, poked her father in the chest with her finger. "You humiliated me."

"I did not."

"You did, too. Standing there like a...a..."

"Father," he finished, and took her chin firmly in his hand. "Do you think I don't know what he's got in mind? His hands were—"

"I know exactly where his hands were," Laura fired back. "They were exactly where I wanted them. I'm not a child, and I'm not going to have the men in my family draw the wagons in a circle around me to protect my virtue. It's my virtue, and I'll do with it what I choose, with whom I choose."

"Not if I beat you and lock you up, you won't."

She snorted. "You never laid a hand on me in your life."

"An obvious oversight which can still be corrected, young lady."

"Stop it." Diana rushed in, closing the door firmly behind her. "Stop this shouting. They can hear you all over the building."

"Let them hear!" Laura and Caine shouted together.

"Lower your voices, or I'm fining you both for contempt of court. Sit down, the pair of you."

"He's the one who's out of order." Laura tossed her head, but she dropped into a chair. "He embarrassed me in front of Royce, and he was rude. He came in here like some—"

"Father," Caine interjected, but sat, as well.

"*Neanderthal* father." Laura sniffed, and turned

her appeal to her mother. "Mama, I'm twenty-four years old. Does he think I've never been kissed before?"

"You'd better not have been kissed like that before," Caine muttered. "Diana, the man had his hands on her—"

"Enough." Diana held up her hands, shut her eyes until she could be certain her own temper was under control. "Laura, if you're a hundred and four, you have no right to speak to your father in that way. And Caine," she continued, just as he began to look smug, "Laura is an adult, a responsible, intelligent woman, and she can kiss whomever she pleases."

"Now, just a damn minute—" Caine began.

"Don't you shout at me," Diana warned him. "If he was rude to Royce, he'll apologize."

"In a pig's—"

"I'll see to it," Diana said between her teeth, searing her husband with a look. "But at the moment, it's more important that the two of you behave yourselves. This is a place of business."

"Tell that to her." Caine wagged a finger at Laura. "She's the one who was conducting personal business, practically on her own desk."

"We were not on the desk," Laura fumed. Though they could have been, she thought, might have been, in another minute. "Royce just dropped by to see if I'd be free for lunch."

"Ha!" was her father's opinion.

Laura slapped a hand on the arm of her chair. "You sound just like Grandpa."

"Oh, that's fine." Insulted, Caine sprang to his feet. "I get yelled at when I have a perfectly reasonable reaction to seeing my daughter being swallowed whole by a strange man, but you have no objection to having your grandfather pick out what he obviously considers a suitable stud for the next line of MacGregors.''

''Caine.'' Diana moaned the word, sinking to the arm of a chair herself.

''What? What do you mean? What are you talking about?''

''It's plain as the burr in the old man's voice,'' Caine told her. ''You're the eldest granddaughter, you're of marriageable age. It's time you were doing your duty,'' he continued, mimicking Daniel's voice, ''finding a suitable husband and getting children of your own.''

Laura's mouth worked for several seconds before she could manage to speak. Then all that came out was a low, whistling scream.

''See?'' Pleased he'd made his point, Caine hitched up the knees of his trousers and sat back.

''He's picked him out.'' Temper had Laura's breath strangling in her throat. ''He sent him to me. He—he selected him so I could...so I could *breed.*''

''Well...'' Satisfied he was off the hook, Caine examined his cuffs. ''That's a bit cruder than he'd have intended.''

''I'll kill him. With my bare hands.''

Caine sat up, enjoying himself now. ''Which one of them?''

''Grandpa. You'd best make funeral arrangements.'' She snatched up her coat and briefcase. ''I'm taking the rest of the day off. I have to drive to Hyannis.''

"Laura—"

"Let her go." Caine grabbed Diana's hand as Laura stormed out. "He deserves it."

"Lord, how did I ever get tangled up in such a family?"

"You wanted my body," Caine reminded her. "Couldn't keep your hands off me." He kissed her fingers. "Still can't."

"I'm going to give it more effort."

"Diana." He turned her hand over, pressing his lips to the palm in a way that both of them knew undid her. "I was just looking out for our little girl."

"She's grown up on us, Caine. It happened too fast." She lowered her head to his. "It's so hard to keep up."

"I just don't want her rushing into anything with some...Cameron Dad's picked out."

"Laura chooses her own," Diana said quietly. "She always has. What did you think of him?"

"I don't know." He rubbed his wife's knuckles over his cheek. "It was hard to tell. I had this red haze in front of my eyes." Then he sighed. "I liked him."

"So did I."

"That doesn't mean he can...right here in the office, Diana. For God's sake."

"Oh, you mean the way we did." She tucked her tongue in her cheek. "Disgraceful."

"That was different." His brows drew together when she continued to smile at him. "All right, all right. Maybe it isn't so different." He slid a hand up her legs. "So, you want to try the desk? See if it still works?"

"I think we've given the staff enough to gossip about for one day." She leaned closer until her lips brushed his. "We'll wait until everyone's gone for the day."

"I love you, Diana." He cupped his hand at the back of her neck to linger over the kiss. "A thousand times more than I did the day you walked into my life."

"We're lucky. All I want is for our children to be as lucky." She brushed her hands through his hair, adoring the way silver threaded through gold. "Caine, she's going to skin Daniel alive."

"I know." His grin was quick and wolfish. "I'm really sorry I'm going to miss it."

Chapter 6

There was nothing, Daniel MacGregor thought as he leaned back in his massive leather chair in the tower office of his personal fortress, like a good cigar.

And since his wife was out of the house for a few hours, he could sneak a smoke without the worry of being caught.

Ah, she had his best interests at heart, bless her. But a woman just didn't understand that a man needed a good cigar in his hand, the roll of it between his fingers, to help him think, to plan.

Which reminded him, he had to bribe one of the children to smuggle in another box. He was running low.

Content, master of his castle, he eased back in the well-worn leather of his favored chair and blew smoke at the ceiling. His life was as it should be, he decided, and he was nearly old enough now to relax and just enjoy it. As soon as he got the grandchildren settled, saw them happily tending to their duties to provide new blood to the MacGregor line, he would be content to while away his days just as he was doing this morning.

With happy thoughts and a good Cuban.

His plans for Laura were working out right on schedule. If the tidbits of information he'd managed to shoehorn out of her cousins were anything to go by. And he'd crowbarred a bit more from Royce Cameron himself.

"Boy thinks he's cagey," Daniel said to himself, and passed some time blowing smoke rings. "Can't outcagey the MacGregor."

Oh, Royce hadn't said a great deal. Yes, he'd met Laura and her cousins. Indeed she was an attractive woman. He'd agreed it was a wonder that some smart man hadn't snatched her up.

Played it close to the vest, had Royce Cameron, Daniel thought now. But he'd read between the lines, he'd watched the boy's eyes.

Smitten, that was what he was, Daniel thought with a chuckle. Hooked good and proper.

He thought a spring wedding would be suitable, unless he could push them into a winter one. Best not to waste time making babies, after all. He missed having babies about.

Laura would make a lovely bride, he mused. She had the look of her mother, and Diana had been radiant when Caine finally talked her into that walk down the aisle. Of course, the boy had taken twice as long to do it than he should have, but it had all worked out in the end.

Now, the next generation needed a bit of a push. He'd give the grandsons a bit more time to season, but it was time to nudge those oldest girls along. Daniel considered himself a wily nudger.

Thinking of Laura, wearing the MacGregor wedding veil and walking on Caine's arm down the aisle, brought a mist to Daniel's eyes. Such a beautiful girl, he thought. Such a sweet-natured child. Such a loving—

"MacGregor!"

The voice boomed out and nearly had Daniel snapping his cigar in two when he jolted. He choked on the smoke he'd just inhaled and frantically waved his hand to clear the haze of it out of the room. With great regret, he stubbed the best part of the Cuban out while his name reverberated through the house.

"I know you're here. I've come to kill you dead."

Grimacing, and moving with surprising speed for a man just past ninety years of age, Daniel shoved the ashtray and stub in the bottom drawer of his desk, flicked the lock, then yanked open the window, still waving at smoke.

"You!" Looking glorious in full fury, Laura strode through the doorway, her finger jabbing. "The nerve of you!"

"Laurie, sweetheart, what a nice surprise." He stood by the open window as freezing air rushed in, a bull of a man whose red hair had gone snow-white, whose beard was full and lush, whose blue eyes had never faded. And who was shaking in his boots.

"Don't you 'Laurie, sweetheart' me." She slapped both hands on his desk. "Pick a stud out for me, will you? What am I, a broodmare?"

"I don't know what you're talking about. You've driven all the way from Boston." He beamed at her while his mind calculated at the speed of light. "We'll go down and have some tea."

"You won't be able to swallow it after I strangle you. Did you think I wouldn't catch on to what you were doing?"

"Doing? I was just sitting here." He waved a huge hand toward the desk, and was careful to keep it between them. "Doing some paperwork."

"I can get my own man when I want one."

"Of course you can, darling girl. Why, you'd have to beat them off with a stick, looking the way you do. Why, when you were no more than minutes old and I held you in my hands the first time, I said to your father, 'This is the most beautiful baby ever born in this world.' So long ago."

He heaved a long, deep sigh, and braced a hand on the back of the chair, as if he needed the support getting into it. "It makes me feel old. I'm an old man, Laura."

"Don't pull that on me. You're only old when you want to be old. Schemer, scoundrel."

He blinked, tried his best to pale as he patted a hand to his wide chest. "My heart. My heart's palpitating."

She only narrowed her eyes. "I can fix that. Why don't I just stop it for you?"

"Maybe it's just breaking." He hung his head. "Breaking in two because my favorite granddaughter would speak to me so. Disrespect," he said weakly. "Nothing carves an old man like the sharp tongue of his favored grandchild."

"You're lucky I'm speaking to you at all. And don't think for a minute you can wiggle out of this by playing that old tune. You're healthy as a horse, and at the moment I think you have less sense than one."

Now his head came up, and his eyes glittered with temper. "Mind that tongue of yours, lass. I'll only take so much, even from you."

"And I'll only take so much, even from you. How could you embarrass me this way? For God's sake, Grandpa, you hired him for me."

"You needed security." His voice wasn't weak now, it boomed out like thunderclaps. "You and my other girls, living there in that city on your own. I protect what I love, and I wasn't having your grandmother fretting herself sick over you. That's that," he said, and thumped his hand on the desk.

"If that was that, it would be a different matter." She shifted to a new tack, walked around the desk and fisted her hands on her hips. "Daniel Duncan MacGregor, you are under oath. Do you swear that everything you say is the truth, the whole truth and nothing but the truth?"

"I don't lie, little girl. Now, if you'd—"

"I'm not finished with my examination of the accused."

"Accused, is it? Accused!" He roared up so that he could tower over her. "Not a year past the bar, and you think you can interrogate me."

"Yes, sit down. Please. And answer the questions. Did you or did you not hire Royce Cameron?"

"I said I did. His company has a good reputation."

"And for this service, you paid him a fee."

"I'd hardly expect a decent businessman to provide his services for free."

"And did you or did you not encourage him to...socialize with your eldest granddaughter, one Laura MacGregor."

"Well, this is nonsense. I never—"

"I'll remind you you're under oath."

"I never said a bloody word about socializing. I might have mentioned that my eldest granddaughter was a beautiful young woman of single status." He sat, sulking a bit. "It's not a crime."

"I say you threw me at him."

"I certainly did not." His smile spread, craftily. "I threw him at you. And if you didn't like the look of him, you were free to throw him back, weren't you?"

"That's—"

"But you didn't throw him back, did you, Laurie?"

She scowled, ground her teeth. "That has nothing to do with it."

"Oh, it does and you know it, or else you wouldn't be here blowing steam in my face. You'd have had a good laugh and pushed it aside." He took her hand before she could snatch it aside, gave it a playful squeeze. "He's smitten with you."

"He is not smitten."

"That he is. A man can see these things in another man. And I had him here for nearly two full days."

She did snatch her hand away. "Bribing him."

Two could play the interrogation game, Daniel thought. "Did he or did he not do satisfactory work at your house?"

"How would I know? And I don't—"

"He did the work, and a fine job, so that your

grandmother and I can rest our minds. Now, if I've a mind to want my own home made safer, more secure, why wouldn't I call on a man who's proven himself?"

How had the argument gotten off track? Laura wondered as she rubbed a hand over her temple. She'd had control of it at the beginning. And lost the grip somewhere along the line. "You know very well it's all a plot."

"Well, of course it's a plot. All of life is." Daniel grinned at her. "He's a handsome lad, that Royce Cameron. Comes from good stock, has made something of himself. His grandfather was a fine man."

That succeeded in distracting her. "You knew his grandfather?"

"Oh, in passing only. A policeman, with a strong sense of duty and a good head for Scotch. And his grandmother was a Fitzwilliams, a strong line. Her I knew a bit better." His brows wiggled. "But that was before your grandmother swept me off my feet. So maybe when I was looking into some small, privately owned companies in the Boston area that a businessman might want to pay heed to, and I saw the name of Royce Cameron—which was his grandfather's name, and took me back a few years—I thought, would that be Millie Fitzwilliams's grandson? And what's he done with himself?"

Defeated, Laura tugged the open window closed before the two of them froze to death. "So you made it your business to find out."

"To satisfy my curiosity, to see about the grandson of old friends. And if, when I discovered he was a strong man with a good mind and a decent head for business, I tossed a bit of work his way..."

"And your granddaughter along with it."

"As I said, I tossed him your way. Nobody held a gun to your head to make you go out dancing with him."

She set her teeth. "How do you know I went out dancing with him?"

Daniel smiled blandly. "I have my ways, little girl."

"I want to choke you."

"Kiss me instead." He took her hand again. "I've missed you, Laurie."

"Ha," she said, and made his heart swell with pride. "You never miss anything, you old schemer." But she kissed him just the same, and it only took the slightest tug on her hand to have her sitting on his lap. "Does he know you tossed him my way?"

"Come now, little girl, I'm better than that. Just what are you going to do about him?"

"I'm going to have a mad, torrid affair."

"Laura!"

The shock and horror in his voice was almost payment enough for the embarrassment. "You reap what you sow, Grandpa. And since you've put such a fine specimen of man at my disposal, I'll use him as I choose, until I'm done with him."

He jerked her back, stared hard into her eyes. "Ah, you're joking."

"Maybe I am." She smiled slowly. "And maybe I'm not. So you just think about that the next time you play laird with me, MacGregor."

"Now then, Laurie—" He broke off when he heard his wife's voice.

"Laura? Daniel, is that Laura's car outside?"

"Up here, Grandma."

"Ssh!" He gave Laura a quick shake to dislodge her. "Don't call her up here. The woman's got a nose like a hound. I only had a few puffs, damn it."

"I'll be right down, Grandma." Laura angled her head. "You owe me, Grandpa. And if you don't remember it, I might just let it slip that I saw a couple of Cubans taped to the back of your file drawer. Under *S* for *Sneak.*"

Now he did pale. "You wouldn't."

She kept that smug smile on her face as she strolled to the door. "Don't bet on it."

But because she adored him, Laura hurried down the stairs before her grandmother could come up. They met on the landing with a long, tight hug.

"I wish you'd told us you were driving up. I never would have gone out."

Laura eyed the small mountain of shopping bags. "Busy morning?"

"I'm determined to have my Christmas shopping done by Thanksgiving this year." She slipped her arm around Laura's waist and led her to the parlor. "Let's sit down. I'll ring for some tea."

"I'd love some tea." Laura sat, watched as Anna called for the housekeeper to brew a pot.

So lovely, Laura thought, as she always did. So sturdy. She thought of her grandmother as a trailblazer, a woman who had pursued her dream of practicing medicine when such careers for women were either laughed at or frowned upon.

She'd not only made the dream reality, she had triumphed, become one of the top thoracic surgeons on the East Coast, while raising a family, making a home.

"How do you do it, Grandma?"

"Do it?" Anna sat, sighing a little as she set her feet on a hassock. "Do what?"

"All. How do you do it all?"

"One step at a time. Oh, I swear, there was a time a morning of shopping wouldn't wear me out." She smiled. "I'm so glad you're here. Now I can sit here and be lazy for a while."

Instantly concerned, Laura sprang up. "Maybe you should lie down. You shouldn't do so much."

"Laura." Her voice was serene, warm as sunlight. "My feet hurt, that's all. Now sit. Tell me, did you drive all the way up here to shout at your grandfather?"

"I..." Laura huffed out a breath. "You know everything."

"I know he's been meddling, and expected you a week ago. Royce Cameron must have had quite some effect on you, for it to have taken you this long to figure it out."

"He's gorgeous."

"I've seen that for myself."

"I just told Grandpa I'm going to have a mad, torrid affair with him."

"Oh." Anna sighed and wiggled her toes. "I supposed he deserved that."

"But I am." Laura wondered how many women could say such a thing to their grandmothers. "I am going to have an affair with him."

Anna said nothing, grateful that the rattle signaled the tea trolley being wheeled down the hall. She waited until the housekeeper left them alone, and poured two cups of tea herself. "I don't have to tell you to be careful. You're a bright, self-aware young woman." Then she sighed. "I'll tell you to be careful anyway."

"I will. Please don't worry. I'm...powerfully attracted to him. I've never been so attracted to anyone. And I like him. I didn't think I would. In fact, I was sure I wouldn't, but I like him a lot."

"And obviously he feels the same way."

"Yeah." She sipped at her tea, then set it aside. "You know, men drive me crazy. I really had no intention of— I've got so much I want to do, and I just don't have time for this kind of complication. Then Grandpa hires him. Hires him, for heaven's sake. You laugh."

"I'm sorry, darling. I shouldn't."

"It might be funny ten or twenty years from now," Laura muttered. "Right now it's just humiliating. And then Ian decides he needs to play chaperon and won't give me five minutes' peace. And you'd think Royce was his best pal ever since he punched him."

"Ian punched Royce?"

"Other way, but it was a misunderstanding."

"Naturally," Anna said calmly, and drank her tea.

"And then Dad barges into my office this morning. *My* office, and bares his fangs just because Royce was kissing me."

"Oh." Anna's smile warmed. "Poor Caine. His baby girl."

"I'm not—"

"You're his baby girl and always will be," Anna said gently, interrupting her. "I suppose you argued."

"We shouted at each other for a while. Mama smoothed it out, mostly. But when he said that Grandpa had... Well, the light dawned on how the whole business got rolling, so I had to come up and yell at Grandpa."

"Naturally." The MacGregors never failed to make their point at top volume, Anna mused, and brushed her hand back to tidy a wave of her sable-colored hair. "But you've made up now."

"You can't stay mad at Grandpa. He wheedles it out of you."

"No one knows that better than I. And no one loves more than Daniel."

"I know." She bit her lip. She was about to say what she hadn't allowed herself to say before. "Grandma...I think I could fall in love with Royce. If I let myself."

"Laura." Anna reached out, took the hand Laura held out to her. "The thing about falling is that you have absolutely no choice. It just happens. Here comes Daniel." She gave Laura's hand a squeeze when she heard Daniel's heavy tread on the stairs. "I wouldn't mention that last part to him just yet."

"I wouldn't give him the satisfaction," Laura said primly, and picked up her tea as Daniel strode in.

"Well, well." He smiled broadly. "Two beautiful women. And they're all mine."

Chapter 7

Laura didn't go home. She drove back to Boston, stopped and ate dinner alone to give herself time to think. As she saw it, she had two choices. She could be stubborn, attempt to teach her meddling grandfather a lesson and never see Royce Cameron again.

That idea didn't make the hot-fudge sundae she had treated herself to go down pleasantly.

On the other hand, she could simply allow her relationship—if it was a relationship—with Royce to progress naturally, over time. She could consider that this blip, this interruption in the forward rush of things, was a sign to slow down, to consider carefully. To look before she leaped.

But MacGregors were leapers, not lookers.

And that was why, at one-fifteen in the morning, she was standing outside Royce's apartment, banging her fist on the door.

The door across the hall opened a crack, just enough for her to see a pair of scowling, bloodshot eyes peering out at her. Laura narrowed her own and hissed. The door shut again with an abrupt snap.

She pounded again, heard a thump and a curse. Then saw a narrow light beam under the door. She angled her head and smiled blandly, certain Royce was staring at her through the Judas hole. An instant later, locks rattled open.

"What's wrong?" he demanded.

"Why should there be anything wrong?" She sailed inside. "Shut the door, Royce, you have a nosy neighbor across the hall."

He shut the door, leaned back against it and struggled to orient himself. She looked as fresh and pressed as she had at ten o'clock that morning in her tidy pin-striped suit and practical heels. He felt as rumpled as last night's sheets in the ragged jeans he'd managed to find on the floor and tug on.

He rubbed his hands over his face, heard the crackle of beard against palm, then dragged his hands back and through his sleep-tangled hair. "Is it one in the morning, or did I oversleep?"

Laura turned her wrist, gave her watch a careful study. "It's 1:17 a.m. To be exact."

"Yeah, let's be exact. What are you doing here?"

Enjoying herself she wandered the tiny living area. "I've never been up to your place." She noted about a week's worth of dust on scarred furniture. Newspapers piled on the floor by a sagging sofa. A small, really excellent watercolor of Boston Harbor on the wall, a high-end stereo system on a set of pine shelves and a Berber rug that was in desperate need of a good vacuuming.

"Now I see why." She arched her brows. "You're a pig."

"I wasn't expecting—" He caught himself. It was one o'-damn-clock in the morning, he remembered. "Yeah, so what?"

"Just an observation. Do you have any wine? I didn't want to have a drink, since I was driving."

"Yeah, I think there's—" He pulled himself up short again. His brain was mush. It had been years since he had to wake alert at a moment's notice. "You came by for a drink?"

"Is that a problem?" She kept the casual, pleasant smile on her face and, judging the kitchen to be to the left, wandered toward it. "Do you want some wine?"

"No." He stared after her, raked his hands through his tousled hair again. "No. Help yourself."

"I will." He obviously stayed out of the kitchen as much as possible, she mused. It was neat enough to indicate disuse. But she did find a decent bottle of chardonnay in the fridge and, after a brief search through cupboards, an unchipped glass. "No frills for you, huh?"

"I don't spend a lot of time here." He moved toward the kitchen, watching her pour the wine. "It's just here."

"And I imagine you're funneling most of your profits back into your business. Which would be wise, and frugal. Are you wise and frugal, Royce?"

"Not particularly. I just don't need a lot of the extras."

"I like the extras." She toasted him and sipped. "I suppose I'm high-maintenance." She studied him over the rim of her glass. His eyes were heavy, she noted. Sleepy, sexy. His mouth was just a little sulky. The jeans weren't buttoned, and rode low on narrow hips. His chest was bare, well-defined, with a thin white scar slicing just under his left shoulder. "Did you get that on the job?"

"Get what?"

"The scar."

He glanced down, shrugged. "Yeah. What's the deal here, Slim?"

"I have a question to ask you."

"Okay, true or false, or multiple-choice?"

"Just yes or no." She made an effort to keep her eyes on his. Too much study of that tough, compact body was bound to distract her. "Were you aware that my grandfather hired you to insure the MacGregor line continues?"

"Huh?"

"Just yes or no, Royce, it's not terribly complicated. I'll rephrase the question. Were you aware when you accepted the job to handle house security for me that my grandfather had selected you, as you fulfilled his requirements, as a potential mate for me?"

"Mate? What do you mean, mate?" His brain was beginning to clear. "You mean— You're kidding."

"I believe that answers the question." She started to move by him, but his hand snaked out and closed over her arm.

"Are you saying that he bought me for you?"

"In the nicest possible way."

"That's bull."

"No, that's the MacGregor." Laura patted Royce's hand. "Some men would be flattered."

"Really." His eyes were narrowed slits of flame blue. "Oh, really."

Because she understood, and appreciated his reaction, she patted his hand again. "You had no idea what he was up to? He's not all that subtle. He thinks he is, but he's not."

Royce dropped his hand, stepped back. "I got the impression—early on—I got the idea that he was trying to set something up. But I figured that was because you were incredibly ugly."

A laugh burst out before she could stop it. "Thank you so much."

"No. Wait." He pressed his fingers to his eyes. Maybe he was having a dream, maybe not. Either way, he had to pick his way through it. "He mentioned you a lot, his granddaughter, Laura. Bright, brilliant, beautiful. Single. I thought he hinted pretty broadly and figured you must be desperate for...well, desperate. Then I got a look at you and decided I'd misread the signals."

She cocked her head. "Now I suppose I should be flattered."

"You're telling me that he set this up so..."

"He wants me married. And raising a family. He thinks you'd breed well."

"That I'd—" Royce held up a hand, stepped back again. "Just hold on. I'm not in the market for...breeding."

"Neither am I. That's handy, isn't it?"

"The old bastard."

"Exactly, but be careful. We can call him that, but we don't take kindly when others do." She set her glass down. "Well, I thought it best to clear the matter up. Good night."

"Just a damn minute." He only had to shift to block her path. "You come here in the middle of the night, drop your little bombshell and stroll off? I don't think so."

"I thought you'd like to know, and to know that I've spoken with him and straightened things out."

"That's fine, that's your family business." He stretched an arm across the doorway, resting a hand on the jamb to hold her in. "And you should know I don't give a damn what your grandfather has in mind." He wrapped her hair around his free hand, tipping her head back. "He's not here, your father's not here, your brother's not here, your cousins aren't here."

Her heartbeat thickened. "No, no one's here except you and me."

"So why don't you tell me what you have in mind, Laura?"

"If I have to tell you, you're not nearly as quick as I thought you were."

"I want you to tell me. Exactly."

There was only one step between them. She took it, closed the distance. "I want you to take me to bed. I want you to make love with me for the rest of the night. Is that clear enough?"

"That's crystal."

He swept an arm under her knees. Her breath caught as he lifted her off her feet. Before she could shift to wrap her arms around him, his mouth was hot and hungry on hers. With a little murmur of pleasure, she sank into the kiss, kicking off her shoes as he carried her toward the bedroom.

The room was full of shadows, the sheets were tangled, and the mattress creaked under their weight. Lifting her arms, she drew him closer and let the kiss spin gloriously through her system.

He yanked her jacket over her shoulders, nipping his teeth over her throat as he dragged it free, tossed it aside. She was slim and eager beneath him, arching at a touch, sighing at a taste. He wanted to savor, moment by moment, inch by inch, but the need he felt was too huge, too strong, as if it had been strapped down and straining for years.

As her mouth slid and angled and gave under his, he ran his hands over her, torturing them both, pleasing them both. He heard her moan, felt her heart trip under his palm, then, unable to wait, tugged her blouse apart. Her bra skimmed low over the curve of her breasts, a shimmering line of satin against silk. He closed his mouth over her, reveling in the mix of textures.

She nearly cried out, just from that, the sensation of lips and tongue on flesh. Oh, but she wanted more, she wanted all, and she curved up to offer, her nails skimming down his back in edgy demand.

It ached, everything he did, everywhere he touched, brought a low, throbbing ache. She hadn't known she could want so much, that the need for anything could be so sharp, so immediate. And when his mouth came back to hers, she all but wept from the sensation.

She rolled with him, her body fluid, energized. Her

breath was sobbing as he dragged off her skirt. Her mouth, seeking flesh, was as greedy as his.

Her flesh was smooth, hot, irresistible. Her hair, all that glorious black silk, wrapped around them as they wrestled over the bed, struggling to free themselves of the last barriers. Soft here, there firm, yielding, then demanding. He filled himself with her, too steeped in her to realize he'd never needed anything, anyone, this desperately.

When he cupped her, her moan was low and long and broken. In the dim light, he watched her eyes flash open, go blind, as he drove her over. She choked out his name, fisted her hands in his hair. And went wild.

She didn't notice that they slid to the floor, dragging trapped sheets with them. The air was thick and heavy, clogging her lungs, his hands were quick and rough, bruising her skin. She flung an arm out, as if for balance. Something crashed.

Then he was inside her, forcing her over the edge again, where there was nothing to hold on to but him. Mindlessly she wrapped herself around him, matched his violent speed, craved more, as the storm raged through her.

She could hear nothing but the roar of her own blood, feel nothing but the unspeakable pleasure his body pumped into hers, see nothing but his face, those lake-blue eyes watching her.

Then, as if he knew it was the final thrill she needed, his mouth crushed down on hers, and they broke free together.

He gathered himself together enough to roll over so that he lay on the cold floor and she was cushioned by his still-overheated body. Then he decided he'd die happy if he could stay, just like this, for the next twenty years or so.

"Are we on the floor?" Her voice was slow and slurred, as if she'd downed the whole bottle of wine, instead of less than one glass.

"Yeah. I'm pretty sure we're on the floor."

"How did we get here?"

"I don't have a clue." He shifted, winced at a small stab of pain. When he found the energy to lift a hand and brush his fingers over the back of his shoulder, he saw the slight smear of blood. "There's broken glass on the floor."

"Uh-huh."

"And there is now broken glass in my back."

"Oh." She sighed, rubbed her face cozily against his chest, than shot upright. "Oh! Did something break? We're naked. We'll be cut to ribbons."

"Whatever happens, I'll always say it was worth it." With a strength that made her blink, he nipped her at the waist and hauled her up until she sat on the bed. "Stay up there until I clean this up."

"I don't think you should— Damn." She squeezed her eyes shut, covered them with her hands when the light flashed on. "Is it glass? Don't step on it."

"I already did." He swore ripely, making her giggle.

"Sorry," she said immediately. "I've never heard those words phrased together quite that way." She opened one eye, and was immediately contrite. "Royce, you're bleeding."

"In a couple of places. It was just a drinking glass. I've got to get a broom."

"I'll tend your wounds," she said with a smile that became dreamy as she watched him walk toward the door. "God, you're built."

Disconcerted, he stopped, glanced back over his shoulder. She was sitting on his bed, all long, slender limbs and tumbled hair. "Same goes, Slim," he murmured and slipped out.

She bent over the bed, and had shaken the glass off the sheet when he came back with a broom and dustpan. "You'll have to launder this. There might still be glass in it."

"Just toss it over in the corner. I'll get to it."

She lifted a brow, glanced around the room. It had a bed, a dresser, a chair. Or at least she assumed that was a chair under the heap of clothing. There was a mirror that needed resilvering, and a desk that was overpowered by a sleek computer and printer.

"All the comforts of home."

"I told you, I don't spend a lot of time here." He dumped the glass in a wastebasket, then left the broom and dustpan tipped against the wall.

"Do you ever actually do laundry?" she asked him.

"Not until I have absolutely no other choice."

She smiled, patted a hand on the bed beside her. "Sit down. Let me see that cut." When he did, she clucked her tongue and touched her lips to his shoulder. "It's just a scratch."

"If we'd fallen off the bed the other way, you'd be kissing my butt."

Laughing, she rested her cheek on his back. "How's the foot?"

"Just a nick. I've had worse."

"Hmm." She shifted, ran a fingertip over the scar high on his shoulder. "Like this."

"Didn't wait for backup. Rookie mistake. I didn't make it again."

"And this?" She touched the small mar on his chin.

"Bar fight. I was just drunk enough not to feel it, and stupid enough to have asked for it. I stopped making that mistake, too."

"Reformed, are you, Royce?" She eased forward to brush her lips against his chin.

"More or less."

"I like that it's more or less." Empowered by the desire darkening his eyes, she knelt to wrap her arms around his neck. "I'd hate for you to be a completely solid citizen."

"Isn't that what you are?"

She laughed, bit his bottom lip. "More or less."

"More, I'd say, than less. Laura MacGregor, of the Boston MacGregors." His hand rode up her side to brush her breast. "What are you doing in my bed?"

"You could say it occurred to me that's exactly where I wanted to be." She nibbled at his mouth. "I have a habit of going after what I want. It's a family trait." Her lips trailed over his jaw. "And I wanted you. I want you. Take me, Royce." Her mouth closed over his, and destroyed any hope he had of thinking clearly. "Take me back where you took me before."

He dragged her hard against him, and took her back.

Chapter 8

Snow buried the East Coast and caused school-age children to dance with joy. Hard winds blew down from Canada and brought bitter cold. Pipes burst, cars stalled, and streets turned to ice rinks.

The brave or the determined crowded the shopping centers and malls to hunt for Christmas presents, to ponder bright wrappings and ribbons. Holiday cards arrived in the mail, and kitchens smelled of baking.

Boston shivered, shoveled out, and watched another six inches of snow fall.

Bundled in layers against the cold and armed with a snow shovel, Laura trooped out to clear the driveway. The sunlight bounced off the white ground and stung the eyes, so she fumbled a pair of sunglasses out of her pocket. The chill air bit her cheeks, burned her throat. She couldn't have been happier.

Beneath her red ski cap, she wore headphones. Music trilled in her ears. Christmas music, as bright and cheerful as her mood. Her life, she thought as she scooped up the first shovelful of snow, couldn't be more perfect.

She'd won her first case the week before. Just a small property-damage suit, of little consequence to the legal world, she thought. But she had faced the judge, argued her points. And she had won. She had two new clients who wanted wills drawn up.

She was just beginning.

Christmas was just around the corner, and she couldn't ever remember looking forward to it more. She loved looking at the colored lights sparkling on houses, at the silly Santas and reindeer flying over lawns, the glimpses of brightly decorated trees behind windows.

She even looked forward to braving the crowds and the madness to do her own holiday shopping. It didn't matter if Julia and Gwen rolled their eyes at her when she burst into song or stared dreamily out the window. She could laugh off their comments about Laura in love.

She wasn't in love, she was simply enjoying the thrilling adventure of a romance with an exciting man. That was entirely different. If she was in love, she'd be worried. She'd sit by the phone and chew her nails, waiting for him to call. She'd think of him every minute of every day, plan every night around him. She'd lose her appetite, toss and turn in bed and suffer from wild mood swings.

None of that was true, she decided, putting her back into her work. Well, maybe she thought of him a great deal, at odd times. Almost all the time. But she didn't sit by the phone, she wasn't off her feed, and her mood was up and steady.

Had she sulked because he refused the invitation to share Thanksgiving dinner at Hyannis Port? Of course not. She'd missed him, and certainly she'd have liked him there, but she hadn't pressed or nagged or wheedled.

Therefore, Laura concluded as she tossed snow over her shoulder, she wasn't in love.

When hands gripped her hips, the shovel went flying. She was whirled around before she could manage more than a strangled scream, and then she was staring into very annoyed blue eyes. She noted that Royce's head was covered with snow, that it coated his shoulders. And that his mouth was moving.

"What?"

He shook his head, took a deep breath, then shoved one end of the headphones off her ear. "I said, what the hell are you doing?"

"I'm clearing the driveway."

He raked a hand through his dark hair to scatter snow. "So I noticed."

"Did I hit you with that last shovelful?" She bit down hard on the inside of her cheek, and struggled to keep her voice sober. "I'm sorry." A laugh hitched out, poorly disguised as a cough, as he narrowed his eyes. "Really, I didn't know you were behind me." She gave up, wrapped her arms around her stomach and let the laugh free. "I really am sorry, but you keep sneaking up on me."

"If you weren't blasting music in your ears, you'd be able to hear the rest of the world. And why the hell are you out here shoveling snow?"

"Because it's there, and so's my car, and I have to get into the office."

He took the sunglasses off her nose, slipped them into the pocket of her coat. "I don't suppose there's a single young boy in this neighborhood who could use ten bucks for shoveling your driveway."

"I'm perfectly capable of doing it myself." Suspicious, she fisted her hands on her hips. "If you're even thinking about saying something insulting, like this is man's work, I'll have to pick up that shovel and brain you with it."

He caught her chin in his hand, drew her face up, close to his. And smiled in challenge. "It's man's work."

She let out a sound like a hissing kettle and whirled. But he beat her to the shovel. "Go inside," he ordered. "Warm up. I'll take care of it."

"I'm doing it." She gripped the handle of the shovel and frustrated herself with a useless tug-of-war. "It's my car, it's my driveway."

"I'm not standing here watching you shovel snow."

"Oh, and I suppose I should take myself off to the kitchen and make you some hot chocolate."

"Good idea." He knew exactly what he was doing, what he was risking when he scraped the shovel under snow. "Hold the marshmallows." He didn't even flinch when the snowball exploded on the back of his head. "We'll play later, as soon as I finish this."

"I am not making you hot chocolate."

"Coffee'd be fine."

"Don't you have anything to do? Don't you work?"

"It's only seven-thirty. I've got time."

And he'd needed to see her, it was as simple as that. He'd told himself he was going into the office early. Then his car had simply ended up in front of her house. He'd sat in it watching her, just watching her. She'd looked like a column of fire against the snow, in that long red coat, the red cap snug on her head.

So he'd sat in the car watching her, wanting her. And it worried him.

The next missile caught the small of his back. He ignored it, kept shoveling.

From the upstairs window, Julia and Gwen studied the scene, their noses pressed to the glass. "How much longer before he grabs her and takes her down?" Gwen wondered out loud.

"Three more hits, tops."

"Agreed. Ten seconds, at the outside, after she hits the ground, he'll be kissing her brainless."

"Five seconds max," Julia declared. "He works fast."

"How long before she realizes she's in love with him?"

"Oh, nice shot, Laura! That's got to be cold, sliding down his neck. I'd say she might be able to delude herself until Christmas, but that's the cutoff."

"I think she already knows." Gwen smiled wistfully. "She's just too stubborn to admit it."

"What about him?"

"Oh, he's hooked. Did you see the way he was looking at her? The way he always looks at her?"

"Like he'd go on looking at her if Boston fell into the bay? Yeah."

Gwen sighed. "Yeah. Oh, here it comes."

The two of them grinned out the window as Royce spun around, as Laura took one step in retreat. "It's going to be a terrific kiss," Julia predicted.

Outside, Laura stopped her backward progress and stood her ground. "I want that shovel."

"You want the shovel? This shovel?" He winged it, distracting her enough to have her watching the flight. Then he tackled her, twisting at the last instant to cushion her fall as they tumbled to the snowy lawn.

"Idiot." She flung out an arm, got a hefty handful of snow. Before she could rub it in his face, he flipped her. She lost her breath, shivered as snow slipped, cold and wet, down her collar. Then found her mouth much too busy for insults.

He was kissing the cold out of her body, the thoughts out of her head, the strength out of her limbs. She attempted one muffled protest for form's sake, then wound her arms around him.

She wondered the snow didn't melt from the lawn and form a lake, and the lake sizzle like a geyser.

"If you think you can get around me that way..." she began when she could breathe again.

"I did." He grinned, kissed her lightly. "Your nose is getting red."

"How nice of you to mention it." This time she did rub snow in his face. Then, giggling wildly, she tried to wiggle away when he swore at her. "Now your whole face is red. Very attractive."

He wrestled with her, pushed her face into the snow. She gave as good as she got, so that within three minutes of tussling both of them were drenched, covered with snow and breathless.

"Let me up, you bully." Her voice shook with laughter as she shoved at him.

"First an idiot, now a bully." He scooped up snow, molded it one-handed.

Her eyes slid to the side, focused on the lopsided ball, then shifted back to his. "Do it and you'll pay."

He tossed the ball, caught it neatly. "Well, now I'm shaking." Playfully he rubbed the snowball along her jaw, up her cheek. She lay still with chin angled and eyes slitted and waited for the worst.

His grin faded slowly. Her pulse began to kick as the laughter died out of his eyes, as his gaze roamed over her face, as his fingers began to trace it.

"Royce?"

"Be quiet a minute." He said it absently, still running a fingertip along those ice-edged cheekbones. Then he lowered his mouth, skimmed his lips over them. She couldn't have spoken if her life hung in the balance.

He wanted to believe it was because she was beautiful, because her face was exotic, unique, her body sleek and arousing. But he knew it wasn't desire that was working in him now. He understood passion, need, hungers. This was more. This was all.

His mouth brushed hers once, lightly, as if testing some new flavor. Then again, and then it lingered.

He'd never kissed her this way. No one had. She'd grown used to the greed, to the urgent demands, even craved them. But this depthless tenderness was new, and it destroyed her.

Her hand slipped limply to the ground. Everything she was, everything she had, yielded to him, to them, to what they had created together.

When he realized she was trembling, he eased back. Shaken, he began to brush the snow off her hair. "You're cold," he said briskly. "Small wonder."

"Royce—"

"You'd better get inside, dry off." He had to get the hell away from her, he thought, nearly panicked. He had to get a grip on himself. He rose quickly, hauled her to her feet. "You've got a yard of hair, and all of it's wet. I'll finish the driveway."

Her stomach was churning into knots, and her head simply wouldn't stop spinning in slow circles. "Yes, all right." She wanted to get inside, wanted to sit down until she could feel her legs under her again. "I'll, ah, make that hot chocolate."

"I'll take a rain check." He moved past her to retrieve the shovel. "Your driveway's nearly done anyway, and I've got things to do."

They weren't going to talk about what had happened, she realized, then let out a quiet breath. Better not to talk about it until she figured out exactly what had happened. "Okay." She began backing up. "You're welcome to come inside and warm up yourself."

"I'm fine. I'll see you later."

"Later." She backed into her car, eased herself around it and fled.

She was out of breath when she got inside and busied herself stripping off her coat, unwinding the scarf from around her neck, pulling off her cap and headphones.

It was too hot, she decided, and yanked off the vest she wore over a cashmere turtleneck. She sat on the landing to pull off her boots, yanked off the first of two pairs of socks.

Still too hot, she thought. She'd gotten overheated. She felt feverish. Maybe she was coming down with something. Flu was going around, wasn't it? Flu was always going around. She'd probably picked up some germ. That was why she felt light-headed and overwarm, why her muscles ached and her limbs wanted to tremble.

She'd take something for it. She'd fight it off.

Then she lifted a hand, touched her fingers to lips that still pulsed from him, that still tasted of him.

Closing her eyes, she laid her head on her knees and admitted the worst. She'd fallen without feeling the jolt, without having the sense to catch herself on the slide.

She had just dropped headlong in love with Royce Cameron.

Chapter 9

"You did very well in court today." Diana smiled at her daughter as they worked together in the law library.

"Thanks." Laura frowned over the wording of a brief, made a notation in the margin. "It felt good. I really appreciate you letting me do the direct on the coroner."

"It's very basic testimony, but still tricky. You handled yourself well. The jury paid attention to you, and just as important, our client trusts you."

Laura worked up a smile. "Only because you do. Amanda's your client."

"You've been a tremendous help to me on this case." Diana scanned the stacks of books piled on the table. "But we're not there yet."

"Are you worried?"

"Concerned," Diana said. "I don't want her to

spend a single day in prison, because I believe she was defending her life. And, Laura, I'm a little concerned about you."

"Why? I'm fine."

"Are you?"

"Absolutely. I'm doing exactly what I've always wanted to do. My life is exciting and rich. It's two weeks before Christmas, and for the first time in history, I've actually finished my shopping. Mostly. What could be wrong?"

"You don't mention Royce."

"He's fine, too." Laura looked back down at the paperwork. "I just saw him last night. We went to dinner."

"And?"

"And it was fine. I enjoy going out with him. I do think it may be best to slow things down a little. We've moved awfully fast to this point, and with the holidays coming up, there's so much going on. It's a good time to step back a bit and evaluate."

Diana let out a sigh. "You're so much like me, it's almost frightening."

"What do you mean?"

"Honey, you haven't once said how you feel about him. What you feel for him."

"Certainly I did. I said I enjoy seeing him, we enjoy each other. He's a very interesting, complex man, and I..." She trailed off, undone by her mother's patient gaze. "And I'm in love with him. I've ruined everything and fallen in love with him. It wasn't supposed to happen. I went into this relationship with my eyes open. I'm responsible for my own reactions, my own emotions. It's supposed to be a physical relationship between two people who like each other, respect each other.''

She cut herself off, squeezed her eyes tight. ''I could kill Grandpa for getting me into this.''

Sympathetic, Diana covered her daughter's hand with hers. ''Is it so bad to be in love with an interesting, complex man you like, you respect, you enjoy?''

''It is when we set ground rules at the beginning.''

''Did you?''

''Not in so many words. It was just understood. We're not looking for love and marriage and family. Royce was every bit as appalled as I was that Grandpa had this harebrained scheme in mind.'' She blew out a breath. ''I'm all right, really. I'm irritated with myself, more than anything. And I can handle it. It's just a matter of slowing things down a little, of refocusing.''

''Of being too stubborn, or too afraid to risk your feelings.''

''Maybe.'' Laura acknowledged the possibility with a nod. ''But I don't want to lose him, and I would if I complicated things. I'd rather have what I have than watch him walk away.''

''And you're sure he would.''

''I'm not sure of anything. But I've decided to keep things fairly status quo, perhaps with a little distance. Once I have a better perspective, I'll go from there. And distance shouldn't be a problem, with the amount of work I have and the holidays.'' She put some effort into making her lips curve up. ''So, to circle back to the beginning, I'm absolutely fine.''

* * *

With his mood light and the small glossy bag in his hand, Caine strolled back to the offices. He'd slipped out to pick up a necklace he'd had designed for his wife. He could already picture her opening the Christmas gift, and himself slipping the collar of gold and colored stones around her throat.

She was, he thought, going to be very happy.

When he caught sight of the man starting up the steps to MacGregor and MacGregor, Caine's mood darkened instantly. Royce Cameron, he thought, the man who was playing fast and loose with his baby girl.

"Cameron."

Royce glanced around, and his own mood, not too cheery to begin with, dropped several levels. Damn MacGregors were everywhere. "Mr. MacGregor."

"Office hours are nine to five," he said coolly. "Laura's assisting on a very important case. If you want to see her, you'd best wait until she's done for the day."

"I didn't come to see Laura. I came to see your wife."

Caine's eyes went sharp and hot. "Oh, really? And do you have an appointment?"

"No, but I think she'll want to see me. It's a legal matter, Mr. MacGregor, not a personal one."

"Diana's caseload is already overburdened. But I've got a few minutes to spare."

For the first time, Royce smiled. "Mr. MacGregor, if I had a legal problem, you'd be the very last lawyer in Boston I'd come to. You'd like nothing better than to see me locked away for ten to twenty, preferably in solitary."

"Not at all. I was thinking more along the lines of hard labor in a maximum-security facility." But because Caine appreciated a man who knew the lay of the land, he opened the door.

He led the way into the reception area, with its antiques and polished woods. "File this under Christmas, Mollie," he asked the woman manning the desk.

"Oh, Mr. MacGregor, it's the choker, isn't it? Can I peek?"

"Just make sure my wife doesn't see it, then buzz her, will you, and see if she has a moment for Mr. Cameron?"

"Right away." But she was already slipping the velvet box out of the bag and opening the lid. "Oh." She pressed a hand against the starched jacket she wore. "Oh, it's the most beautiful necklace I've ever seen. She's going to love it."

Distracted, Caine eased a hip on the desk and took another look himself. "You think?"

"Any woman who found this under the Christmas tree would know she's adored. Just look how the sunlight catches these stones."

Baffled, Royce watched the dignified former attorney general of the United States grin down at a piece of jewelry the way a giddy boy grinned at a jar full of lightning bugs. And it struck him that this was a man completely besotted by a woman he'd been married to for a quarter of a century.

How did that happen? Royce wondered. How did it last? How did two people possibly live together for a lifetime and still love?

"No comment, Cameron?"

Royce jerked himself back and took a look at the necklace. It was exotic, deeply colored stones glinting against thick gold. He imagined it would suit Diana MacGregor perfectly. And undoubtedly her daughter, as well.

He shifted, felt remarkably foolish. "It's impressive," he said. "I don't know much about glitters."

"Women do." Caine winked at Mollie. "Right?"

"You bet we do." She slipped the bag into her bottom drawer and turned a small key. "I'll just buzz Mrs. MacGregor now, Mr. Cameron. If you'd like to have a seat."

"He can come up with me. Ring my office if and when Diana's free, Mollie." Caine's wolfish grin spread as he turned to Royce. "Suit you?"

"Sure." Deliberately cocky, he shoved his hands in the back pockets of his jeans as he followed Caine up straight, uncarpeted stairs with a brass-and-wood rail that gleamed with a mirror shine.

The place smelled rich, was all he could think. Subtle scents, thick rugs, leather, polish. The wainscoting in the hall they walked down had to be mahogany. But, more, it had the feel of a home, rather than a place of business. It impressed him that anyone could accomplish that, or bothered to even try.

Caine stepped inside his office, his turf. Wanting to set the tone, his tone, he sat behind his desk. "Have a seat, Cameron. Want anything? Coffee?"

Royce chose a wing-backed leather chair in deep navy. "I haven't been a cop for while now, but I remember how to set up an interrogation. I'm probably as good at it as you are."

"I've been at it a lot longer. Let's just cut straight to the heart of the matter, shall we? What are your intentions as to my daughter?"

"I don't have any. No intentions, no plans, no designs."

"You've been seeing her for nearly three months now."

"That's right. I'd imagine she's dated a number of other men."

But this was the only man Caine had ever worried about. "Her social life didn't begin with you. Laura is a beautiful, outgoing young woman. A wealthy young woman," he added, keeping his eyes level on Royce's. The flash of heat, the snap of insult, pleased him enormously.

"You don't want to go in that direction."

"It's an undeniable fact."

"Do you think I give a damn about her portfolio?" Royce's temper snapped, shoving him to his feet. "Do you think a man could be with her for five minutes and think of anything but her? I don't care what you think of me, but you ought to think better of her."

"I do." Relaxing now, Caine leaned back in his chair. "And now I know you do, as well."

"You son of a bitch."

"As you say, what we think of each other doesn't really matter. I love my daughter. I also trust her judgment in most cases, and have always found her to be a good judge of character. She sees something in you, and I'm going to try to accept that. But hurt her..." He leaned forward again with eyes that gleamed.

"Cause her one moment's unhappiness, and I'll come down on you like the wrath of God."

When his phone rang, he answered without taking his eyes from Royce's. "Yes, Mollie. Thanks." He hung up, inclined his head. "My wife will see you now. Her office is across the hall."

Because he didn't trust himself to speak, knew whatever came out of his mouth at that moment would be bitter and vile, Royce turned on his heel and walked out.

"Control," Caine murmured, and felt a first twinge of sympathy for the man. "Admirable."

"Royce." Diana opened the door herself, and her smile was a telling contrast to her husband's frost. "How nice to see you. Please come in and sit down. Would you like some coffee?"

"No, I don't want anything." He set his teeth. "I don't want anything."

Fury, Diana mused, barely leashed. She flicked a glance at the office across the hall and controlled a sigh. "All right, then, what can I do for you?"

"Nothing. I don't want anything from any of you, and I never did. I've got some information you may be able to use on the Holloway case."

"Oh? Please, sit down."

"I don't want to sit," Royce snapped out. "I just want to get this over with and get the hell out of here." He stopped himself, forced himself to take one long, calming breath. "I'm sorry."

"It's all right. I imagine Laura's father was difficult."

"I don't think we'd better discuss Laura's father. Or Laura, or anyone named MacGregor just now."

"Then why don't we discuss Amanda Holloway?"

"I don't know her, I never met her. I knew her husband slightly when we both worked out of the same house. Precinct," he elaborated.

"Did you work with him directly?"

"Only once. We took a call together. I hate this," he said, and finally sat. "Look, cops back each other, because when you go through the door together you've got to know the one going in with you is with you. All the way.

"We took a call, domestic dispute. The worst. Guy had been pounding on his wife, kids were screaming. I restrained the man, Holloway took the woman. Her face was bashed up, bleeding, and she'd gone over. I mean, she was going after her husband now. She wasn't going to take it anymore. I remember her screaming that when Holloway took hold of her.

"He hurt her," Royce continued. "I had the man on the floor, cuffing him, and I heard the woman cry out. I saw Holloway yank her arm back, it's a wonder he didn't snap a bone, and he shoved her back against the wall. I told him to ease off, and he said something like 'The bitch is asking for it.' That her husband had a right to teach her a lesson. And he slapped her, backhanded her. I had to leave the husband on the floor to drag Holloway off the woman."

Royce paused a moment, tried to gather his thoughts. "He had a rep as a good, solid cop. The men liked him. He did the job. I told myself he'd just snapped that day, just lost his grip for a minute. But I kept seeing the way he looked when he hit that woman, and I knew he'd gotten off on it. And I knew if I hadn't been there, he'd have done worse. So I reported the incident to the lieutenant."

"Would that be Lieutenant Masterson?"

"Yeah."

"There's no mention of an incident such as you described on Holloway's record."

"Because the lieutenant ordered me to forget it. Holloway had been defending himself against a violently hysterical woman. Bottom line, he brushed it off, and a few weeks later I was transferred. I was ticked off enough to do a little digging. In the six-month period before I transferred, three 911 calls were logged in from Holloway's house. Domestic dispute. Officers responded. No charges filed, and the reports were buried."

"They closed ranks," Diana murmured.

"Yeah. And Holloway moved up them, beating on his wife whenever he felt the urge."

"You'll testify to the incident you were witness to?"

"If I have to. It doesn't change the fact that she whacked him. You're going to go for diminished capacity, and this doesn't add that much to the medical records that she was abused continually over the course of years."

"It speaks to the character of the man, the despair of the woman and the complicity of the police. She'd called for help, and no one helped. She did what she could to survive. There was no one else to take her part."

"You have. Laura has."

"Yes, and now you have. Why?"

"Because maybe it'll make a difference, and I'd

stopped thinking I could make one. And because it's important to Laura."

"And she's important to you."

"She...matters," he said, after a moment. "If you need to go over this again, I'll be available. I've got some things to do."

"I appreciate you coming in." She offered her hand. "I very much appreciate it."

She watched him go out, and knew the instant the door across the hall opened. "Well?" Caine demanded.

"He just gave me some weight to add to the Holloway defense." She looked at Caine. "And he's in love with Laura. She's in love with him."

"Diana, she's just... She's only a..." He leaned against the door.

Understanding perfectly, Diana crossed the hall and cupped Caine's face in her hands. "She'll still be ours. Nothing changes that."

"I know. I know." He let out a windy sigh. "Trust Laura to pick a guy who'd like nothing better than to kick my ass from here to Canada."

She laughed, kissed him. "And that, Counselor, is one of the reasons you like him."

Chapter 10

Two days before Christmas, Laura rushed up the steps to Cameron Security. As usual, Royce's secretary was away from her desk. Laura all but danced to the door of the inner office, and knocked briskly.

"Got a minute, Mr. Cameron?" She poked her head in, saw him on the phone. He gave her a come-ahead curl of his finger.

"If you're sure this time, I can start right after the first of the year. No," he said firmly, then again, with a hint of exasperation, "No, Mr. MacGregor, I can't do that. I appreciate— No," he said again, and rubbed at the headache brewing behind his eyes. "I understand, thanks. Yes. Merry Christmas."

"It had to be my grandfather," Laura said when Royce slapped the receiver back on the hook. "Of all the Mr. MacGregors, he's most likely to cause that reaction."

"He's finally decided on the system he wants. At least he's decided, again, for the moment. I think the man wants to keep me on a string for the rest of my life." He looked over, saw her beaming smile. "What are you so happy about?"

"Oh, a number of things. We really turned a corner on the trial today, Royce. Your testimony yesterday made an enormous difference."

"Good."

"I know it wasn't a happy day for you, but it helped. And I'm hearing rumors that IAD and the district attorney's office are going to investigate Masterson. Amanda Holloway is going to get justice." She leaned over the desk and kissed him. "Thank you."

"I didn't do anything to speak of. I thought you'd be on your way to Hyannis."

"I'm just on my way home to pick up my bags. I wish you'd change your mind and come with me. You know you're welcome." She lifted a brow. "And I know Grandpa has been nagging you for weeks to come up for the holidays."

"I appreciate it, but I can't. Besides, I'm not a family-gathering type. Christmas is for kids and families."

She shook her head. "You didn't even put up a tree."

"You bought me that ugly little ceramic one."

"It's not ugly, it's tacky. That's entirely different." She wanted so much to ask him again, to find the right words to persuade him to spend Christmas with her, to be part of her life. But she'd resolved to make do and accept what she had. "I'll miss you."

"You'll be surrounded by people." He smiled a little as he stood up. "Hordes of MacGregors, even the thought of which unnerves me. You won't have time to miss me."

"I'll miss you anyway." She kissed him lightly. She pulled a brightly wrapped box out of her pocket, handed it to him.

"What's this?"

"A present. It's traditional. I want you to open it Christmas morning."

"Look, I don't have—"

"Royce, say thank-you."

Though he was as miserable as he'd been in his life, he made his lips curve. "Thank you."

"Now say Merry Christmas."

"Merry Christmas, Slim."

"I'll see you in a few days." She hurried out, telling herself it was the sentiment of the season that misted her eyes.

Royce sat where he was, continued to sit as the sun slanted lower through his small window, as the light dimmed and darkness fell.

He couldn't avoid it any longer, he thought. He couldn't keep denying what had happened to him, what had become of him. It had probably happened the first moment he saw her face, when she stood there wearing next to nothing and prepared to hold him off with a kitchen knife.

How could a man not love a woman like that?

But it didn't matter how he felt about her. Hadn't he already argued with himself for days about this single point? She didn't just come from a different world, she lived in one. She was the niece of a president, the granddaughter of a financial legend. An heiress, as her father—who hated the sight of him—had so acerbically pointed out.

Just in case he'd missed those facts, he had only to note that she wore diamond studs in her ears, lived in a house in the Back Bay filled with arts and antiques, and drove a spiffy car that would cost a year of his annual income. In a good year.

She was Harvard Law and he was community college, and he hadn't even finished that. It couldn't possibly work. He was deluding himself by even fantasizing about it.

But he'd discovered something in the past few weeks. He understood now what put that bedazzled look in Caine MacGregor's eyes when he spoke of his wife. He knew now what caused a man to fall so deeply in love it never ended.

It was finding the unique woman, and what knowing her could do to your heart.

Forget it, he ordered himself. Forget her and move on.

He turned back, telling himself he would lock up, go home. The office looked so empty, and his apartment would be even emptier. Why hadn't that ever bothered him before? He'd liked his lone-wolf status. He wanted to come and go as he pleased, when he pleased. Now even the thought of sleeping alone depressed him.

He rubbed his hands over his face and wondered when he'd become such a coward, so afraid to take a risk. He'd gone after her, hadn't he? He'd made the moves. And now he was going to let her go because he was afraid she wouldn't want him, couldn't want him, as much as he wanted her.

That was bull. He dropped his hands. He wasn't going to sit around brooding over his beer and feeling sorry for himself. He still had some moves to make.

He grabbed his coat on the way out.

Royce had been right about one thing. The house in Hyannis was crammed with MacGregors. And MacGregors made noise, and lots of it. Music blasted from the stereo in the parlor. In the music room down the long hall, Laura's youngest cousin, Amelia Blade, pounded out Christmas carols on the piano and added her strong, rich voice to Daniel's booming baritone.

From somewhere upstairs, male voices carried down. An argument in progress, Laura mused. It sounded like the oldest grandchild, Mac, and either D.C. or Duncan. Hardly mattered, she decided. Whoever was fighting would bicker the point to death, then find something else to wrangle over.

She walked into what the family affectionately called the throne room, in honor of the huge high-backed chair Daniel presided in during family events. There, before the wide windows that opened onto a view of the cliffs, the Christmas tree soared, fifteen feet of glossy pine, every bough and branch heavy with ornaments and twinkling with lights.

It would stay lit, day and night, until Epiphany.

Beneath it were mountains of gifts. At midnight, following family tradition, there would be a minor riot of ripping and laughing and love. Most of all love, she thought. No matter how they fought, no matter how much noise and confusion there was, this house was always filled with love.

And how she hated to think of Royce alone on Christmas Eve.

"I don't know how they do it," Caine said from behind her. He stepped up, laying his hands on her shoulders to rub. "Every year they manage to find the perfect tree. Ever since I was a boy, there's been a tree right there at Christmas. And it's always been the perfect tree."

"When we were little, before we were old enough to stay up to midnight, we always used to sneak down, huddle on the stairs and watch for Santa to come down the chimney over there." Laura leaned back against him. "I don't have a single bad memory in this house, and it's only occurred to me just lately how lucky I am. I love you so much." She turned into his arms, rested her head on his shoulder.

It was the catch in her voice that had him lifting her chin, and smoothing back her hair when he saw the tears swimming in her eyes. "What is it, baby? What's wrong?"

"Nothing. I'm feeling sloppy and sentimental. It's the season for it. I've decided I don't get sloppy and sentimental nearly often enough. You were the first man in my life, the first man to ever pick me up. And I wanted to tell you that you've never, not once, let me down."

"You're going to make me sloppy," Caine murmured, and gathered her close.

There was a thunder of footsteps behind them as a horde of people raced down the stairs. Shouts, threats, insults, laughter.

"Ian and Julia have instigated a snow battle." Laura gave her father a hard squeeze. "Another fine MacGregor tradition."

"Interested?"

"Yeah." She tipped her head back and grinned. "We can take them. Why don't you go issue the challenge, and I'll be out in a minute?"

"You're on." He kissed the tip of her nose. "You've never let me down, either, Laura. I'm proud of who you are."

"Good blood," she said with a smile. "Strong stock."

She smiled as he went out, raising his voice over the melee to challenge a former president of the United States to a snow war. Chuckling, Laura sat on the arm of her grandfather's chair. She'd go out and join in, but she wanted a moment to herself first.

She would make a wish on the tree, she thought, as she often had as a child. Now it would be a woman's wish, the hope that one day, on some snowy Christmas Eve, the man she loved would stand in this room with her.

"Laura."

Her head jerked around, and for one foolish moment she thought she was dreaming. Then her smile bloomed. "Royce! You changed your mind. That's wonderful." She rushed across the room to take his hand. "God, your hands are freezing. Where are your gloves? Here, let me take your coat, and you can warm up by the fire."

"I need to talk to you."

"Of course." She continued to smile, but her eyes went cool as she glanced beyond him. It was no less crowded in the hallway than it had been moments before, but it was dead silent. "My family," she began.

"I'm not going to be introduced to a half a million MacGregors, at least not until I've talked to you."

"Fair enough." She skimmed over several interested faces. "Beat it," she ordered. Without waiting to see if the order was obeyed or ignored, she closed the door and tugged Royce into the throne room. "Don't worry, you've already met a portion of them, and you'll sort the rest out over the next couple of days."

"I don't know if I'm staying."

"Oh, but—"

"You may not want me to when I'm finished."

Something skittered in her stomach, but she ignored it. "Well, at least take off your coat and let me get you a glass of Christmas cheer. Will brandy do you?"

"Sure, fine. Whatever." He stripped off his coat while she walked off to lift a decanter. "Some tree."

"Well, it's no ceramic tabletop, but it does the trick." She walked back, then tapped her glass against the one she gave him. "I'm glad you came."

"That remains to be seen."

She had a hunch she should sit, and without thinking, she chose Daniel's chair. It should have dwarfed her, Royce thought. Instead, she looked regal, a queen prepared to rule. But he'd be damned if she'd lop off his head without a fight.

"If something's on your mind," she said carefully, "you should just say it."

"Yeah, that's easy for you to say." He began to

pace, remembered he didn't care for brandy and set the snifter down. "I'm the one who had to drive up here, into enemy territory."

She had to laugh. "Enemy territory?"

"Your father hates me."

"Oh, Royce, he doesn't. He's just—"

"Doesn't matter." He waved her amused protest aside and kept pacing. "And why shouldn't he? I didn't go to Harvard, I don't own a house, I'm an ex-cop with a struggling business and I'm sleeping with his daughter. In his place, I'd have arranged for a quick, quiet murder."

"My father isn't a snob."

"He doesn't have to be. The facts are there, right there. That's reality. And even if you push all that aside, this wasn't the deal. It wasn't the deal."

"What deal?"

He shook his head, paced, stopped, stared at her. "I want to— I have to— I need a minute here." He walked to one of the windows. Outside on the rolling lawn, at least half a dozen people were pummeling each other with snowballs. "I don't know anything about this kind of family. It's not where I'm from."

"I'd say this family is unique by almost any standard."

"I'm not poor." He said it almost to himself. "The business is holding its own. I know what I'm doing." He turned away from the window, but he decided it was easier to keep moving. "I don't care about your money. It doesn't mean a damn to me if you've got five dollars or five million."

Now she was completely baffled. The words themselves were puzzling enough, but he looked miserable, angry and, though it seemed unlikely, nervous. "I never thought otherwise."

"Just so you know." He muttered to himself, then shook his head. "I can support myself. I've been doing it for most of my life. You're used to more, and that's not a problem for me. You should have what you're used to having."

"Good, I'm glad you think so, because I certainly intend to." She stood up. "Royce, I wish you'd get to the point."

"I'm working on it." His eyes heated, glinted dangerously. "I'm working up to it. You think this is a snap for me? I never planned on this. I never wanted this." He stalked up to her, fury bubbling in his eyes. "Get that clear, Slim. I never wanted this."

"Wanted what?"

"To not be able to go one lousy day without you inside my head. To start reaching for you at night when you're not even there. To need to hear your voice, just hear it. To be in love with you."

"In love with me?" she repeated, and sank slowly back into the chair. "You're in love with me."

"Now, you hear me out, all the way. I know you have feelings for me, or you wouldn't have let me touch you. Maybe it started out as just chemistry, but it's more. It's a hell of a lot more, and if you'd give it a chance—"

"Royce—"

"Damn it, Laura, you'll hear me out." He had to move away, pull back his control. He felt as though he were three stories up and toeing his way across a very thin and shaky wire. "We're good together, and

I know I can make you happy." He spun back. "Your grandfather's on my side here."

The warmth flowing through her heart was cut off in a snap. "That's the wrong button to push."

"I'm pushing it. He figures I'm good enough for you, so why shouldn't I think the same?"

"Good enough for me," she repeated, almost sputtering.

"That's right. I've got a strong back, I've got a good mind, and I don't cheat. And I love you, I love everything about you. And I'll even give learning to live with your family a shot. That should be enough for anyone."

He dug a hand into his pocket and came out with a small box. "Here," he said, and shoved it at her.

Laura reached for it, bobbled it, then holding her breath opened the lid. Her heart took another spin on the roller coaster he'd brought with him, this time shooting straight up and shouting for joy. The deep red ruby gleamed seductively against a circle of gold.

"I figured a diamond was too predictable for you," he muttered. "For us."

"Are you proposing to me, Royce?" She was pleased that her voice could sound so steady, so mild, when her heart was still somewhere in the stratosphere.

"It's a ring, isn't it?"

"Yes, it certainly is. And a lovely one." She lifted her gaze from it, stared into his eyes.

"What? It's not big enough?"

"Idiot. I'm waiting."

"You're waiting? *I'm* waiting."

She sighed. "All right, let's try this. I didn't plan

this, I didn't want this. It wasn't the deal. But I'm in love with you."

He'd opened his mouth, his arguments ready. "Huh?"

"Hear me out." Enjoying herself now, she sat back in the chair, laid one arm out. "You're an extraordinarily attractive man. You have your own business, and though apparently you occasionally undervalue yourself, you have a healthy ego, a good brain." She pressed her lips and nodded in a considering way. "And you come from strong stock. I believe—if we're going to use your idiotic turn of phrase—you're good enough for me."

"You're in love with me" was all he could manage.

She wondered if she would ever again, in the long life she planned for them, have him at such a disadvantage. "Yes, I am desperately in love with you, Royce. And I've been very brave and stoic, I'll have you know, accepting that you weren't in love with me. But since you are, it's different. And if you had the sense to ask me to marry you instead of shoving a box in my hand, I'd say yes."

He was still staring at her, but his brain was clearing. And his heart...his heart was lost. "I had really good arguments planned to talk you into it."

"Do you want me to hear them now?"

"No." He took another breath. "I'm not getting down on my knees."

"I should hope not." She got up, handed him the box. "Try again."

It wasn't hard to say it, he realized, when your heart was full of the words. "I love you, Laura." He touched her hair at the temple, kept his eyes on hers. "I love you. I want a life with you, a family with you. I want to spend the next sixty Christmas mornings with you. Will you marry me?"

"Oh, that was really good." For the first time, her vision blurred. "I want my ring, and I want you to kiss me. Then it'll be perfect."

"Say yes first."

"Yes, absolutely yes." She leaped into his arms, found his mouth with hers. It was more than perfect. "I'm so glad I found you. So glad I found you when I wasn't even looking for you. I wished for you." She let the first tear fall as he slipped the ring on her finger. "I wished for you just a little while ago. And here you are."

"Here we are," he murmured. The front door crashed, someone shouted as footsteps thudded down the hall. "Surrounded."

"They're going to love you." She laughed, lifted a hand to his cheek. "I do. And you do have the MacGregor on your side." Her eyes danced as she leaned into him. "Let's go tell him. Ordinarily I'd want him to suffer awhile, but it's Christmas. He'd just love the gift of being right."

From the Private Memoirs
of
Daniel Duncan MacGregor

A man's family is his most prized possession. It is also his most solemn responsibility. I never shirk my responsibilities, and I tend well all that is mine.

I've seen my first granddaughter married. What a beautiful bride she was, glowing, luminous in her long white gown, with the veil worn by her grandmother over her shining dark hair.

Such a picture did our Laura make that I had to hold my Anna close and soothe her. The woman gets emotional at such times.

It was, for me, a moment of great joy and private satisfaction. Oh, I watched my son Caine beam—the proud papa—as he escorted Laura down the aisle to the man who would be her husband. The man *I* personally selected. But we'll just keep quiet about that.

Children tend to become surly at what they mistakenly see as meddling. Tending is what it is, and make no mistake.

And on that perfect spring day, I stood and watched Caine grin, chuckled to myself as he exchanged manly backslaps with his new son-in-law, even dashed a stray tear from my own eye when Ian, as brother of the bride, made a toast to the new bride and groom.

Oh, a happy day it was for the Clan MacGregor.

My work there is done. Laura and Royce will be happy, and they'd best be seeing about giving their grandmother new babies to bounce on her knee. Anna is already fretting for a great-grandchild.

Now I can turn my attention to my sweet Gwen. Pretty as a princess is my Gwen, with a strong spine, a serious nature and a romantic heart. And a brain? God love her, the child is bright as the sun. Still, she's like her grandmother and doesn't see that she needs a man beside her, children to bring her joy.

So it's up to me to see that she has the right man, a man of substance. I've already picked him out for her. Good solid stock. He has a good mind, a fine heart. I'd settle for nothing less for Gwen—and be damned if I'd let her settle for any man who didn't measure up.

This will take a bit of time, but I've time yet. A man who's lived as long as I knows all about choosing his moments. I can be patient. I'll take a few months to lay the groundwork. I'm a man who appreciates the importance of a good, strong foundation, when you intend to build something that will last.

I'll wager my Gwen will be planning her own wedding by Christmastime. And I won't ask for any thanks there either. No, no thanks will be necessary. I look after my own.

But I wouldn't have to if they'd look after themselves.

Part Two

Gwendolyn

Chapter 11

"On three. One, two, three." Gwen and the emergency room team lifted the two-hundred-pound man from gurney to table. Well trained, they moved in synch, almost a blur of motion as she called out orders.

"Intubate him, Miss Clipper." Gwen knew the fourth-year medical student was eager and had good hands. But she watched those hands in training as they worked, while the head trauma nurse cut away the bloody, tattered jeans of the unconscious man.

She watched, and assessed the patient, storing his vital signs in her mind, relaying orders to the others, while her own hands worked swiftly. "Motorcycles," she muttered. "Hello, death."

"At least he was wearing a helmet." Audrey Clipper let out a short breath as the tube slid in. "Intubated."

"He should have been wearing body armor. Let's get blood gases, toxicology. Smells like he'd been partying." Gwen adjusted her protective goggles and went to work on the leg.

She had to work fast, but her hands and her mind were cold and steady. The gash on the left leg ran from ankle to knee, exposing bone. And the bone had snapped clean. It was her job to piece the patient back together and get him up to surgery. Quickly, efficiently. And alive.

From the next room, a woman continued to scream and sob, calling out for Johnny over and over in a voice pitched to shatter eardrums.

"This Johnny?" Gwen asked, flicking a glance through the glass that separated the two treatment rooms.

"John Petreski, age twenty-two," one of the orderlies informed her.

"Okay, we'll make sure he can dance at his next birthday. Lynn, call up to OR, tell them what we've got coming up. Fyne, take over here while I check on the screamer in room two."

She swung out through the connecting doors, stripping off gown and gloves. "Status," she snapped out while she yanked on fresh protective gear.

"Contusions, lacerations. We're waiting for pictures. Dislocated shoulder." The resident had to pitch his voice over the woman's hysterical screams.

"What's her name?"

"Tina Bell."

"Tina." Gwen leaned over until her face dominated the hysterical woman's vision. "Tina, you have to calm down. You have to let us help you."

"Johnny. Johnny's dead."

"No, he's not." She didn't wince when the young woman grabbed her hand and squeezed, bone against bone. But she wanted to. "He's going up to surgery. We're taking care of him."

"He's hurt, he's hurt real bad."

"He's hurt, and we're going to take care of him. You have to help me out here, Tina. How much had he been drinking?"

"Just a couple beers." Tears leaked out of Tina's eyes, to mix with street grime and sweat. "Johnny!"

"Just a couple? We need to know so we can treat him properly."

"Maybe six or seven, I don't know. Who was counting?"

Gwen didn't bother to sigh. "Drugs? Come on, Tina."

"We shared a couple of joints. Just a couple. Johnny!"

Through the glass panel of the door, Branson Maguire watched what he thought of as a ballet. Motion, teamwork, costumes and lights. And the strongest light, he decided, was on the delicate blonde in the incredibly ugly pea green scrubs and clear plastic gown.

He couldn't see her eyes. The wide protective goggles covered them, and half her face, as well. Still, he knew what she looked like, Dr. Gwendolyn Blade, heiress, prodigy, daughter of a part-Comanche gambler and another prodigy heiress. A MacGregor.

He'd seen Gwen's picture in newspapers, in tabloids, on television, during her uncle's years of campaigning and the eight years he'd lived in the most important house in the country. He'd seen her photograph, crammed with other faces on the massive desk of her grandfather, Daniel MacGregor, builder of empires.

Though Branson considered himself to be a keen observer, he hadn't expected her to be so...slight, he decided. She looked as though she should be wearing gossamer and granting wishes, not encased in a blood-smeared tent and fighting to save lives.

She moved like a dancer, he mused. Her gestures filled with personal grace, effort and efficiency. Her hair, somewhere between red and gold under the bright lights, was gamine-short, with spiky bangs across the forehead. For style, he wondered, or practicality?

It would be interesting to find out.

He stood where he was, hands comfortably in the pockets of stone-gray chinos, and watched her, watched everything. It was one of his finest skills, this watching. And he didn't mind waiting for whatever happened next.

Gwen noticed him—the face behind the glass. Dark blond hair that fell to the collar of a navy crewneck sweater. Cool gray eyes that rarely seemed to blink, an unsmiling mouth.

He made a statement just by existing, but she didn't have time to wonder, or to give him more than a passing thought.

But when she had both her patients stabilized, through the door, and on their way to treatment, he was still there. She had to pull up short when he blocked her way.

"Dr. Blade? Gwendolyn Blade."

He smiled now, just a quick, crooked lift of lips. And she saw she'd been wrong. The eyes weren't cool, but smoky-warm, like his voice.

"Yes, can I help you?"

"That's the idea. I'm Branson Maguire."

She took the hand he offered automatically, had hers squeezed and held. "Yes?"

"Ouch." His grin was both charming and self-deprecating. "There goes my ego. I guess you don't have a lot of time to read."

She was tired, and wanted five minutes to sit down and fuel up with coffee. And she wanted her hand back. "I'm sorry, Mr. Maguire, I don't—" Even as she tugged her hand free, she placed the name. "Oh, yes, Detective Matt Scully, Boston PD. I have read your books. You've created an interesting character."

"Scully's doing a good job for me."

"I'm sure he is. I don't have time to discuss popular fiction just now. So if you'll—"

"They're lavender."

"Excuse me?"

"Your eyes." His stayed steady and focused in what would have been a rude stare in another man. In him it merely appeared a natural state. "I'd wondered if it was just a trick of the light. But they're not blue, they're lavender."

Prickles of irritation scraped at the back of her neck. "It says blue on my driver's license. Now, as I said, I'm a little pressed for time."

"Isn't your shift over at two? It's nearly three."

The temperature dropped as she drew back—an automatic defense for a woman who, due to family, had lived most of her life in the spotlight. "Why would you know my schedule?"

Not just ice, he thought, impressed. Sharp, jagged ice. This pixie could grow fangs. "Ah, I take it you weren't expecting me?"

"No, should I have been?" She glanced back as Tina was wheeled out.

"Doctor. Doctor. I want to see Johnny. I have to see Johnny."

"Excuse me." She turned her back on Branson and walked over.

All he heard was the tone, the way that frosty voice immediately warmed and soothed. The young woman on the gurney subsided into muffled sobs and nodded.

"Nice bedside manner, Doc," Branson commented when she approached him again.

"You were saying I should have been expecting you this morning?"

"Your grandfather told me he'd set it up."

"Set it up?" And because she was tired, she closed her eyes. "I need coffee," she muttered. "Come with me."

With a swing of her lab coat, she turned and marched down the hallway. She bore left, shoved through a door and into the lounge. Branson looked everywhere, noting, filing in his mind the dull colors, the cheap chairs, the stingy lockers, the noisily humming refrigerator, the smell of stale coffee that didn't quite mask the underlying stench of hospital.

"Cozy."

"Do you want coffee?"

"Sure. Black."

She took a pot from the warmer, filled two insulated cups. And, because she knew just what the filth disguised as coffee tasted like, added a heap of sugar to her own.

Branson sampled the cup she gave him and shuddered. "Good thing I'm in a hospital. You pump stomachs, right?"

"It's one of my greatest joys. I need to sit down." She did so, crossed her legs and tried to wiggle her toes inside her flat, practical shoes. "Look, Mr. Maguire."

"Bran."

"Look," she repeated, "I'm sorry you were misled. My grandfather is...well, he is what he is."

"He's the most incredible man I've ever met."

She had to smile at that, and it warmed her eyes as he sat on the threadbare sofa beside her. "Yes, he's an incredible man. He is also set in his ways, in his methods, and in his goals. I'm sure you're very nice, and as I said, I enjoy your work. But I'm just not interested."

"Uh-huh." He risked another swallow of coffee. "In what, exactly?"

"In being set up." She skimmed long, slender and unpainted fingertips through her hair. "Grandpa doesn't think I give enough attention to my social life, but I give it the attention I believe it warrants. Dating just isn't very high on my list right now."

"Oh?" Intrigued, Branson lifted a brow and settled back comfortably in the corner of the couch. The shadows under her eyes nearly matched the fascinating color of the irises, and made her seem as delicate and appealing as spun glass. "Why?"

"Because I'm a second-year surgical resident and

I have other priorities. And because,'' she added with a snap, ''I don't choose to date men my grandfather has hand-selected for me. And you don't look like the type who needs a ninety-one-year-old man to set you up with women.''

''Maybe that was a compliment,'' Branson said after a moment. ''I think that was a compliment, so thanks.'' Then he grinned, a lightning flash of humor that had a dimple winking at the corner of his mouth. ''I wasn't planning to ask you out, but now I'm going to have to. Just to soothe my ego.''

''You weren't—'' She drew in a breath, struggled to adjust. Her brain was starting to shut down, she realized. The double shift was catching up with her. ''What are you doing here?''

''Research.'' He smiled again, charmingly. ''At least that's the plan. I'm starting a book—I need some hospital and medical data, some background, some atmosphere. Color and buzzwords and rhythm, that kind of thing. Daniel said you'd help me out, let me hang around for a couple weeks, play things off you, annoy you with questions.''

''I see.'' She let her head rest against the back of the couch, let her eyes close. ''Well, this is embarrassing.''

''I think it's great. So, how about it? You want to go out with me, get some decent coffee, have sex, get married, have three kids, buy a big house and an ugly dog?''

She opened one eye and nearly smiled again. ''No, thanks.''

''Okay, you don't want the coffee. I'm flexible. But

I still want sex before we get married. I'm firm on that."

She did smile, let out a weary sigh. "Are you trying to make me feel better, or more ridiculous?"

"Either way." He set the coffee down. The caffeine kick just wasn't worth the loss of stomach lining. "You're beautiful, Gwendolyn. I'm telling you that so if I end up hitting on you, you won't think it's because I'm trying to score points with the old man."

Her smile remained in place, but sharpened like a scalpel. "Men who try to hit on me often end up requiring medical treatment. I'm telling you that in case you need to renew your insurance."

He puffed out his cheeks. "Okay. How about the research assistance? I observe in the ER a few weeks, keep out of everybody's hair. I ask questions when it's convenient for you and the staff. I run certain angles I hope to use for the story by you. You're free to shoot them down, to suggest how they can be adjusted to ring true."

She wanted a pillow, a blanket and a nice, dark room. "You're free to observe. Even if I objected, you could go over my head—which you already, in essence, have. My grandparents have a lot of influence with the administration of the hospital."

"If you don't want to cooperate, I can go to another hospital. There are plenty of them in Boston."

"I'm being rude. I'm tired." She lifted her hands to rub at her temples and struggled to adjust her mood. It wasn't his fault he'd caught her at the end of a particularly hideous day. "I don't have a problem giving you a hand with your research—as long as you don't get in my way or anyone else's in the ER. I'll answer your questions when I have time, and instruct the staff on my shifts to cooperate with you—when they have the time."

"I appreciate it. And if, after we're done, I ask you out to dinner or buy you a small, tasteful gift to show that appreciation, are you going to hurt me?"

"I'll try to restrain myself. I'm on the graveyard shift for the next three weeks."

"No problem. I like the night. You're exhausted," he murmured, surprised by the urge to tug her down so that she could rest her head in his lap and sleep. "Why don't I give you a lift home?"

"I have my car."

He angled his head. "How many people have you patched up who've fallen asleep behind the wheel?"

"Good point. I'll sleep here."

"Suit yourself." He rose, looked down at her. Her eyes were heavy, nearly closed. The delicate shadows beneath them seemed to deepen as he watched. "Try for eight straight, Doc. I'll be back tomorrow."

He started for the door, paused, turned back. "One last point—I have full coverage on my medical insurance."

He stepped into the hall, noting that for tonight, at least, the ER was quiet at 3:00 a.m. He headed out, filing away the position of the admitting desk, the number of computers, the sound his own sneakers made on the tiles of the floor.

The November wind slapped hard at his face when he stepped outside. His hair blew into his eyes as he jingled keys out of his pocket.

One other point, Dr. Dish, he mused. A man would

have to be an idiot not to hit on you. And Meg Maguire's son Branson was no idiot.

He climbed into his classic Triumph convertible, the seat already adjusted to accommodate his long legs as best it could. He turned the key, smiled at the purr. He was a man who loved a well-tuned engine.

And for all her resemblance to a fairy princess, Branson had already decided Gwendolyn Blade was a well-tuned engine.

He flipped on the CD player, hummed along with Verdi. And, driving away, he began to plot in a way that would have made Daniel MacGregor proud.

Chapter 12

It was after ten in the morning when Gwen unlocked the door to the house in the Back Bay. A thin, icy rain was falling, making her hurry inside to shiver in the warmth.

She didn't bother to call out. She knew her cousin Julia would be out, wheeling some real estate deal. And her third housemate, Laura MacGregor, had moved out months before, when she married Royce Cameron.

Gwen still missed her. The three cousins had roomed together for years and had all but grown up together before that. They'd been a threesome from college campus to apartments to the houses Julia had begun to acquire.

Knowing Laura was wildly happy was everything she wanted, but Gwen still caught herself glancing up those curving stairs off the foyer and expecting to see Laura come flying down them.

Gwen draped her coat over the newel post. She had the entire afternoon free, she realized, and there were dozens of things she could catch up on. Including a long, hot bubble bath. But that was going to be her second order of business, she decided. Food was first.

She headed back into the kitchen, rubbing at the ache she'd worked into her neck by spending four hours sleeping on the lounge sofa instead of getting into one of the cots.

She'd get one of the physical therapists to give her a neck-and-shoulder massage before she started her next shift.

She smelled the roses before she saw them. There must have been three dozen, pale as snow, long stems tucked into a gorgeous crystal vase, then spearing up to end in tightly curled buds.

One of Julia's men, she assumed, and indulged herself by sniffing, then sighing over the mass of blossoms. Her romantic heart had a weakness for roses, and for foolishly extravagant gestures.

She crossed to the refrigerator with little hope. Since Laura had moved out, the pickings were invariably slim. They'd often said Julia never ate, Laura always ate, and Gwen herself ate only when food was shoved in front of her.

Without much enthusiasm, she pulled out a carton of yogurt, checked the expiration date on the bottom. Well, what was a week when it came to curdled milk, anyway? she decided, and pried off the lid. She closed the door, then tugged the note attached to it down to read while she ate.

Gwen, hubba-hubba on the roses. What other secrets are you keeping from me? Will interrogate you later. Messages for you on the machine. Grandpa. Don't ask me. And some sexy voiced man named Bran. Flower guy? Hmm. Well, as a doctor you'd know bran's good for you. Back by six. Maybe. Jules.

Frowning, Gwen read the note again, then glanced back at the flowers. She stared at the little envelope tucked among the stems. She plucked it off the clear plastic holder, tapped it consideringly against her palm. Then, with a shrug, tore it open.

They looked like your style.
Thanks in advance for the help.

Bran

"Oh." She couldn't quite suppress the giddy little thrill as she looked at the roses. "Mine," she murmured and, leaning over, inhaled deeply. Then she caught herself, stepped back. Three dozen long-stemmed white roses in November was definitely an overstatement. A terrific one, but nonetheless...

She was going to have to be more direct in discouraging Branson Maguire. Grandpa, she mused, just what are you up to and what have you done?

She turned to the answering machine, punched for messages, and had to grin as Daniel's voice boomed out.

"Hate these damn things. Nobody talks to anybody, just rattles away to machines. Why aren't you girls ever home? Gwen, I've a young friend who needs a bit of help. He's a writer, spins a good tale. But then, he's an Irishman, so what would you expect? Does well murdering people right and left and tracking down mad killers. You'll give him a hand, darling, won't you? A favor to your old grandpa. He's a nice boy. His mama went to college with yours, so he's not some strange man off the street. Julia, I spoke with your father. He said you're buying another house. That's a lass. And would it hurt either of you to call your grandmother now and again? She worries."

Gwen chuckled, combed her fingers through her hair. A typical Daniel MacGregor message, she thought, delivered at full volume. But it seemed harmless enough. The son of a friend of her mother's. All right, then, there seemed to be no plot or scheme behind it. Just a favor, an easily granted one.

Satisfied, Gwen picked up her yogurt again, got out a spoon, then hit the button for Branson's message.

"Gwendolyn."

She paused, with the spoon nearly to her lips. There was something about the way the man said her name, she thought. Using the romantic whole of it, rather than the quick and easy Gwen.

"It's Branson Maguire. I hope you got some sleep. And I hope you like white roses. I was thinking, if you had the time to spare, I'd appreciate an hour, anytime today. I'd offer to buy you lunch or dinner, but I don't want to put your back up again. I'd just like to run a couple things by you—plotwise. If you can manage it, give me a call. I'm planning on being in all day. If not, I'll see you tonight."

She didn't bother to note down the number. She'd remember. Thoughtfully, she spooned up yogurt. It was a reasonable request, she supposed. There'd been nothing really flirtatious in the content or the tone. Laughing at herself, she scooped up another spoonful. Just listen to yourself, analyzing every nuance. It was exactly the attitude that had caused her such embarrassment the night before.

The man was a professional, and so was she. She could certainly give him an hour—if for no other reason than to secretly apologize to him, and to her grandfather, for being so suspicious.

She picked up the phone, punched in his number. He answered on the third ring. "Maguire."

"Hello, it's Gwen Blade. Thank you for the roses, they're lovely."

"Good. Did they work?"

"Work?"

"Did they soften you up enough for you to give me an hour?"

"No. But the message I got from my grandfather did. I didn't realize our mothers went to college together."

"A couple semesters, I'm told. Mine went on to interior design, and yours, apparently, went on to a variety of things. My mother says that Serena MacGregor was interested in everything."

"And still is. I can meet you at two. Downtown would be best. I've got some shopping to take care of."

Two, Branson mused. After lunch, before dinner. Clever woman. "Two's fine. How about meeting me at the Boston Harbor Hotel? They serve a pretty great tea."

"Yes, I know." She looked down at the yogurt, thought of rich, creamy pastries. Her neglected stomach growled. "Fine. Two o'clock, in the main lobby."

Gwen was exactly on time, a habit her cousin Julia called her most irritating. She'd taken that long, hot bubble bath, which had done wonders for the stiffness in her neck. And had paged through a paperback copy of *Die a Fine Death* by Branson Maguire. She'd read it before, but she'd wanted to familiarize herself more with his style of writing before the meeting.

She would have given precisely the same review and thought with a patient's history before treatment, or an acquaintance's personality before buying a gift. She was a thorough and meticulous woman, one who had graduated from medical school years before the norm and was now the youngest surgical resident to ever serve on the staff of Boston Memorial.

She'd worked for it, and she knew she'd earned it. There was no discounting the advantages she'd grown up with. Her family was loving, supportive, generous. They had backed her in every decision she made along the way. She also understood that wealth, the kind the MacGregors could claim, smoothed many bumps in many roads.

But it was the love of medicine, the mystery, the art, the science, of it that had sealed her destiny.

She wandered through the hotel lobby, appreciating the grandeur, the grace of the ornate coffered ceiling, the huge urns filled with towering and exotic flowers, the marble and the gilt.

And she looked, Branson thought as he stepped off the elevator and saw her, like a rich man's college-age daughter come to town. She'd changed into a tailored gray jacket and slacks, and she had a black overcoat draped across her arm. Minimum and classic jewelry, he observed. Heirloom-quality locket-style lapel pin, small, scallops of gold at her ears, slim watch with black leather band.

She also looked alert, refreshed, and not nearly as fragile as she had the night before.

"You're prompt," he said as he walked to her.

"Yes, an annoying habit of mine."

"I like prompt women." He took her arm and turned her toward the elevators. "Wasting time should be saved for when it can be most enjoyed." He used a small key to access a floor, then turned to smile at her as the doors slid shut. "You look great. Got some rest, I'd say."

He was wearing a soft navy sweatshirt, arms shoved up to the elbows, over dark jeans. His high-top sneakers appeared to have seen many a mile. "Thank you, yes. Where are we going?"

"Up to my suite."

Her eyes deepened, her lids lowered. "Oh?"

He had to laugh. "Gwendolyn, you really shouldn't be so trusting and naive. People will take advantage. Relax," he added before she could speak. "I've ordered tea. We'll sit in the parlor. It's very conventional, and it's more convenient for me to take notes and avoid interruptions from hovering waiters. No hidden agenda."

"All right, since I happen to be very hungry. I thought you lived in Boston."

"I do." He took her arm again, to lead her off the elevator. "I live here. The press figures it's an eccentricity, the writer living in a hotel. What it really is is a high-class apartment building, with daily maid service, room service, and a really quick turnover of tenants. You've got a great smile. Why are you finally giving it to me?"

"My parents essentially lived in a hotel until after Mac, my oldest brother, was born. And they often still do. Both of my brothers live in hotels, year-round, and my younger sister, Amelia, would if she could get away with it. I don't consider the choice the least eccentric."

"Right, I'd forgotten. Casinos. Vegas, Atlantic City, New Orleans, Europe. Your family's cost me some money—indirectly."

"There's nothing we enjoy more." She waited for him to unlock one of a pair of wide double doors, then walked into the spacious and smartly appointed parlor. She noted the sleek little laptop, with full-size monitor attached, on the end of the walnut dining room table. There were stacks of books, papers, coffee cups.

"I'd say this would be a very quiet and convenient place to work."

"It does the job for now. Occasionally I get a low-grade itch to buy a house, mow a lawn, paint some shutters. It usually passes, but I expect it's going to stick one of these days."

"If it does, you should call my cousin Julia. She's an expert on real estate."

"Ah, the First Jule."

Gwen angled her head. "Yes, the press dubbed her that when Uncle Alan was president. She thought it was amusing. Even at seven, Julia had a well-developed sense of the ridiculous."

"Would have been a kick growing up in the White House. Let's see, her brother D.C.'s an artist. Then there's the lawyer cousins. One of them just had a big, splashy wedding last spring."

"That's right. Are we here to discuss my family or your book?"

"Just making small talk." Prickly, he thought. Protective. "Daniel likes to brag. I've heard enough about his kids and grandkids that I feel as though I know them. He's very proud of you."

"I know." Gwen's eyes softened again. "I tend to be defensive about my family. Another habit."

"An attractive one. That'll be food and drink," he said when the bell sounded. "Just make yourself at home."

She decided the most efficient place to sit was at the dining room table, at the opposite end from his workstation.

She smiled at the room-service waiter, listened to Branson joke with him, argue good-naturedly over some football game, then watched a folded bill slide discreetly from Branson's palm to the waiter's.

"How the guy can live in this great city and be a Dallas Cowboy fan is beyond my understanding." Branson lifted a bottle from an ice bucket. "Champagne?"

"No."

"Just covering the bases." He screwed it back into the tub of ice. "We'll put it back for another time. Dig in." He swept a hand over the plates of sandwiches, scones, pastries. "You said you were hungry."

"And you said you wanted to discuss your book with me." She picked up the teapot, poured two cups.

"Yeah, okay, so what I've got," he began as he sat and piled something of everything on a plate, "is a psychopathic doctor."

"Lovely."

"She is. Just a stunner."

"She?"

"Yeah. I figure you don't see enough good female psychopaths today. What I want to do is a kind of play on Jekyll and Hyde, with a twist of black widow and Lizzie Borden." He took a bite of a lady-size tea sandwich. "You're really perfect."

"Am I?"

"Absolutely. You've got the looks—not just the beauty, I mean the air of fragility, the delicate bones. The grace and the efficiency. I'd been thinking of making her tall, lush and deadly," he continued, his eyes slate-colored, narrow and intense on Gwen's face, "but now I realize the contrast is better. Much. I couldn't ask for a better prototype."

She decided to be amused, rather than insulted. "For a psychopath?"

"Yeah." He grinned, and his eyes went from cool to warm smoke. "Do you mind?"

"I think I'm oddly flattered. So your villain is a doctor, a woman, who heals with one hand and kills with the other."

"There you go. You're quick." He slid forward a bit in his chair, his fingers tapping idly on the edge of his plate. "She's absolutely in control, knows exactly what she's doing. She enjoys it. The power of healing, the thrill of destroying. Of course, she's insane, but that's a different level. So if I made her a surgeon, what would her life be like? She'd be older than you. I don't want to complicate it by having her be a genius on top of everything else."

"I'm not a genius. I'm just a good student."

"Gwendolyn, you're in med school at Harvard years before you're old enough to drink in most states, you're a genius. Live with it." He reached for another sandwich as she blinked at him. "So, how much pressure is she going to have to deal with as a female surgeon? That's still primarily male territory, right? The boys' club. Then there's the God complex, that arrogance and ego that comes from having your hands inside the human body."

"Arrogance and ego?"

"You've got them. I could see it when I watched you work on those kids yesterday. You snap out an order, it never occurs to you that it won't be obeyed—immediately obeyed." He saw it in his head again, a perfectly cued loop of film. "You stride from one room to the next, and people come to attention. You don't notice, because you're used to it. You expect it. I want that for her, that expectation of absolute respect and obedience, that confidence in herself. While on the other hand she's boiling with rage and frustration. You have much rage and frustration, Gwendolyn?"

Good Lord, he moved fast. "Now, or in general?"

He beamed at her. "I really like your voice. High-class, frosty sex. Anyway, what I'm after is the female take on what you have to do to get ahead in the field. How you handle both the subtle and overt sexual harassments and advances on the job. See, I figure she moonlights mutilating men because she finds them inferior, irritating, obstructive and obnoxious."

Her smile bloomed again, coolly amused. "I'm beginning to like her."

"Good, I want you to. I want the reader to, even while they cringe." He piled more food on her plate as he spoke. "She's bright, she's ambitious, she's unapologetic. A couple of the guys she takes out in the beginning are slime, so that makes her more sympathetic. Then she gets into it, gets to enjoy it a little too much. That's when she'll turn the corner. And the demands, the pressure, the stress of constant life-and-death issues and decisions—I figure that'll be what finally snaps the connection she has on her humanity."

Gwen decided it was more productive to be amused and intrigued than to be annoyed. She selected a watercress sandwich from the hodgepodge he'd served her. "Well, the pressure is outrageous. A number of good doctors wash out simply because they can't handle hospital work, the vicious hours, the miserable bureaucracy. Emergencies, budget cuts, interrupted personal lives. She won't have much time for play unless she's very flexible. I'm assuming she's on staff at a major Boston hospital."

"Right." He pulled a notebook over and began to scribble. "How many hours would she put in a week?"

"Oh, forty to a million."

He smiled at her, put a gorgeous, glossy chocolate éclair on her plate where the sandwich had been. "Keep going."

The hour had run to ninety minutes before she remembered to look at her watch. "I'm running behind. I have to go, if I'm going to finish my Christmas shopping before my shift."

"Finish? It's November."

"I'm an obsessive overachiever." She rose, got her coat.

"Listen, I'll go with you."

"Shopping?"

He was up, helping her into her coat, before she could do it for herself. And if he took the opportunity to sniff her hair, roll his eyes in approval over the top of her head, she didn't know the difference. "I have excellent gift-buying taste. And I can pick your brain some more while we're at it. Then I can run over to the hospital with you."

"Another obsessive overachiever."

"There you are. I love my work." He grabbed his coat, took Gwen's arm again. "You know, I was thinking of having her fall for Scully. They could have some pretty great sex, complicate their lives, break each other's hearts."

He paused, took a moment to study Gwen's face, to enjoy it. "So, do you think he's her type?"

Gwen cocked her head. She knew a line when she heard one, however cleverly it was delivered. "Rough, tough and cynical, with an affection for poetry? He might suit her...and she'll undoubtedly enjoy trying to kill him."

"That's what I thought." He slipped his hand down to hers, linked their fingers and pulled her out the door.

Chapter 13

"So when am I going to meet him?"

Because she was cutting wrapping paper with a surgeon's precision, Gwen didn't glance up. "Who?"

Julia picked up a silver bow from the color-coordinated piles Gwen had stacked on the dining room table. "The guy who's good for you." She briefly considered hauling out some of her own gifts and getting to work on them. But it was only the Sunday after Thanksgiving. And she was feeling lazy.

"Good for me." Gwen laid the shirt box on the paper, neatly folded the edge of the wrap under, then brought the sides up to overlap exactly one inch.

"Flower guy." Julia yawned, and sipped her coffee.

"Branson?" After applying the tape, Gwen began to fold the first end. "You want to meet him?"

"Well, you've been seeing him for nearly three weeks and I haven't even gotten a peek."

"I'm not seeing him." Gwen turned the box around to deal with the other end. "I'm just helping him with some research."

Julia sat back in her chair. She adored Gwen, her innate tidiness of habit and mind, her generosity of self, her quiet humor, her unshakable loyalty—and her amazing lack of self-awareness. "He's very attractive."

"Hmm."

"That wasn't a question. I've seen his photo on the back of his books, caught a couple of his interviews on the morning shows. He's *very* attractive."

"I wasn't going to disagree." After a brief debate, Gwen decided on the red ribbon and began to calculate the proper length.

"So, you're not interested in him on a personal, man-woman type level?"

"I haven't thought about it."

"Gwen."

With an impatient sigh, Gwen set the ribbon aside. "I'm not interested in being interested. And you're beginning to sound just like the MacGregor."

Julia grinned, dark eyes dancing. "Is that a compliment or an insult?"

"You know very well Grandpa'd like nothing better than to see all of us married and raising a dozen children. He thought he was sly at Thanksgiving dinner, all those questions about what boys we might be seeing. Boys!" She rolled her eyes, then gave up and laughed. "He'll never change."

"Who'd want him to? He was a little more specific with you. 'Ah, Gwennie love, how are you getting on with my young writer friend? A fine boy that Branson, clever brain. And the Irish know the value of family.'''

Gwen shook her head and neatly tied the ribbon over the box. "He's obviously fond of Branson."

"He set you up."

"No, that was my first reaction, but I realized I'd misjudged the situation. It's harmless."

Julia opened her mouth, then closed it with a snap. "Okay, if that's the way you want to look at it. You ask me, he'd have pinned you to the wall over it, if Laura and Royce hadn't announced they were expecting. Then he was too busy wiping his eyes, making toasts, slapping Royce on the back and beaming to remember his plots."

Gwen picked up a huge red bow and sighed. "We're going to be aunties. Laura looked so happy, didn't she?"

"Yeah." Feeling a bit misty herself, Julia sniffled. "And a year ago, she was telling herself—and us—that she wasn't the least bit interested in a relationship. Just like you're telling me you're not right now."

"For heaven's sake—"

"Door." Julia bounced up, grinning. "Finish off that patient, Doc. I'll get it."

Doesn't have a clue what's going on, Julia decided as she made her way through the house. The woman could cut open and sew up people from morning to night, list every bone in the body in alphabetical order, diagnose a multitude of diseases, conditions and traumas, but she didn't know when she was becoming involved in a relationship.

Julia opened the door and saw the other half of that relationship holding a glossy white bakery box.

"Doughnuts or Danishes?" she demanded.

"Both."

"Well, come right on in."

Branson stepped inside, studying with interest the curvy woman with wild red hair, eyes the color of rich chocolate and skin as pure and smooth as top cream. She was wearing a thick chenille robe in dizzying stripes, and fuzzy bunny slippers.

"Branson Maguire, nice to meet you." Julia smiled and held out a hand that glittered with rings. "I recognized you."

"Julia MacGregor, nice to meet you." Branson took the long, narrow hand in his. "I recognized you."

"Isn't that fun? I like you already. Any man who shows up at the door at eleven o'clock on a Sunday morning with baked goods instantly becomes my friend."

"How do you feel about Bavarian cream with chocolate frosting?"

"My *best* friend. Gimme." She snatched the box out of his hand. "Take off your coat, stay awhile. I think I can find some coffee to go with these."

"That was the plan. I thought if Dr. Dish was—" He broke off, grimaced. "Oops. Little slip."

"Dr. Dish?" Julia's eyes danced with delight. "I like it. And since you brought me a few million calories, it can be our little secret."

"I'd appreciate it." He laid his coat over the newel post. "Is she around, or do we get to eat all of those ourselves?"

"She's operating in the dining room. This way."

"Great house," he commented as they started down the hall.

"It's my favorite. That's why we live here."

"That's right. You like to buy houses."

"Buy, sell, rehab, restore. You like to tell stories."

"Mmm." They moved through a room with cozy sofas, a small stone fireplace. A large flute-edged bowl in bleeding blues and greens caught his eye, had him stopping to take a closer look.

"My mother's work."

"Fabulous. She'll have an interesting place in history, won't she? Both as a brilliant artist and a dynamic First Lady."

"I really like you."

"I did a report on your father when I was in high school." He flashed a smile. "I aced it."

"Former president Alan MacGregor always had a strong stand on education. He'll be very pleased." And because she was, too, Julia took Branson's hand and led him into the dining room.

"Look who's come bearing gifts," she announced.

Gwen's head came up. The scissors she had in her hand snapped closed. "Oh." The little lurch in her stomach surprised her, as did the quick urge to fuss with her hair. "Hello, Branson."

"He brought us pastries, so I've decided I'm in love with him. I'll get some coffee, put these on a plate. Don't let him get away, Gwen. I think I might want to keep him." Julia winked at Branson and carried the box out into the kitchen.

"Actually, I think I might be in love with your

cousin, too." Without waiting for the invitation, he pulled out a chair and sat beside Gwen.

"Well, that was quick."

Was there a faint edge of irritation in her voice? Branson wondered. Hoped. "Don't you believe in love at first sight, Doc?"

"No." That was a lie. She believed in all manner of foolish things, when it came to the heart. "Why did you bring us pastries?"

"You don't eat unless someone supplies it." Idly he picked up a blue bow, studied it. "And it's my small way of thanking you for the time you've been giving me."

"It's very nice." When he set the bow down in the pile of gold, she automatically removed it and set it in its proper place. "And unnecessary. It hasn't been any trouble."

His lips twitched. Deliberately now, he picked up a red bow. "Trouble or not, it's your time, and you've been a lot of help." He set red on green.

"Is the book going well?" She shifted the bow.

"Well enough." He grinned when Julia came back in with a tray holding a coffeepot, cups and a dish piled with his pastries. He signaled her by a wiggle of brows, then moved silver ribbon onto the red. "That looks great."

Julia tucked her tongue in her cheek as her cousin meticulously realigned ribbon. "You're telling me. I hope you don't mind, but I've already culled out my share to take upstairs. I've got a few calls to make. Drop by anytime, Bran. Bring chocolate."

She gave him a thumbs-up sign behind Gwen's back and sailed out.

"So can I give you a hand with your wrapping?"

"No, I have a system."

"No kidding." He poured the coffee himself and put a glossy cruller on a plate. "Have some sugar."

"I will. Just a second." Her focus was on exact alignment as she folded down the corners of the paper.

"How was your Thanksgiving?"

"Noisy, confusing, greedy. Wonderful. Yours?"

"Pretty much the same." He watched her thumb slide over the paper, form an edge as straight and sharp as a razor. And found her intense concentration to detail utterly adorable. "I'm sorry about this, Gwendolyn, but it just has to be done."

He put a hand on the back of her head, angled it, and brought his mouth to hers. She didn't jerk, barely stiffened, but he felt her surprise. Deciding to use that to his advantage, he brought his other hand to the edge of her cheek and slid it around her ear into the soft, short gold of her hair.

She tasted fresh, he thought, like the first warm breeze in early spring. He'd wondered, spent three weeks wondering, and he had to ask himself why he'd waited so long, when she was just so...perfect.

He coaxed her lips apart, slipped inside. The sound that hummed in his throat was pure approval.

This had to stop, she told herself. Immediately. Oh, God, she felt dizzy, hot, helpless. Her blood pressure must be... Her pulse had to... Then his teeth scraped gently over her bottom lip and she didn't think at all.

"Sweet," he murmured, losing himself. "Sweet, gorgeous Gwendolyn." His hand slipped down so that his fingers could stroke over the back of her neck, make her shiver. "What have we got here?"

"Wait." She put a hand to his chest, surprised that his heart beat as fast as hers, when he'd seemed so much in control. "Just wait."

"I don't want to." Branson deepened the kiss before either of them could prepare for it.

He wanted to pull her down into his lap, move his lips from hers to her throat, from throat to shoulder, and keep working his way down until he got to her toes.

"I said wait." She broke free, fought for breath, for composure, for rationality. "We have an arrangement."

"Are you involved with someone else?"

"No, that's not the point."

He only lifted his brows. "Do you have a problem with mystery writers of Irish extraction?"

She raked a hand up through her hair, causing it to spike like a sunflower. "Don't be ridiculous."

"Do you consider kissing an unhealthy habit?"

Suspicious, she slanted a look over at him. "You're making fun of me."

"Maybe of both of us. And since I'll take that for a no, I'll confess I think kissing you could become a habit." He lifted a fingertip to trace her mouth while his cool gray eyes skimmed over her face. "I'm developing a thing for you."

"A thing?"

"I haven't figured out the definition yet. But I'm working on it. Or maybe I should call it a condition. You'd relate to that." His fingers trailed down to trace her jaw. "Maybe you'd help me explore it, study it."

His eyes met hers, curiosity gleamed in them. "You're nervous," he realized with a jolt of surprise and pleasure. "I would have sworn you didn't have a nerve in your body, with the things I've watched you do these past weeks. You never flinch, you never hesitate, you never sag. But you're nervous right now, because I'm touching you. And that, Gwendolyn, is incredibly arousing."

"That's enough." Abruptly she pushed back her chair, sprang to her feet. "Just stop it. I'm not nervous. I just don't want to pursue this."

"Now you're lying." He chuckled when her eyes went dark with temper. "That's ticked you off, and I can't blame you. But the fact is, when a woman melts in my arms the way you did, a claim of indifference just doesn't ring true."

"I didn't claim indifference," Gwen said coldly, and made him laugh.

"No, you're right, you didn't. My mistake." He took her hand, ignoring her tugs for freedom. The mouth that had so recently seduced her smiled arrogantly. "Don't worry, I'm not going to kiss you again until…well, until."

"Branson, I'm busy."

"Gwendolyn, I'm persistent. And I want you. It can't be the first time you've heard that."

It was the first time she'd heard it delivered with a cocky grin and an overabundance of confidence. She hated the fact that the combination excited her. "If you want me to continue helping you, you're going to have to understand and acknowledge the conditions and restrictions."

"No, I don't. I don't like conditions and restrictions."

"You arrogant, insufferable—"

"Guilty. You're afraid I'm going to seduce you," he declared. "Because we both know now that I can. We'll just hold off on that a bit."

If her voice had been frosty before, it now dipped to subzero. "If you think I'm a pushover, an easy mark, you couldn't be more mistaken."

"I don't think anything of the kind. I think you're incredibly strong, even valiant. I'm amazed by you every day. You're selling yourself short if you think the only reason I want you is because you have beautiful eyes and a wonderful body."

"I—" She lifted her hands, let them fall. "You've succeeded in confusing me."

"That's a start. Why don't I let you think it over for a while, since that's what you're going to do anyway? I'll see you at the hospital later."

She let herself relax again, nodded. "Yes, all right."

He caught her face in his hands, pressed a firm, brief kiss to her mouth. "I guess that will have to hold me until then," he told her, and strolled out.

Chapter 14

She was back on the day shift the first week in December. Over the years, Gwen had learned to adjust her body clock as her schedule demanded. When it was time to sleep, she slept, and slept deeply. When it was time to wake, she woke, and woke quickly.

Since she decided to follow her grandmother into medicine, into surgery, she'd allowed nothing to distract her. Family and work were the focus of her life. Everything else was incidental.

Including men.

Including, she told herself firmly, Branson Maguire.

He'd been conspicuously absent for three days. She'd decided that he'd gathered enough information and atmosphere that her help was no longer necessary. And she'd concluded that her lack of encouragement for a personal involvement had finally penetrated his undoubtedly hard head.

She was determined not to be disappointed by that fact.

Carefully she continued suturing a three-inch gash on the calf of a patient who had had a nasty meeting with a tree.

"I was really moving down the hill," he told her, looking anywhere but at the sterile field and the needle. "Just thought I'd take the sled for a test run before my kids hogged it." He winced at the tug on his flesh. "Guess I'm a little old for sledding."

"You've just got to watch out for those trees jumping in the way."

When the door opened and Branson walked in, her stomach shimmied. She completed the next suture without a tremor. "You're not allowed in here," she said mildly.

"I won't get in your way." He walked over to look down at the wound. "Ouch," he said with a sympathetic smile.

"You're telling me. Bled like a son of a bitch."

"Hold still, Mr. Renekee. We're nearly done here."

"Sorry. Say, you look familiar," he said to Branson, seizing on the distraction.

"People are always saying that to me." He pulled up a metal folding chair and sat companionably. "So, how'd you end up having the prettiest surgeon in Boston sew you up?"

"Ah..." Renekee glanced at Gwen, noted she remained focused on him. "It was me, a Flexible Flyer and a tree. The tree won."

"It's a great day for sledding. And if you had to lose to a tree, you couldn't do better than Dr. Blade.

Tell me, since you've gotten to know her a little bit, what do you think I have to do to get her to have dinner with me tonight?"

"Well, I..."

"Branson, go away." She didn't blush, but embarrassment was a hot little ball in her stomach.

"Just a nice, quiet dinner," he continued. "She forgets to eat, so I'm just thinking about her health."

"That could work," Renekee decided, enjoying himself. "You know, a doctor, proper nutrition, that sort of thing."

"Exactly. Wine—in moderation, of course. Candlelight—restful on the eyes. A relaxing meal after a long day. It's all a matter of taking care of yourself."

"Don't make me call security, Branson. Mr. Renekee, I'm going to dress this now. You'll want to keep it dry. I'll give you a list of instructions, and you need to come back in a week to ten days to have the sutures removed."

"She's got great hands, doesn't she?" Branson commented. "I tell you, if I needed stitches, I wouldn't have anyone else touch me. You know, I was thinking of this French place—they do some really impressive flaming desserts. Do you think Dr. Blade would go for that?"

"My wife sure would."

"And I'm sure she's a very discerning woman. How about it, Doc?"

"You're done here, Mr. Renekee." Gwen shoved back in her chair, wheeling it over to a table and selecting a printout of instructions for caring for sutures. "I'd stay off Flexible Flyers for a while."

"Yeah, thanks." He took the sheet, smiled at her.

"You ought to give him a break," he told her, and walked out.

"I am not having you distract me or my patients while I'm working." Incensed and working her way toward being outraged, Gwen stripped off gloves and gown. "You are not to enter treatment or examining rooms unless you require treatment or examination. And you will most certainly not hit on me while I'm on duty."

He couldn't have stopped the grin if he wanted to. Her voice was all New England frost. "Is it any wonder I can't get you out of my head?"

She made a strangled sound and tossed her gloves away. "Do you require treatment or examination?"

"Darling, if you want to play doctor—" He stopped himself this time. After all, there were a lot of sharp implements close at hand. "Okay, bad joke. I've been working around the clock for the past couple of days. When I came up for air, you were the first thing that came to mind. I figure there's a reason for that, and I'd like to take you to dinner."

"I have plans."

"Flexible or inflexible?"

"An inflexible hospital fund-raiser."

"I'll go with you."

"I have an escort."

"An escort." He didn't know whether to chuckle over the term or snarl over the idea of her going out with another man. "Sounds tedious."

"Greg is a friend, an associate, and a very charming man." Who she could admit privately defined the term *tedium*. "Now, if you'll excuse me I have work."

"How about breakfast?"

She had to close her eyes. "Branson."

"Do you really think I'm going to give up because some guy named Greg is escorting you to a hospital fund-raiser?"

She tried a new tack, giving him a slow, challenging smile. "Perhaps I intend to have breakfast with Greg."

There was a little flare of something directly under his heart, quickly banked. "Now you're trying to make me mad. Okay, forget breakfast. When's your break?"

"Why?"

"We can run over to my hotel, have a quick bout of hot sex, and I can get it out of my system. You're driving me crazy."

She surprised them both by laughing. "Take two Prozac, call me in the morning, and go away." She started for the door.

"Did you mean the call-you-in-the-morning part?"

She shot a glance over her shoulder, and let the door swing in his face.

All right, Gwendolyn, Branson thought as he rocked back on his heels. He was just going to have to start playing dirty, pull out the big guns. And he knew just where to find the big guns.

A light, wet snow was falling in Hyannis Port. It coated the grand old trees that graced the sloping lawn of the castle the MacGregor had built.

Branson loved the house, with its gleaming stone, its elegant windows and its fanciful turrets. He'd often wondered how he could work it into a book. What murder or mayhem would bring the world-weary Scully to such a place? he mused. Or, as it was for his creator, would it be a woman that drew him here?

A woman, Branson admitted, who was definitely under his skin, on his mind, and beginning to sneak into his heart.

He'd always figured if he fell for a woman, it would come in an explosion of recognition, of certainty, of passion, lust and madness. But this was a nagging tug, a gentle pull that was drawing him slowly along from basic attraction and into unexplored territory.

A mystery, he thought as he climbed the steps to the great front door, with the prideful crest of the MacGregors. He couldn't resist a mystery, needed to pick it apart, layer by layer, until he found the core.

If he was indeed falling for Gwen, he needed to be sure, to compile the facts, as well as the emotions. And, damn it, he needed a little cooperation.

It didn't surprise him that Anna answered herself, or that she looked lovely and trim. Her dark eyes warmed with pleasure, her fine hands reached out for him. "Branson, how wonderful. Daniel will be just delighted."

"I was hoping he wasn't here, so that I could convince you to leave him and run off with me to Barcelona."

She laughed and kissed his cheek.

"Get your hands off my wife, you Irish dog." His grin fierce and deadly, Daniel MacGregor, wide of build and huge of voice, descended the grand stairs. "Barcelona, is it? You think I'm deaf, as well as blind? Coming around flirting with my wife right under my nose.''

''Caught. Well, you're a better man than I, MacGregor, to have caught and held such a woman all these years.''

''Ha!'' Pleased, Daniel caught Branson in a bear hug, with an energy, Branson managed to think as the wind rushed out of him, that belied more than ninety years of living. ''That silver tongue of yours saved you again. Come in and sit, we'll have us a drink.''

''Tea,'' Anna said firmly, angling her head at her husband.

He rolled his bright blue eyes. ''Anna, the boy's driven from Boston on a cold, snowy day. He'll want whiskey.''

''He'll get tea, and so will you. Go into the parlor, Branson. I'll be right along.''

''I tell you, a man can't get a whiskey in this house anymore until the sun sets, and then he's lucky if he gets more than two fingers, with that woman around.'' He had his arm around Branson's shoulders, propelling him into the parlor, with its roaring fire, gleaming antiques and art-filled walls.

''Tea will do me,'' Branson told him. ''I want both our heads clear for the matter I've come to discuss.''

''The day a glass of whiskey clouds my brain—or that of a good Irishman—is a dark day in the world.'' Daniel sat, stretched out his long legs, stroked his soft white beard. ''A matter to discuss, you say?''

It was the gleam in the twinkling blue eyes that clinched it. ''You know, it took me a while to realize that Gwendolyn was right with her first instincts.''

''Gwen?'' All innocence, Daniel folded his big

hands. "Ah, that's right, she's been helping you a bit with your story. And how is that going?"

"The help, or the story?"

"Whichever. Both."

"The story's going very well, and she's been a tremendous help so far."

"Good, good. A bright girl, my Gwennie, diamond-bright. Takes after her grandmother—a woman you seem to have more than a decent affection for."

"You old meddler," Branson murmured. "'Go by the hospital, lad. Gwen's just the one you need.'"

Daniel smiled broadly. He'd never thought Branson Maguire slow. If he had, Daniel would never have picked him for his granddaughter. "And wasn't she?"

Branson sat back. "And what do you think she'd have to say to your scheme? Do you think she'd thank you for dumping me at her feet?"

"I'd say that depended on you."

"What have you done, Daniel?" Anna wheeled the tea tray in herself, shooting her husband an exasperated look.

"Nothing. I've done nothing at all."

"He's matched me up with your granddaughter," Branson told her, rising to see to the tray himself. "Gwendolyn."

"Daniel." Anna lifted her chin. "Didn't we discuss this type of thing? Didn't we agree that you would not interfere in the children's lives?"

"It's not interfering to see that Gwen is introduced to a fine young man like Branson here. It's interest, it's..."

"Meddling," Branson finished, and poured tea for Anna. "And I appreciate it."

"It's not meddling to—" Daniel broke off, and his eyes went shrewd. "There, you see. He appreciates it. And why shouldn't he? A beautiful girl like our Gwen. Smart, tidy, loving, good bloodline."

"You needn't list her virtues," Branson said dryly, and poured a cup for Daniel. "And I hope you'll resist listing whatever you consider mine to her and messing this up before I've got it started."

"Got it started." Daniel thumped a fist on the arm of his chair. "You've had the best part of a month already. You're dragging your feet."

"Daniel." Patience, Anna warned herself. Surely after a lifetime with the man she had accumulated a mountain range of patience. "Leave him alone."

"If I leave him alone, it'll be the next century before he comes up to the mark."

"That's why I'm here."

"See." Daniel thumped his fist again, this time in triumph. Then he frowned. "What do you mean?"

"Your granddaughter isn't cooperating."

"Cooperating." Daniel rolled his eyes. "Well, why aren't you charming her, romancing her? Do you need it written down, boy, what a man needs to do to court a woman?"

Branson shifted in his chair. "*Courting* is, perhaps, the wrong term."

"Oh, is it?" Those blue eyes became sharp, deadly. "And just what is the term you had in mind when it comes to my granddaughter?"

"I don't have one, exactly." Branson held up a hand for peace. "I'm very attracted to her, I'm very interested in her.'' What the hell, he thought, he was among friends. ''I'm halfway in love with her.''

''What's wrong with the other half?''

This time Anna only laughed. ''Oh, he is never satisfied.''

''Well, what the devil good is halfway about anything?''

''It's far enough for me, until I see if she's even going to catch up. I've gone a long time without having my heart broken,'' Branson told Daniel. ''And I'm hoping to keep it that way. My point is, you haven't gotten to where you are without being an expert at the art of a deal, without being able to read people, judge their strengths and weaknesses. And I know you love your family. So, you had to consider the pros and cons before you decided I'd suit Gwendolyn.''

''There's a smart lad, Anna. Is it any wonder I'm so fond of him?''

''Don't get too excited,'' Branson warned. ''*I* haven't decided if we'll suit yet. But,'' he added before Daniel could explode, ''I want very much to explore the possibility. Since you've known Gwendolyn—''

''He calls her Gwendolyn,'' Daniel said, misting up a little. ''See how he calls her by her full name, Anna, the romance in it?''

''Hush, Daniel,'' Anna murmured, because indeed she had.

''You've known her all her life,'' Branson continued. ''I've only had a few weeks. So how about a little insider information, some pointers?''

"She respects honesty," Anna said, with a telling look from man to man.

"I'm not planning on being dishonest." A dimple winked charmingly as Branson smiled. "I'm planning on taking advantage of a situation already in place."

"The girl needs to be swept off her feet," Daniel claimed. "She was always one for fairy tales."

"She needs to stand on her own feet," Anna corrected. "Gwen prides herself on her strength and independence."

"She needs moonlight and roses and wooing."

"She needs integrity, partnership and respect."

Branson blew out a breath. "Well, this is all very helpful." Then he shook his head in confusion as both Anna and Daniel burst into laughter. "Did I miss the joke?"

"You weren't a gleam in your father's eye, nor your father a gleam in his father's," Daniel said, reaching for Anna's hand. "So you've missed it right enough. I told you Gwen took after her grandmother, and so she does. The things we've said Gwen needs are what she needs. Just as lovely Anna Whitfield demanded them sixty years ago from a clumsy Scotsman who fell madly in love the minute he saw her in a rose-colored dress at the Donahues' summer ball."

"And though it took quite a bit of work," she murmured, "I managed to get them all from him. And more. Just be yourself, Branson, and let her be what she is. That's how you start."

Gwen, profoundly grateful that she'd insisted on taking her own car, pulled into her drive at midnight.

If she had ever, in the whole of her life, spent a more boring evening, she'd have to have been comatose.

She didn't object to hospital functions, she didn't object to Greg. But the combination of the two of them in one endless evening had been a study in tedium.

And if his hand found its way up her leg under the table one more time, the surgeon would have required surgery.

She imagined Branson would have made pithy, whispered comments about the pompous speeches. And have made her struggle not to laugh and lose dignity.

He'd have had plenty to say about the lukewarm and rubbery chicken Kiev she'd pretended to eat.

And they'd probably have danced, rather than discussed laser surgery for ninety minutes before she finally made her excuses and escaped.

Why was she thinking about Branson? She shook herself, climbed out of the car. She hadn't wanted to be with him, either. What she'd really wanted was to be home, curled up in front of the fire with a nice brandy and a good book. Since it was too late for that, she'd settle for a warm bed and oblivion.

She was almost at the door before she saw the little potted tree sitting on the stoop in the porch light. Baffled, she crouched down, stared at the little stuffed bird attached to a branch from which golden silk pears dripped.

Since the attached card carried her name, she tugged it free and ripped it open.

Consider this the first day of Christmas.

Bran

He'd sent her a partridge in a pear tree, Gwen thought, and, pressing the card to her breast, sighed hugely. How incredibly sweet. She skimmed her finger over one of the glossy pears and set it swinging, smiled foolishly at the colorful, plump bird.

And realized, with a suddenness that had her sitting down hard beside the silly little tree, that she was in deep and serious trouble.

Chapter 15

Gwen walked out of OR three rubbing cramps out of her fingers. The surgery had been long and complicated, but she'd been pleased to be allowed to assist. She'd spent the past ten hours on her feet, and figured if she was lucky she could clock out shortly and leave the hospital on a high note.

She saw Branson waiting in the corridor and decided the odds of that high note had just improved.

"They told me you were up here, sewing some guy back together."

"Assisting," she corrected. "But sewing him back together's close. Thirty-six-year-old man who was very, very careless with a chain saw."

"Ouch."

"I think he's going to keep his arm." She rolled her neck as she pushed the button for the elevator. "Dr. Merit is the best in the state. I don't know anyone else who could have done what he did in there. The massive blood loss and trauma, the muscle and nerve damage. And the patient wasn't the best candidate for a long surgery—a good hundred pounds overweight. But he could very well be swinging a chain saw to cut down his Christmas tree next December."

"Did you get yours yet?"

"Our tree?" She stepped out into the ER, relieved that it seemed to be quiet. "This weekend." She took a quick look at the board, saw she wasn't needed. "I'm going to grab some coffee."

"You're off shift, aren't you?"

"In ten minutes." She swung into the lounge, headed straight for the pot. "I didn't think you'd be by today."

"I had a few things to deal with." He pulled a box out of his pocket. "Here's one of them."

With the pot in her hand, Gwen stared at the pretty silver box and bow. "Branson, you have to stop this."

"Why?"

"You can't keep giving me presents."

"Why?" He grinned at her. "You liked the others, and I've got a theme going here."

The pear tree, she thought, the lovely little brooch of two turtledoves, the silly trio of china hens, and four ridiculous chirping plastic windup birds. She adored all of them. "When your theme hits nine dancing ladies, you're going to be in trouble."

"I've got plans for that. Come on, open it up."

He took the pot from her, handed her the box, then poured two cups himself. She was charmed, and they both knew it. He heard her helpless little sigh as she took off the lid and saw the long chain with five rings intricately braided into it.

"How do you manage this?"

"Patience, determination. Persistence." He set the cups down. "Here, let me put it on for you." He took the necklace out and draped it over her head, where it glowed against her dull green scrubs. "Quite a fashion statement."

She ran a hand down the chain. "I shouldn't take it."

"Of course you should. You want it."

"Of course I want it," she said with a hint of exasperation. "It's lovely and it's charming."

It made no sense. They barely knew each other. She'd given him no encouragement. He simply wasn't the next step she'd planned for her life. "Why are you doing this?" she demanded.

"Because I've still got that thing for you." He leaned down, brushed his lips to hers, adoring that mix of confusion and annoyance in her eyes. "And it seems to be spreading. Why don't you change into something a little less intimidating, and we'll go out?" He slid his arms around her waist. "Try that candlelight dinner this time."

"I'm not dressed for dinner."

"You look wonderful. Lovely. Perfect." He could feel her hesitate, soften, sway toward surrender. "I want to be with you, Gwendolyn. I want to make love with you. I can't remember wanting anything quite so much, and there are a great many things I've wanted."

She felt herself sliding into the kiss, into him, before she could stop herself. "I've barely had time to catch my breath since you walked into my life."

"Don't catch it," he said, suddenly, fiercely, impatient. "Let it go. And come with me." His mouth demanded now, possessed, severing any thought of protest. The thrill whipped through her as he dragged her into the heat, under the dark. "For God's sake, Gwendolyn, let me touch you."

"I want—" She had her hands on his face, threaded her fingers through his dark blond hair, fisted them. "I want you. I'm not being coy or playing games." She eased back so that she could meet his eyes. It was vital to her to be honest, and to be logical. "I haven't wanted anyone else enough to let them touch me."

It took a moment for his head to separate itself from the storm rising in his body. A moment to cool the mind and understand what she was telling him.

Untouched. Innocent. She was the fairy princess after all.

Instinctively he gentled his hold. "You can't possibly know how much that means. I don't want to hurt you."

"I'm not afraid of that." She stepped back, pushed a hand through her hair. "I'm a doctor, I—" Her eyes narrowed when he chuckled. "What are you laughing at?"

"Some matters may have to do with the anatomy, Dr. Dish, but nothing at all to do with medicine."

"Doctor *what?*"

"You heard me." Lord, but it was a pleasure in itself to shock her. "And believe me, you won't be thinking like a doctor when I make love with you."

"I haven't said you will yet," she told him evenly. The cocksure grin and all-male ego irritated her enough to have her regain some balance. "And if you continue to find my lack of experience in this particular area so amusing—"

"I don't find your lack of experience in this area amusing at all. I find it erotic. Unspeakably erotic. And I'd like to exchange the dinner for a late supper. Very late. I want to spend a great deal of time giving you—" he reached out, closed his hand over the chain and tugged her closer "—all manner of experiences in this particular area."

"I haven't decided," she began, and felt a gush of relief as her beeper sounded. "Excuse me." She stepped back, angled the beeper she wore on her hip so that she could read the code. Turning, she pushed through the doors and hunted up the chief resident on duty.

"Good, Blade, I saw you hadn't clocked out. We've got a drive-by. Gunshot wounds, chest and abdomen. Twelve-year-old male. ETA two minutes."

Branson watched her transform in front of his eyes from an aroused and irritated woman to cold and sturdy steel. She moved fast, heading for the heavy double doors even as the sound of sirens punched through the quiet.

The paramedics hustled the boy in on a gurney, with Gwen rushing beside them, filing away the shouted information on vital signs and treatment that they snapped out at her. She yanked on gloves and gown while a nurse strapped goggles over her eyes. In seconds her hands were covered in blood.

The kid wore a Bruins' line jacket, Branson noted,

black high-tops. A man and woman rushed into the room behind the gurney, both of them crying, both of them shouting demands, pleas, questions.

"You can't be in here," Gwen snapped out as she slid the endotracheal tube into place. "We have to help him now. Wallace," she ordered, jerking her head at an orderly. "Get me six units of O-neg, stat. He needs whole blood."

"He'll be all right. Won't he be all right?" The woman fought against the orderly on the way to the door. "He was just walking home from a friend's. He was just walking home. My baby. Scotty."

The smell of grief and terror hung in the air, overriding even the blood.

"Scotty's in good hands now," Wallace said as he urged the parents away from the door. "Dr. Blade's the best. You have to let her do her job."

Her hands moved quickly, her mind remained cold. A stream of blood shot out, striking her across the breasts. "We've got a pumper. Clamp."

"BP's dropping. I'm losing the pulse."

She ordered IVs, tests, a type and crossmatch on the victim's blood. Her words punched the air even as her hands fought to heal. But in her mind, in the cold, clear logic of it, she already knew it was useless.

"Irrigate this, I can't see what the hell— I found the exit wound. Somebody get out and push for the pictures. I want to know how many bullets went into this boy. Come on, Scotty, come on, stay with me."

She fought for him, sweat sliding down her back unnoticed. Her eyes were fierce and warrior-bright. Sometimes, she knew, death could be beaten. Or, if not beaten, cheated.

So much damage in such a small body. But she didn't allow herself to think of that, only to focus on each step, each need, each answer.

Time sped by with gowned staff rushing in and out of the doors.

When he coded, she never broke rhythm. "Let's zap him. Now!" She snatched the pediatric paddles, waited for the tone. "Clear." His body jerked, but his heart didn't respond. "Again. Come on, damn it, come on." With the second shock, the monitor registered the beat.

"Slow sinus rhythm."

"Get him a bolus of epi. That's the way." It was only the two of them now in her mind, just the two of them challenging the inevitable. "Just a little longer. Is OR ready for him?"

"Standing by."

"BP dropping. No pulse."

She swore now and hitched herself onto the table to straddle him. "Bag him. Hurry up," she ordered as she began CPR. "We're losing him."

His hair was glossy black curls, he had the face of a sleeping angel. Gwen ordered herself not to notice, not to think, just to act. "I need another two units of blood. Get it in him. Let's go, move, let's get him upstairs."

They shoved the gurney through the doors with Gwen still atop it, working the boy's chest. Even as the parents rushed up, tried to cling to the gurney, she never took her eyes off the boy's face.

The last glimpse Branson had was of the fierce determination in her eyes before the elevator doors closed.

* * *

And when they opened more than two hours later, he saw her eyes again, and the boy's death in them.

"Gwendolyn—"

She only shook her head. She walked past him to the lobby desk. Very deliberately, she picked up her charts, completed her notations and clocked out. She said nothing, simply walked into the lounge and to her locker.

"I'm sorry," Branson said from behind her.

"It happens. He was gone when they brought him in. He was gone when the bullet cut into his heart." She pulled off her scrubs, took out a wool blazer. "You shouldn't have waited, Branson. I'm too tired to socialize tonight. I'm going home."

"I'll take you."

"I've got my car." She took out her coat, her purse.

"I'm not leaving you alone when you're churned up this way."

"I'm not churned up. This is hardly the first patient I've lost, or the last I will lose." She shrugged into her coat, found her gloves in the pocket where she had tucked them hours before. "We did everything we could. We used all of the skills available to us. That's all we can do." Her fingers were numb and stiff as she pushed open the door.

He waited until they were outside, until the light snow whirled around them and clung to her hair. "I'm driving you home."

"Leave me alone." She shoved his hand from her arm, rounded on him. The pressure in her chest was hideous, unbearable. "I'm perfectly capable of driv-

ing myself anywhere I want to go. I don't want you, I don't need you. I don't—''

Appalled at herself, she stopped, pressed her fingers to her eyes. "I'm sorry. I'm so sorry. No, please." She shook her head quickly before he could touch her again. "I need to walk."

He slipped his hands into his pockets. "Then we'll walk."

Chapter 16

The breeze was brisk, the snow a whirl of white flakes. In silence, they walked toward the river with the sound of traffic a steady whoosh. Streetlights gleamed, Christmas bulbs glowed. On the near corner, a streetside Santa rang his bell monotonously as pedestrians hustled by.

Christmas, Gwen thought, was a time for children's laughter, for family, for secrets and for joys. But to fate—if one believed in it—one day, one season, was the same as the next.

"You can't let it inside you," Gwen said at length. Her hands were so cold and so tired. She tucked them in her pockets instead of taking the effort to pull on her gloves. "If you do, you lose your edge, you start to doubt yourself, your instincts, your abilities. Then, the next time, the next patient, you're not focused. You can't let it in. I know that."

"But if you don't let any of it inside you, you lose your humanity, what makes you care enough to fight the next time, for the next patient."

"It's a difficult line," Gwen murmured in response. "No matter how straight you try to walk it, you end up teetering over one side or the other at any point." She stopped to look out over the water.

She loved this place, this city, with its insane traffic, its lovely old buildings, its graceful waterways. She loved its history and its pride. But just now she found no comfort in it. It was part of a world that could be cold and cruel to the defenseless.

"I didn't want to lose him. In my head I knew I would, the minute I saw how badly he was damaged. But sometimes you get a miracle. And sometimes you don't."

She closed her eyes, grateful that Branson said nothing, that he understood she needed to get it out. "I can take it. I can take the hours, the stress, the pressure. I wanted it. I trained for it. I can take the paperwork, the bureaucracy. The rude patients, the drug addicts and the self-abusers. I can take the wasted lives. You see so many of them, you almost stop noticing. And then, suddenly..."

Her voice shuddered, and she pressed her fingers to her eyes. "He was only twelve years old."

He spoke now, saying the only thing there was to say. "You did everything you could do."

"That doesn't seem to matter when it's not enough."

"You know better than that." He turned her to face him, could think of nothing but her as he watched a tear spill out of those soft lavender eyes. "How many lives did you save today, this week, this year?"

"I know when I see people in pain or distress that I can fix it, most of the time—I can fix it, or at least help."

"And you do," he said quietly. "Whatever it takes out of you, that's what you do."

"That's what I need to do. And I know that sometimes, no matter what you do, or how hard a team works, you'll lose. That's rational, that's real, and still part of me just can't accept it. I know that only this morning, that little boy got out of bed, ate his breakfast. Maybe he ran for the school bus and daydreamed in class. Then, because he walked down the wrong street at the wrong moment, his life is over. Everything he might have done won't be done."

She turned to walk again. "I had to call it," she continued. "He was my patient, and I had to call it. You have to decide to accept the moment when there's nothing else to be done. You look at the clock and note the time. Then it's over. I had to go out and tell his parents."

"Gwendolyn, what you do is courageous. It's miraculous." He took her hands, rubbing and warming them instinctively. "What you feel is courageous. And miraculous." He brought her hands to his lips. "It takes my breath away."

With a sigh, she let herself be gathered close, let her head rest on his chest. "I'm sorry I snapped at you before."

"Shh." He lowered his lips to her hair.

Here, she thought, was comfort. A man to lean on. Needing him, she lifted her head, found his mouth with hers and soothed herself. The warmth he gave back eased the ache, smoothed the raw edges.

"Branson." She tried to smile when he brushed tears from her cheeks with his thumbs. "If you want me, I'll come with you now."

His stomach muscles knotted tight. The hand on her cheek stilled, and with an effort, he made it slide down to stroke her shoulder. "Of course I want you. But I can't ask you to come with me now."

"But—" She closed her eyes when he pressed his lips to her brow.

"You inspire me to play by certain rules. You're shaky and you're vulnerable. It would be easy to convince myself I'd be comforting you, taking your mind off things."

"Wouldn't you be?"

"I'd also be taking advantage of the moment. I won't do that with you." Couldn't do that with her, he realized, because he wanted much more than just the moment with her.

"I don't understand you. I thought you'd prefer having the advantage."

"Not this way. Our first time together isn't going to happen because you're unhappy, or feeling grateful because I listened. When I touch you, when you let me, it won't have anything to do with anything but the two of us."

"If you're being careful because I haven't been with a man before..."

"I'm being careful because it's you. You matter, Gwendolyn." He touched his lips to hers again. "You very much matter. That's why I'm going to see that you have dinner, then I'm taking you home and, if necessary, I'll tuck you into bed myself to make sure you sleep."

Now she did smile. "I don't need to be taken care of, Branson."

"I know. That's what makes taking care of you so appealing. Tonight I'm not going to give you any choice in the matter. You're cold," he added, and slipped an arm around her shoulder before walking back toward the hospital.

"I appreciate the gesture, but I'm all right now. And I do have my own car, so—"

"You need to eat."

"I'm not hungry."

"You'll eat," he said simply, just as he caught sight of the little restaurant a half block from the hospital. "Right here is just what you need. Solid, simple, American food."

"The service is surly here, and the food quality spotty."

"Good. That'll add a bit of adventure into it." His hair glinted gold in the dark as he swung her toward the door. "Dr. Blade, I believe we're about to have our first date."

She looked up at him as he pulled open the heavy smoked-glass door. Scents and warmth rushed out over her. Foolishly garish Christmas balls dangled from the ceiling and cheered her. "All right. Why not?"

They were three deep at the bar, and voices were a flood of noise in the overheated room. She didn't hear what Branson said to the hostess, but she did see a folded bill pass from his hand to hers. And they were seated in the dining section, in a corner booth, in under ninety seconds.

"This isn't the kind of place where you bribe the maître d'," Gwen told him as she slid over the worn leather seat.

"Worked, didn't it?" His dimple winked. "You needed to sit down, and you needed to do it as far away from the meat market in there as possible."

"It's a popular singles spot," she said, and let her head rest against the high seat. "A lot of the hospital staff comes here to flirt or cruise for action." She laughed at his lifted brow. "And no, I don't come in often, because I rarely have the energy to flirt or cruise."

"It wouldn't hurt my feelings if you put a little effort into the first part of that tonight." He took Gwen's hand firmly in his and looked up as the waitress wandered over. "We'll order drinks and dinner now," he told her, and rattled off his choice of wine, appetizers and entrées while the waitress scrambled to pull out her pad.

"Medium rare on the steak," he repeated, "and we'll need a bottle of mineral water for the table. What did you say your name was?"

"Crystal," she muttered, brows knit, as she noted down his order.

"Crystal, we'd appreciate it if you'd snag a basket of rolls from the kitchen when you bring the drinks by. The lady's had a rough day, and she's tired. You'd know how long, rough days go."

He beamed at her, looking so sympathetic that Crystal's irritated scowl smoothed away. "I'll say I do. Sure, I'll take care of that for you."

Gwen waited until the waitress walked off, then drew in a breath. "Branson, did you just order for me without consulting me?"

"It won't become a habit," he said easily. "Your brain is tired and it's too overworked to be asked to make decisions. You need relaxation, red meat, and time to recharge. I'm providing them. And to show my heart's in the right place, next time we have dinner, you can order for me."

"Really?" She smiled blandly. "How do you feel about sweetbreads?"

He grimaced. "I could probably live my entire life happily without sampling internal organs."

"Remember that the next time you decide what I'm going to have for dinner."

"Deal. When's your next day off?"

"I've got a half day Saturday and all of Sunday."

"Will you go out with me Saturday night? You pick the when, you pick the where."

She arched a brow. "*The Marriage of Figaro* is playing at the Conservatory. How do you feel about opera?"

"I feel very warmly toward opera."

She blinked twice. "You do?"

"It's rewarding to surprise you occasionally." He smiled up at the waitress. "Thanks, Crystal." He took a roll out of the basket, broke it in two and buttered it before passing half to Gwen. "And I'm particularly fond of Mozart. I'll pick you up at seven. We'll have a late supper afterward, if that suits you."

"Yes, I suppose it would."

"Good. Then I'd like you to stay with me, let me make love with you. And I'd like you to sleep with me and have a very late, very indulgent breakfast in bed Sunday morning. If that suits you."

She swallowed bread, chased it with the sparkling water he'd poured into her glass. "Yes," she managed, "I suppose it would."

"Let me see," Julia demanded the moment Gwen stepped into the house. "Oh, I wish I could have gone shopping with you. Laura, Gwen's back and she's got shopping bags."

"Is Laura here?"

"Raiding the refrigerator. Of course." Julia grabbed a bag and hurried with it into the parlor. "She claims Royce dragged her out this morning to shop for baby things, and that she finally pleaded exhaustion."

"What did they buy?"

"Nothing yet. Apparently they just mooned. I'd love to have seen Royce mooning over bassinets."

"We whittled it down to three choices." Laura stepped in, scooping up spaghetti from a bowl. "But we're having a major style clash over cribs."

Gwen dropped onto a chair across from the heavily decorated Christmas tree, and curled up her legs. "You don't look the least exhausted," she said accusingly. If anything, she thought, her cousin radiated vitality and health. Laura's dark eyes shone, her golden skin glowed.

"I'm not, but he was making noises about scouting for electronics, and I escaped."

"Well, I'm exhausted." Gwen rubbed the bottom of one foot. Drawing in a deep, satisfied breath, she smelled pine and cinnamon and sizzling apple wood.

She smelled home. "Serves me right for waiting until the eleventh hour to look for a new dress. I didn't need a new dress."

"You certainly did, which I pointed out to you." Julia dived into the first bag. "A major date deserves a major dress."

"That's the wrong bag."

"Oh?" Julia tucked her tongue in her cheek as she separated tissue paper and drew out a lacy pink garter belt. "I'd say that depended on your point of view."

"I'm always running my panty hose," Gwen began. "I thought it would be more practical if I..." Then she laughed, shrugged. "All right, I wanted to knock his socks off."

"Believe me, when he gets a load of you in this, he's not going to be wearing socks, or anything else, for long." Julia slipped out the matching bra. A tiny white rosebud decorated its front hook. "Oh, honey, you'll destroy him."

Laura set her bowl down, sat on the arm of Gwen's chair. "He's the one?"

"I want him to be."

"Anyone who sends you seven crystal swans would be hard to resist."

"He'll be here in a couple hours," Julia began. "Why don't you hang around and get a load of him?"

"I would, but I have a hot date with my husband. Come on, Gwen, let's see the dress."

"All right, but remember, I spent four hours hunting it down, so be kind." She took the box out of the shopping bag and, rising, opened it to pull out a long velvet column in deep rose velvet.

"It's beautiful," Julia murmured.

"You don't think it's too much, with the jeweled band at the neck and cuffs?"

"I think it's perfect for you." Laura reached out to run her fingertips over the smooth material. "Classic, elegant."

"It's not terribly sexy. I tried to find something with a little more...less, I guess...but I kept coming back to this."

"It's plenty sexy," Julia disagreed. "High neck, long, snug sleeves, the drape to the ankles. He'll wonder just what's going on under it. Then, when he finds out... Well, you know CPR, so he'll probably live through it."

"Are you nervous?" Laura wanted to know.

"No." Gwen smiled, carefully folding the dress in the tissue again. "It's the right time, it's the right man—it's just right. Now I'm going to go up and indulge in an incredibly long bubble bath and spend twice as long as necessary on my makeup and hair." She gathered up her bags and left the room.

"Are you sure about this guy?" Laura asked Julia once Gwen had headed up the stairs.

"I'm telling you, he's cross-eyed over her. And he's the first man to ever put that foolish look on her face."

"Yeah, it is nice to see her look dreamy." Feeling lazy and content, Laura stretched her arms. "Where did the MacGregor find him?"

"Old family connection. Gwen doesn't think Grandpa pulled the strings."

With a laugh, Laura picked up her bowl again. "Foolish woman. He always pulls the strings." She cocked her head. "And you know, Jules, if she ends up in a serious relationship with this man Grandpa picked out for her, he's going to turn all his attention on you before much longer."

"I'm on to him." Julia smiled smugly, and for her own amusement picked up a windup Santa that looked strikingly like Daniel. With a few quick twists of the wrist, she had him ho-ho-hoing. "Forewarned, pal," she said to Santa, "is forearmed."

Laura snorted at the smug, knowing grin on the cheery and bearded face before grinning at her cousin. "You go right on believing that."

At precisely seven o'clock, Gwen started down the stairs. She felt calm, steady, relaxed. The diamonds her parents had given her when she graduated from med school shot fire at her ears and gave her confidence. The froth she wore under the quietly elegant gown made her feel female, secretive, and amused.

She laid her wrap over the newel post just as the doorbell rang.

And her steady system took a quick, shuddering leap as she opened the door and saw Branson in a formal tux, with a spray of white roses in his arms.

"Oh, how lovely."

"Wait." He stood just where he was and simply looked at her. "You are perfect. Gwendolyn, you leave me breathless."

"Then I won't tell you how hard I worked at it." She smiled, took the roses from him. "I want to put these in water before we go. You don't mind waiting."

"No." He took her hand and, with his eyes on hers, lifted it to his lips. "I don't mind waiting."

Chapter 17

The parlor of Branson's hotel suite was filled with white roses just opening their fragile petals, white candles already softening the air with delicate light and scent. A small table was tucked under the window, where the drapes were drawn wide to allow the city to twinkle behind the glass. Silver and crystal gleamed against white linen.

Gwen's heart gave a long, long sigh.

"Do you have elves?" she murmured.

"Just a very efficient hotel staff." He slipped her wrap from her shoulders. "I called just before we left the theater so they could have everything set up."

"You've gone to a lot of trouble."

"No, I haven't. Setting scenes is something I enjoy." He set her wrap aside, lifted her hand to press his lips to the palm. "And I did this for both of us. Of course, I ordered food without consulting you."

"I think I can let that slide this time."

"Cold dishes, so we won't have to worry about it. Are you hungry, or should we just work on the champagne for a while?"

"Champagne sounds perfect."

"Perfect is exactly what I want for you tonight." He took a single rosebud from the table, handed it to her before lifting the bottle of wine from the silver ice bucket. "The first time I saw you, I thought of a ballet, efficiently choreographed."

She angled her head, smiling a little at the muffled pop of the cork. "Dancers are much more sturdy than many people think."

"The best are strong, dedicated, tireless. You also made me think of fairies and storybook princesses." He handed her the wine. "Also stronger and more resilient than most people think. Still, it's difficult not to want to rescue and cherish a princess."

"What would you rescue me from, Branson?"

"For a night, one night, from reality." He touched his glass to hers. "To fairy tales and happy endings."

"All right." She sipped, letting the wine bubble excitedly on her tongue. "But this is real, and I don't need to be rescued from it. Or want to be rescued from it. You don't have to seduce me, Branson. I'm here because I want to be here. Because I want you."

"Seducing you, Gwendolyn, is my very great pleasure." He touched a hand to her cheek and lowered his mouth to hers for a quiet kiss.

She wasn't nervous, not yet. And he wanted her to be. He wanted to watch those wonderful eyes go dark with nerves, with needs, with knowledge. He would, layer by layer, slide away the practical, until he uncovered the romantic she hid inside.

It was the romantic he would awaken and pleasure. And cherish.

When he found her, he would give her everything he had, everything he was.

"Here." He plucked a strawberry from a bowl, swirled it into white chocolate. "Taste."

She opened her mouth as he brought the berry to her lips, let the mixture of textures and flavors linger on her tongue. "It's wonderful."

"Have more."

He fed her small bites, slipping nibbling kisses between samples. And felt her first small shudder.

"You've only to tell me what you like. When you want more. When you want less." Still touching only her face, he deepened the kiss, degree by aching degree. "When you're ready for all."

"I'm not fragile." But her voice shook. He was taking her somewhere she'd never been, and the first steps were dizzying. "You don't need to worry."

"Not fragile, perhaps, but precious." He took her glass from her unsteady fingers, set it aside. His eyes were dark and intense in hers. "And mine, tonight."

Her heart did a slow spin in her chest when he lifted her into his arms. Perhaps it was foolish, but the image slipped into her head of a knight, armor glinting silver in the sun, lifting her astride his white stallion. Her lips curved as she pressed them to his throat. "You're overwhelming me."

"I want to. I need to."

The bed was turned down. The rose petals strewn over it made her heart stutter. Candles burned here, as well, soft, shifting light. "There's no time here," he told her when he set her on her feet beside the bed. "No world but this one. No one but us. Only you, Gwendolyn, and me."

She believed him. This world he'd created for her was the only reality she wanted or needed tonight. She lifted her arms, wound them around him and let herself slide into it. Into him.

His mouth was patient, persuasive, possessive one moment, teasing the next. She swayed, dizzy from the onslaught, and the fragile scent of roses and candle wax swirled in her head.

Touch me.

As if she'd spoken it, his hands skimmed up her sides, cruising over velvet, tracing curves.

More. Still more.

His mouth traveled down her throat, nuzzling gently, to where the jeweled band circled. And slowly, inch by inch, he drew the zipper down her back for the first sampling of flesh.

Silk beneath velvet, he thought. And already warm. It was no effort for him to take care, to take time. Desire for her was an equal match with his need to give. He turned her until his mouth could savor the wonderful line, the back of her neck, the slope of her shoulder. When her arm lifted, hooked around him, his blood took a quick, hard leap. But his mouth remained patient, his hands gentle.

She shivered, arched backward, when his hands cupped her breasts, when his thumbs brushed the swell and curve of them. Their moans mixed when he eased the gown from her shoulders and it slipped down to pool at her feet.

"God." He'd never expected to find such a fantasy beneath. He'd prepared himself for her body, the wonder of it, the punch of desire. But the pink silk slip, the froth of lace, had his fingers flexing hard on her shoulders as he turned her to face him again.

That sudden leap of lust in those smoky eyes had her heart slamming into her ribs. When his gaze left hers, traveled slowly down, she felt her skin go hot, her head go light.

"I wanted to...surprise you," she managed, then took an instinctive step back as those eyes, nearly black now, whipped back to hers. There was something not quite civilized in them.

She was all pink and white, like something deliciously forbidden behind thin glass. He wanted to smash the barrier and ravish, plunder, devour. He yanked a choke chain on desire and skimmed, fingertips only, over the subtle swell just above pink silk.

"You stagger me."

How could he touch her so gently, and look at her with such simmering violence? Her hand trembled as she loosened his tie, fumbled a bit as she undid his studs. "I want to see you."

There were the nerves, he thought. Tiny fears flickering in her eyes, even as she stood her ground. And seeing them, feeling the tremor of those skilled hands, he tumbled the rest of the way into love.

"Look at me," he murmured when she spread the formal white shirt apart. "I want to see your eyes when I touch you. I want to see what you feel when my hands are on you. Like this."

He ran his hand over her skin above the sheer

stocking. Her eyes went wide and her breath caught in her throat as he unsnapped the front garter.

"You're shivering. I want you to." He flicked the next garter free. "And more than anything, I want...surrender."

He eased her onto the bed, covered her body with his. His mouth crushed down on hers, giving her hints of dark and dangerous needs, hot-blooded urgency. Then it gentled, leaving her confused and unsteady.

If the first steps into this world he'd created for her had been dizzying, these were staggering.

His lips traveled down, savoring flesh. His hands traveled up, caressing it. A sharp lance of heat stabbed her, pleasure coated pain, as he took possession of her breasts, slipping her bra aside.

Then the sharp flare of fire died to warmth.

No one had ever touched her so. No one had ever incited such conflicting and overpowering sensations. Rose petals clung to her skin, sweet, romantic kisses. Candlelight glowed against her heavy eyelids, soft, romantic light. He murmured to her, approval, promises, his voice mesmerizing. Yet somehow his gentle hands had her pulse pounding like a drumbeat, and the lazy brush of his mouth stole each breath before she could draw it in.

He wanted to give her everything he had to give. And he wanted to take everything she was. He rolled the stockings down her slim thighs, thrilling when her breathing grew thick and her movements restless.

When she touched him, those elegant and competent hands roaming over him, fingers seeking, flexing, he had to take her mouth again or die.

She moaned when his shirt was tugged away, when

his flesh slid over her flesh. This was what she wanted, this intimacy of body to body and mind to mind. Her earlier nerves forgotten, she smiled against his mouth, framed his face with her hands.

Pleasure was cool and silky. She wrapped herself with it.

He knew that she floated, drifted. Her lazy sigh was another thrill for him. Slowly, slowly, he took her higher, until her sighs were gasps, until her eyes flew open in shock. Beneath his, her body arched instinctively, seeking more.

Sensation spiked into sensation. She shook her head once, as if to deny what was happening inside her. His eyes were on her face, intense, concentrating on every flicker of emotion that passed over it. And his hands…oh, his hands were so quietly relentless.

Heat slammed into her, a ball of lightning. The breath strangled in her throat. Pleasure was suddenly sharp and fierce, and endlessly thrilling. She heard her own moan, all but felt it rise up through her and thicken the suddenly heavy air.

She shot to a peak, over, then shuddered down again.

"Branson."

"Again." He didn't want her to catch her breath, to clear her mind. Watching her, dazzled by her, he urged her to the next wave. And when he was sure she was ready, when he was certain there would be more pleasure than pain, he let himself ride with her.

He was inside her, filling her, and moving with him was as natural as breathing. She gave herself, yielded herself. When his mouth came back to hers, she met it eagerly. When his hands closed over hers, she gripped them tightly to complete the union.

Slowly, silkily, spinning it out, savoring it. They were mated, and they were matched. In his eyes she saw her own wonder. And her heart filled with joy the moment they rose and fell together.

He pressed his lips to her throat and knew he'd never really made love before. He'd been as innocent as she, because he'd never known what it was to be in love with a lover.

It was everything.

"Gwendolyn. Beautiful, strong, outrageously sexy Gwendolyn."

She felt happiness bubble. "Branson," she said, in the same sleepy tone. "Beautiful, strong, outrageously sexy Branson."

He lifted his head. Her eyes were heavy and dark, her skin was glowing, her lips were softly curved. "I'm going to have a hard time ever letting you out of this bed."

"Was I going somewhere?"

"Not far, anyway." He traced the shape of her face with his finger. "There's a whirlpool tub in the next room."

"Is there?"

"I'm thinking I could let you get just that far. How would you feel about a hot, bubbling bath, a glass of icy champagne, and a man who already wants to make love with you again?"

"I'd feel very interested. Wait." She took his face in her hands, brought his mouth to hers. The kiss was warm and deep. "I'd wondered what it would be like, the first time. How I would feel after knowing I'd shared myself with a man. Nothing I ever hoped for, no foolishly high expectation I ever built up, was as wonderful as tonight.''

Swamped with emotion, he lowered his brow to hers. ''I don't know what to say to you now.''

''Tell me the night isn't over.''

''I'll tell you it's only beginning.'' And he would tell her, when the time was right, that he wanted a lifetime of nights with her. If he told her now, he thought, the romantic in her would want to believe it. But the practical woman within would doubt.

When he told her he loved her, he wanted no doubts.

And if he told her now, while she was still soft and pliant from loving, the romantic in her might give him the answer he needed. And then the practical woman would step back, assess and decide she'd been swept up in the moment.

When she told him she loved him, he wanted no doubts.

''What are you thinking about?'' she asked him.

He brought himself back, smiled. ''I was thinking what I could do to persuade you to put that little...surprise you were wearing back on.''

''Right now?''

''No.'' He rubbed a finger over her bottom lip. ''After the tub. You could wear it while we have that cold supper.''

She chuckled. ''You want me to wear a garter belt while we're eating?''

He bent down to nibble the lip he'd just rubbed. ''Oh, yeah.''

She considered, remembered the way he'd looked

at her when he discovered what she'd been wearing under the velvet gown. "Tell you what. I'll give you a chance to talk me into it, in the tub."

"I'm really good at water sports," he warned her, and she laughed.

"I'm counting on it."

Chapter 18

She awoke luxuriously, as if sliding through layers of shimmering silk. Her sigh was low and indulgent as she shifted, reaching out, then soft and sulky when she found herself alone in bed.

She'd wanted him to be there, just there, so that she could touch that firm, warm flesh. So that he would turn to her again. If they could survive one more again.

She didn't open her eyes yet. It was so nice just to float and dream. To feel her system slowly hum to life again.

She'd had no idea the body could be so miraculous. None of her studies, her training, her work, had taught her just what marvelous reactions the human system had to sensory stimulation. Nothing had prepared her for what she was capable of, given the right… incentives.

She rubbed her hand over the sheet, found it cool, and wondered how long he'd been gone. And when he could come back.

He'd promised her breakfast in bed, she remembered. And she intended to collect. Reluctantly she opened her eyes, blinked owlishly at the clock. Well, perhaps it was a bit late for breakfast, she decided. But it was the perfect time for brunch.

Rising, she found a soft terry-cloth hotel robe on the bathroom door and she bundled herself into it and went to find him.

He was working at the laptop on the table in the parlor. His brow was furrowed in concentration, his eyes seemed just a little irritated. Odd, she thought, she'd imagined him writing with little or no effort, words simply flowing out. Everything he did seemed to come so naturally to him. But now he had the look of a man who was struggling with something, and was not entirely pleased with the results.

She raked a hand through her hair to smooth it. Her body was already tingling. It was exciting, she realized, to watch him work, to see him think, to know he wasn't aware she was watching. Part of the excitement might have been that he wore only black sweatpants. And, to her own surprise, she had already imagined how easily she could dispense with them.

His head came up suddenly. He looked at her—through her, really. Then his gray eyes cleared, warmed, and he smiled at her. "Good morning. I didn't want to wake you."

"I'm disturbing your work."

"It's not going well anyway. It was, for a while." When he held out a hand, she crossed the room, threaded her fingers with his. "I woke up early," he told her, kissing her fingers one by one. "I thought you could use a little more rest."

"I don't think I've ever been so relaxed in my life." She laughed when he tugged her into his lap. "Or more rested," she said, lifting her mouth to his.

"I didn't let you get much sleep."

"And I appreciate it."

He found that sweet spot, just at the curve of her neck, and nuzzled. "We can crawl back into bed and order breakfast."

"Mmm. This is fine for now." She shuddered when his hands slipped under the robe and found her. "And that's even better."

It was nearly noon before she could think again. They were sprawled on the floor of the parlor, with her head on his chest. He had to smile when he felt her fingers on his wrist. "Taking my pulse, Doc?"

Laughing at herself, she drew her hand away. "I suppose I was. It's still a little fast."

He pressed his own fingers to the beat in her throat. "So's yours." He drew her with him as he sat up. "If I don't feed you, we won't be able to even crawl into bed."

"I enjoyed the floor." She picked up the robe she'd been wearing, studying him as he rose. "As a doctor, I'd like to say you're in excellent shape. As a woman," she continued as he hauled her to her feet, "I'm compelled to say you have a great butt."

"Thanks. On both counts."

"I was watching you work after I woke up. You looked so serious and annoyed."

"Certain parts of a story are nothing but an annoyance."

"What part is this?" She shifted to try to look at the screen of the computer he'd left on when she distracted him. "Can I read it?"

"No." Briskly he leaned over and, flicking a few keys, turned the screen to black.

"Well, that's definite." She frowned at him. "And rude."

"Yeah. Want me hanging over your shoulder giving opinions when you remove your next gallbladder?"

She was very close to pouting, which appalled her. "Who said I was going to give any opinions?"

"You would have. You wouldn't have been able to help yourself. The trouble here, darling, is while few believe they can perform brain surgery, nearly every living soul believes they can write. If only they had the time and opportunity."

He kissed her lightly. "Nobody reads my work until it's done, except my editor. I keep more friends that way."

"Well, if you're going to be touchy about it..."

"I am. What would you like for breakfast?"

She jerked a shoulder. "Whatever. You've already told me what the story's about," she reminded him.

"No, I told you the basic conflict and gave you an overview of one of the main characters." He knew better than to grin, but couldn't help himself. "Are you going to sulk? It's very attractive, actually."

"I'm not sulking." Her eyes went dark and moody. "I never sulk."

"Nobody warned me about this," he murmured. "Gwendolyn doesn't like to be crossed. She pouts."

"I certainly do not. Are you going to order breakfast, or shall I?"

"I'd be happy to." He found it just one more facet of her to enjoy. The simple illogic of it. Feeling cheerful, he ordered twice as much food as they could possibly eat. "You'll feel better when you have some coffee."

She set her teeth. "I feel perfectly fine."

"And I think I have something else that might smooth your feathers."

"They're not ruffled," she said evenly, "therefore they need no smoothing."

"Just the same." He strolled off, and came back in with a big gold box tied with red ribbon.

She huffed out a breath. "Branson, I'm not a child who needs to be placated with presents. And if I were irritated with you, a gift would hardly change the matter."

"This one might." He smiled charmingly. "And you don't know until you open it."

She didn't want to be placated, but found herself too curious to resist. It would be the eighth day, by his odd and unpredictable calculations. The box was heavier than she'd expected, so she set it on the table and toyed with the ribbon.

"It's awfully small for eight milkmaids," she commented.

"Maybe I switched themes." The quick distress in her eyes that she didn't quite manage to hide delighted him. "Open it and find out."

She pulled the ribbon, opened the lid.

The bowl was gorgeous, the interior a glossy summer blue. Around the outside, eight pretty maids sat on buckets and milked foolishly cheerful spotted cows. She didn't need to see the signature on the bottom to know whose work it was.

"Aunt Shelby," she murmured. "How did you manage this?"

"I begged. Actually, I begged Julia, and she used her influence on her mother. I'm told the former First Lady found the request amusing."

"She would. I love it." She spoke quietly as her heart swelled. What was he doing to her? she wondered. How could he make her feel so many different things in so short a time? "I don't think you'll be able to top this one."

"I've an ace or two up my sleeve yet."

"It's still a week till Christmas," she said, then, on a strangled sob, threw herself into his arms. "I don't know what's happening to me. It's all so fast, I can't keep up."

"Just hold on to me. Wherever we're going, we'll get there together."

"I need to find my balance. You keep throwing me off." She clung to him. "It's as if you know what I'm thinking, what I'm feeling. Even before I do. It's unnerving." She sighed and rested her head on his shoulder.

She didn't know why what he'd said earlier played back in her head at just that moment. Why the words rang in her ears like an alarm. But the eyes she'd closed opened. "What did you mean, no one warned you?"

"Hmm?"

She eased back slowly, until they were no longer touching, and studied his face. "Who have you been talking to about me?"

"I don't know what you mean. That'll be breakfast." Grateful for the delay, he went to the door.

She remained calm as the waiter set up the food. And she began to think, to backtrack, and to come to a few logical conclusions.

"You've studied me, haven't you, Branson?" she asked when they were alone again. "A prototype, you once said."

"Of course I've studied you." He poured the coffee carefully. "On a professional level. We agreed to that at the beginning."

"But we're not on a professional level here."

"And one has nothing to do with the other. Absolutely nothing to do with the other." Temper simmered in his eyes. "Do you think I'm using this, using what's happened between us, for a book? Is that what you're accusing me of?"

"I'm not accusing you, I'm asking you."

"Then the answer is no." His gaze narrowed. "You're not sure you believe that."

"It just seems odd that you know me so well, as if you've outlined me as a character."

"I outlined your profession, your gender, your focus. I mixed in Audrey—the blond med student—her ambition and competitive streak, and the body language of the head ER nurse. That's what I do. I wasn't taking notes for the damn book when Daniel and Anna told me about you."

The wave of shame that had started to crest receded. "Told you what about me?"

He could, quite happily, have sawed off his tongue. Temper always undermined control, he reminded himself. "Just about you. The food's going to get cold."

"You asked them about me?"

"What's wrong with that?" he demanded. The chill in her voice put his back up, and he knew he was in a corner. "I was interested in you. I wanted to know more about you."

"When?"

"Shortly after we met. For heaven's sake, they didn't divulge any state secrets," he said impatiently. "You could just as easily have asked them about me. Daniel would have been more than happy to fill you in with every detail. I imagine he knows all there is to know, or I wouldn't have gotten within a mile of you."

She held up a hand, took a breath. "He did set it up, didn't he? He arranged it all. You knew."

"No, I didn't, not until after I'd met you. And I didn't get the full drift until I'd gone up to see him. What difference does it make?"

"I don't like being manipulated, maneuvered, deceived."

"I haven't deceived you, Gwendolyn."

She nodded slowly. "But manipulated, maneuvered?"

"No. The situation, but not you." Frustration darkened his eyes, his voice. "I was attracted to you. Was I supposed to walk away from that because Daniel MacGregor decided I should court his granddaughter?"

Humiliation and temper waged a war inside her.

"He shouldn't have interfered, and you should have told me when you discovered he had."

"All he did was arrange for us to meet. If there'd been nothing there, I would have researched my book, giving you a nice acknowledgment in the front of it, and it would have ended there."

She shook her head and walked to the table for her coffee. She would have to think about this carefully, she decided. When she was more calm. "I don't know how you can defend him. He manipulated you every bit as much as me."

"I'm grateful to him. If he hadn't have arranged it, I'd never have met you. I wouldn't have fallen in love with you."

She went very still, stared at him when he laid his hands on her shoulders. "I love you, Gwendolyn. However it came to be doesn't change the result. You're what I've waited for without ever knowing I was waiting."

"You're going too fast." Her stomach jittered as she stepped back. "We've been steered into this, and we haven't had time to think."

"I know what I feel."

"I don't." She said it desperately. "I don't. I've just found out all this was going on behind the scenes. I need time to think. This needs to slow down. We need to slow down."

"You don't believe me." Seeing the doubt in her eyes hurt unbearably. "Do you know how insulting it is for you to stand there and doubt my feelings? For me to wrap them up like another gift for you and you to hand them back?"

"That's not what I'm doing." Terrified, she rubbed

a hand over her thudding heart. "I'm telling you we need time, both of us."

"No amount of time is going to change the fact that I'm in love with you. And since you're already dealing with the shock of that, I'll tell you that I want to marry you. I want to have children with you."

There was nothing loverlike in his tone. But it wasn't the bite of anger in his voice that had her going pale, it was the words themselves. "Marriage. Good God, Branson, we can't possibly—"

"Because your grandfather started it?"

"No, of course not. Because we've barely had time to—"

"Why did you sleep with me?"

"I—" Her head was reeling. She lifted a hand to it, surprised to find it was still on her shoulders. "Because we wanted each other."

"And that was all? Just want, just sex?"

"You know it was more."

"How can I, when you won't tell me?"

She stepped back again, fighting for calm. "You're more clever with words than I, Branson. You know how to use them. Now you're pushing me with them, when I need time to think."

Because he couldn't deny it, he nodded. "All right. But I can't take back what I said, and I can't change what I feel. An hour, a year, a lifetime, I'm still going to be in love with you. You'll have to get used to hearing it."

She wasn't certain she ever could, not when her heart swam into her throat every time he said it. "If we could just take this a step at a time."

In an abrupt change of mood, he smiled. "All right,

but you're already several steps behind." He leaned down to kiss her lightly, though his stomach was raw and his heart aching. "Try to catch up."

Chapter 19

Gwen all but limped into the house. She'd missed her dinner break and worked nearly three hours over her shift. She wanted to believe her miserable mood was due to that, and not because Branson hadn't been by the hospital in two days.

If he was angry with her, it couldn't be helped. She'd reminded herself of that dozens of times since she left his hotel on Sunday. She was doing the right thing, the only thing. Being sensible, slowing down, thinking things through.

She'd even resisted calling her grandfather to scold him for his machinations. And that, she told herself, had taken an enormous act of will.

Besides, she would be in Hyannis Port on Christmas Eve. It would be much more satisfying to give him a piece of her mind face-to-face.

Relieved to be out of the bitter cold, she tugged off

her gloves, scarf, wool cap. "Julia? Jules? You home?" And sighed when there was no response. She and her cousin had barely time enough to bump into each other as they came in and out of the door.

She needed someone to talk to, Gwen admitted as she bent down to pull off her boots. She needed someone who'd listen while she vented, someone who'd tell her that she was right to be angry, she was right to be cautious, she was right to step back and analyze the situation she'd been maneuvered into.

"Ninety-year-old men playing matchmaker," she muttered, and she headed back to the kitchen. "Thirty-year-old men falling right in line. It's calculating and it's insulting and it's unacceptable. Someone has to make them understand life isn't a game."

Feeling righteous, she shoved through the kitchen door. And when she saw the big bright box on the table, her heart dropped to her knees.

"Oh, Branson." She caught herself before the dreamy sigh was complete, sucked it firmly back in. She was not going to be softened up by some silly gift.

Turning her back on it, she headed to the refrigerator. Julia's note was a bold scrawl in Christmas red.

> I think you can guess who sent the box. By my calculations we're up to dancing ladies. I have earned huge points for resisting easing it open myself for a quick peek. Dying to see, but I won't be home till late. Thank God we're out of here in a couple of days for the riot that is our

family at Christmas. Jules
P.S. Bran is one in a million.

Gwen read the postscript and jammed her hands in her pockets. "Damn it, you're supposed to be on my side. Well, I'm just not going to open it. This has to be stopped, readjusted. After the holidays both of us will be able to think more clearly."

She decided she wanted wine more than food, and snatched a glass out of the cabinet. And stood there, glass in hand, staring at the box.

"I'm not opening it," she repeated. "If we're going to put things back on some reasonable, sensible level, then I… I have to stop talking to myself," she decided, rubbing a hand over her face. "Or I'm going to end up in the psych ward."

She got out the wine, poured the glass. She would have sworn the box at her back was singing her name. After one sip of wine, she realized she didn't want any after all. What she needed to do was go upstairs, put on comfortable clothes and…

"All right, all right, all right, I'll open it." She spun around, scowling at the box as she yanked off the cheery red-and-green ribbon. "It's not going to make any difference," she muttered. "I will not be charmed, I will not be swayed." She tossed the lid aside. "I will not be… Oh."

Nestled inside the tissue paper were music boxes. A ballerina, an ice skater, a Southern belle, a flapper, an Irish colleen, a Scottish lassie, a tambourine-tapping Gypsy, an elaborately gowned lady poised for a minuet, and a fiery-eyed *señorita.*

Nine dancing ladies waiting for her to give them

their cue. She couldn't stop herself from taking each out, admiring each of them in turn, lining them up on the table. Giving in, she wound them and stood back grinning foolishly.

Waltzes and Charlestons and reels tinkled and clashed and rang as her nine ladies whirled and spun.

She didn't realize she was crying until her hands covered her damp cheeks.

"Oh, this has to stop. How am I supposed to think when he keeps muddling up my head?" As the music slowed and died, she wiped her cheeks dry. "It has to stop," she said again, more firmly, then marched out of the kitchen.

Branson let the scene flow through his mind, out through his fingers and onto the screen. The hard-bitten Detective Scully was about to be singed by the sexual sparks flashing between him and Dr. Miranda Kates. His objectivity would be lost for a time, his career compromised and his heart battered before it was done.

It would be good for him, Branson thought. It would humanize him. Scully had been too much in control in his three previous outings. This time he was going to fall, and fall hard. And it was just his bad luck that the woman he tumbled for was a cold-blooded killer.

He'd suffer, Branson mused, and be a better man for it.

He stopped typing, pressed his fingers to his gritty eyes. Whoever had said suffering built character should be dragged out in the street and shot, he decided.

Who the hell needed character, anyway? he wondered. What he needed was Gwendolyn.

He'd played it wrong. There was no doubt about that. Needing to move, Branson pushed back from the table and prowled the hotel suite he'd made his home. He should have told her about the setup the minute he figured it out. They might have laughed about it then shrugged it off.

But it hadn't seemed important or necessary. And it hadn't seemed like good strategy, he admitted. He hadn't wanted to risk her bolting with her principles before he had a chance to romance her.

Then he'd been in too deep, and he'd nearly forgotten how it had all started because he was so steeped in her.

Then he'd still ended up blowing it, he thought in disgust. He'd known she wasn't ready to hear that he was in love with her. But, damn it, he was ready. Didn't that count for something? Was she really so stubborn, so pigheaded, that she would let the one small, insignificant fact that her grandfather had matched them up stop her loving him back?

Jamming his hands in his pockets, he stalked to the window. What did he want with a woman like that anyway?

He stared out at the city, the gleam of lights glinting on snow and street, the glint of the dark water of the harbor. Boston was blanketed in holiday spirit, he thought. Friends and family were gathered together, out of the cold and wind.

And he was alone, because the woman he wanted wouldn't admit she wanted him.

He should have bought a third ticket, he thought,

gone along with his parents on the gift cruise he'd given them for Christmas. He could have worked on the ship and enjoyed a nice sail in the Greek Isles.

That would have given Gwendolyn her time and her distance.

He scowled at the knock on the door. He hadn't ordered dinner yet, and the last pot of coffee that had been sent up didn't need replenishing yet. Whoever it was could go the hell away, he thought, stalking over. He looked through the security peep, saw Gwen and shut his eyes.

Great, he thought. Perfect. He hadn't shaved in two days, and he was as surly as a bear woken out of hibernation. The doctor sure picked her moments. He took a moment to compose himself, raked his fingers through his untidy hair and opened the door.

"House call?" he said, and even managed to smile at her.

"You look like you could use one. You look exhausted. Did I wake you? Did I come at a bad time?"

"No, you didn't wake me." He stepped back, cocked his head as she hesitated. "Coming in?"

"Yes, all right." Her eyes widened at the disarray in the elegant parlor. Cups, glasses, bottles, were strewn everywhere. The dining table was heaped with books, papers, more cups.

"I kicked the maid out for a couple days," Branson told her, getting a clear look at the mess for the first time. "I guess I'd better let her back in. I've got coffee, we can wash out a cup."

"No, I don't need anything." Her mission took a back seat now to concern. "You look completely worn out."

''It hasn't been letting me sleep.'' He gestured toward his laptop. ''Or much of anything else.''

''Meaning food, exercise, fresh air.'' The doctor in her stepped forward. ''Branson, you'll make yourself sick. I'm sorry if the book's not going well, but—''

''It's not going well. It's going terrific. I'm just riding the wave.''

''Oh, so this is what happens when you're not having trouble with the story.''

''If it wasn't going well, I'd tell myself I really needed to take a walk, get a haircut, learn to speak Japanese. Sure you don't want coffee?'' he asked as he headed for the pot.

''Yes, I'm sure, and you should order up some food. Some soup.''

''I'll get to it, Doc.'' His system was already wired, he decided. What was one more hit of caffeine in the vast scheme of things? ''You look a little tired yourself.''

''We got most of the victims from the bus wreck into ER this afternoon.''

''What bus wreck?''

She blinked at him. ''On the Longfellow Bridge? Icy roads, thirty-five people injured? It's been all over the news most of the day.''

''The news hasn't been part of my little world today.'' He studied her over the rim of his cup. She looked a little pale, he noted, but steady, as always. And she had yet to take off her coat. ''Why don't you sit down? I'll order something up.''

''No, not for me. I can't stay long. I've got a double shift tomorrow—making up for taking three days off for the holidays.''

"The ever-conscientious Dr. Blade."

Because he smiled when he said it, she relaxed. "I wanted to thank you for the music boxes. They're charming. And they were unexpected. I thought you were angry with me."

"Did you?"

"I know you were. I'm glad you're not anymore. Now that things are smoothed out, I hope we can talk about it—after the holidays, when life calms down a bit."

"We want to be calm," he said quietly. "We want to be reasonable."

"Yes." Relief flooded her as she walked to him, took his hand. "I'll be back on the twenty-seventh. If you're free—"

"Oh, I'm free. I put my parents on a plane tomorrow for Athens."

"Your family's leaving town?"

"They've always wanted to go to Greece, so I'm sending them on a cruise."

"That's a lovely thing to do, but you shouldn't be alone at Christmas. You know you'd be welcome to come to Hyannis. My grandparents would love to have you."

He stared at her for so long she felt her heart begin to bump erratically. "You really don't have a clue, do you?" he murmured. "You figure everything's just clicked back into an acceptable position."

"No, I only thought since you weren't angry—"

"I am angry."

He didn't raise his voice, didn't throw or break anything, didn't threaten to do her bodily harm. It was only more confusing. She'd grown up in a family that had expressed every passion and emotion at full volume.

"It all has to be spelled out for you, doesn't it? If I shouted, if I shoved the table over, smashed some crockery, then you could logically conclude that I'm angry. Well, I don't work that way. My actions and my feelings aren't always simple, and they're not always logical."

"All right." She was more frightened, more stupefied, by his cold control than she would have been by a violent display. "You're still angry, so obviously we still need to talk."

"You hurt me."

The quiet statement had her eyes filling, her heart ripping. "Oh, Branson. I'm so sorry. I never meant to. I want—"

"That gets to you." He shut his eyes and turned away, furious with himself for having admitted it. "The compassion takes over. I don't want your compassion, or your sympathy or your guilt." He turned back, and the violence in his eyes was all the more compelling in contrast to the absolute calm of his voice. "I want you to tell me you love me, because you do. If I didn't know it, if I couldn't see it in your face, if I hadn't felt it when I touched you, I'd walk away. Do you think I enjoy humiliating myself like this?"

"No, I don't. Please, let's sit down and talk this out."

"Haven't I said everything already? I'm in love with you. I want you to marry me, raise a family with me. What part of that don't you understand?"

"Understanding and accepting aren't always the

same.'' Couldn't he see that she needed to decide, and decide lucidly, what was right and sane and necessary for both of them? ''Maybe you believe you love me, and maybe I...'' She shook her head, moved back quickly. ''I came here tonight to tell you I won't be pressured, I won't be pushed.''

He moved fast, had her locked in his arms in less than a heartbeat, had his mouth on hers in less than two. Her practical words rang hollowly in her ears as her heart simply melted.

''Tell me what you feel now,'' he demanded against her mouth. ''Tell me what you're feeling now, this instant.''

''Too much. I can't think past it. Please don't do this.''

He knew that he could have her, that she would yield. And that whatever he took would leave him empty. He drew away. ''You'd better go. I'm not feeling reasonable.''

She nodded, ordered her shaky legs to walk to the door. And there, with her hand on the knob, she felt shame for being less than honest, for giving him less than he'd asked.

''I'm out of my depth with you, Branson,'' she said quietly. ''I feel out of control. I don't know how to function that way, and I need to decide what that means for me.''

She opened the door, but made herself turn so that their eyes met across the room. ''I need to decide what to do about the fact that I'm in love with you.''

She rushed out. He was halfway across the room before he stopped himself. No, she wouldn't listen now, he told himself, and fought to calm his speeding pulse. She would fight him every step of the way if he tried to press the advantage she'd just given him.

He'd made enough missteps without making another.

Slowly he rubbed a hand over his heart. The ache was gone, that dull, nasty throb. The doctor had healed him, he thought with a slow smile. He was going to have to work very fast to complete plans for her payment.

He was going to order up a meal, a huge meal, a banquet. God, he was starving. He needed a shower, a shave, a long walk.

Then he had to get to work. There was only a matter of days before Christmas.

"She loves me," he said, and laughed out loud.

You say you're out of your depth now, Doc, he thought. Believe me, you ain't seen nothin' yet.

Chapter 20

Daniel MacGregor scowled fiercely, huffed out a breath. "Well, what's wrong with the boy?" he wanted to know.

"Nothing's wrong with him." Gwen barely resisted throwing up her hands. She'd made certain she got to Hyannis early, and cornered her meddling grandfather before the rest of the family could distract her. "That's not the point."

"What is the point, I'd like to know? I'll tell you what the point is," he continued, jabbing out a finger before she could speak. "The point is, you met a nice young man of good family. A young man with a fine and clever mind and of strong and steady heart. If he's been romancing you, what have you got to complain about?"

"If he's been romancing me," Gwen said evenly, "it's because you tossed us in each other's faces, and under false pretenses."

"False pretenses." He rolled his bright blue eyes. "Did he want to research his murder book or not?"

"Yes, but—"

"Are you a doctor with some know-how in the medical field?"

"Grandpa—"

"And if you're both young, healthy, single people, what harm is there in having you meet? You don't like him, you toss him back."

"He's not a trout," she said between her teeth.

"So, you do like him, don't you, Gwennie?"

She had to shut her eyes, had to wonder why she'd believed, even for an instant, that she would get anywhere with the MacGregor. "My feelings for Branson have nothing to do with this conversation."

"Of course they do, they're the point." He beamed at her. "Has he asked you to marry him?"

"I'm not going to discuss it."

"He has." Triumphant, Daniel banged his fist on the arm of his chair. "I knew young Branson Maguire was a sharp lad, a man of taste and character."

"Which is why you picked him for me?"

"Exactly. I—" He stopped, hissed between his teeth. She'd caught him there. "Now, Gwennie, it's just that your grandmother worries so that you're alone there in the city."

"I'm not alone."

"And that you might meet the wrong type of individual. That Gilbert doctor, for instance."

"His name is Greg," she said wearily. "And he's a perfectly nice man."

"But he's no Bran Maguire, is he? Tell the truth and shame the devil."

Her lips twitched, forcing her to press them into a firm line. "Perhaps I prefer the sober, serious type."

"Ha. In a pig's eye, kin of mine would prefer a dull dog to a purebred. George would bore you to death within a year."

"Greg. And you're not going to turn this around. You interfered with my life, with Branson's life, and if you think either one of us is going to thank you for it—"

She swore when the front door slammed and voices rolled down the hall.

"That's my Rena." Grateful for the interruption, Daniel hauled his bulk out of the chair. "Rena!" He bellowed it. "Your daughter's in here."

"Gwen?" Still shaking snow off her sleek bob of red-gold hair, Serena MacGregor Blade rushed into the room. Her eyes lit, and her face, as lovely as any Gwen knew, glowed with pleasure. "You're here early." Laughing, she threw open her arms. "Oh, I've missed you."

Gwen flew into her mother's arm, and her hug was just desperate enough to have Serena lifting a brow and aiming a narrowed look at her father.

"What have you been up to?" she demanded of Daniel.

"Just having a nice chat with my granddaughter." No one, he knew, could cut through his bluster as quickly or as keenly as his daughter. He admired her for it, and was greatly relieved when Justin Blade walked in.

"Dad." Gwen turned to embrace him, held tight. He was tall and strikingly handsome, his thick dark hair glinting with silver, his green eyes sharp as gemstones. Those eyes met his wife's over their daughter's head, then, as a unit, both pairs shifted to Daniel.

"What we need here is hot food and drink." Calculating quickly, Daniel decided on retreat. "I'm going to see to it. The rest of the family will be along any minute. I don't know what your mother's up to, Rena," he said as he strode out. "Always fussing, always worrying."

"He never changes," Justin commented, and laughed. "Thank God for it." Then he tipped up Gwen's chin. "Hello, beautiful," he murmured. They were the exact words he'd said to her when she was placed in his arms at birth.

"I'm so glad to see you both. Where's Mac, Duncan, Mell?"

"Mac's flying in from Vegas. He'll be here in a couple hours. Duncan and Mell are driving up from Atlantic City. They're probably an hour behind us."

"Why don't I help you get your bags upstairs?"

"There's time for that." Serena led Gwen to the sofa, drew her down. "Just how angry with your grandfather are you about Branson Maguire?"

Gwen blew out a breath as her father sat on her other side. "I should have known word would travel."

"It always does—this route was Julia to Shelby to me to your father. How impossible has he made it for you?"

"He's made it uncomfortable," Gwen muttered.

Justin ran a hand over her hair. "If you're not interested in this Maguire, that's the end of it."

"I am interested."

Justin's hand paused. "I see. How interested?"

"Justin." With a laugh, Serena shook her head at him. "What's he like?" she asked Gwen. "Tell us about him."

"He's a writer. I suppose you knew that."

"He's a good one," Justin admitted.

"I haven't seen him since he was a baby." Serena sighed over the passage of time. "His mother and I lost touch. It's a shame. I'll have to call her."

"He's been to the Vegas casino." Justin took out a slim cigar, studied it. "Mac knows him slightly."

"Really. Well, it's interesting how things work." Serena smiled at her daughter. "But you haven't told us what he's like."

"He's charming and gentle. He's very intense about his work. He likes French food and Italian operas. He's got a wonderful smile and gray eyes that look right inside you."

"You're in love with him." Serena's eyes stung as she reached for her husband's hand. "She's in love with him."

"I might be." Gwen sprang up, too restless to sit. "How do I know? I've never felt this way before. How can I be sure? He wants to marry me. He insists on it as if it's a given, something that's bound to happen sooner or later, so why not sooner? And Grandpa set the whole thing up."

Deciding he would deal with all the conflicting emotions spinning inside him later, Justin lifted Serena's hand to his lips. "He's done it before, with excellent results."

"So I should just fall in line?"

"Of course not." Justin rose, put his hands on

Gwen's shoulders. "You have your own mind, your own heart. You'll follow them."

"They're telling me different things. And it's all happening so fast. Being swept off your feet is fine in storybooks, but in reality it's frightening. How can I marry him?" she demanded, turning to her mother. "How do I know I'll be good at it? That I'll be able to handle all those demands and responsibilities? My career, a husband, children. How do I know I can do as good a job with all of that as you have, as Grandma did?"

"You don't. You decide if you're willing to work at it every day for the rest of your life. Darling, you've achieved everything you've ever gone after. Maybe that's a problem for you now." Serena patted the cushion beside her. "You were always such a serious child. Not without humor and a sense of the ridiculous, but always responsible, and very goal-oriented."

"I've hurt .him," Gwen murmured. "And I'm afraid if I'm not careful, if I'm not cautious, I'll end up hurting him again."

"By marrying him."

"Yes, and failing at it."

"Then you should take the time you need. But let me give you a hypothetical case—medically speaking. You have a cool doctor's mind. If you had a patient, a strong, heathy patient, and there were two choices for her. With one she could go on exactly as she had been. She would be content, successful, even happy. Nothing would have to change for her. The other choice involved a certain risk, an adjustment in life-style. If she took this choice, took this risk, she might gain a great deal. Not a longer life, but a richer one. Not a healthier body, but a fuller heart. Which prognosis would you wish for her?''

"You're very wise,'' Gwen murmured.

"MacGregors are, very wise.'' Serena leaned over to kiss her. "I can't tell you what choice to make. You have to make it for yourself. And I won't tell you whether to follow your mind or your heart. In the end, if it's right, you'll follow both.''

"You're right, absolutely right. I have to decide. And I will.'' She rose again. "I love you, both of you. I'm going to take a walk, do some thinking before the horde descends and I won't be able to hear myself think.''

Justin waited until they were alone, then walked to his wife. Taking her hands, he drew her to her feet. "There are two things I need to do.''

"And what are they?''

"I have to go smuggle the cigars in my suitcase to Daniel, to thank him for his daughter, who is the most incredible woman I've ever known. And then—'' he lowered his head to brush his lips over hers "—I have to take his daughter, my wife and the mother of my children upstairs and make love with her.''

Serena wound her arms around his neck. "Why doesn't his daughter, your wife and the mother of your children go upstairs and wait for you?''

Justin kissed her again, lingered over it. "Why doesn't she?''

Gwen barely slept. It had been nearly 3:00 a.m. before everyone stumbled off to bed. She had lain there, staring at the ceiling, willing the right answer to come. But she'd only been able to see Branson's face.

And to yearn for him.

Just before dawn, she drifted off, but even that thin sleep was ragged with dreams. She saw him in the hospital corridor, his eyes focused on hers as he told her who he was and what he wanted. Now, smiling, that quick, charming grin, as he shopped with her downtown. Holding her when she cried over the loss of a patient. Kissing her breathless at her front door. Carrying her to a bed strewn with rose petals.

And that dark and desperate look in his eyes when he'd told her he loved her.

Then the dream became less memory than wish. She saw herself smiling back at him, holding out her hands. Accepting, giving, embracing.

Pipes were playing as he swept her up, onto a gleaming white stallion. She felt not helpless, but powerful. Her laugh mixed with his as they thundered off, bagpipes singing high and bright.

She stirred, sighing with the dream, the romance, the rightness of it. And she was murmuring his name as she woke.

The pipes played still.

She sat up, rubbing her eyes clear. Bagpipes, she thought in confusion. And the steady beat of drums with it. She yawned, laughed and swung her legs off the bed. Grandpa, she thought, had cooked up something special for Christmas morning. Early Christmas morning, she noted with a glance at the clock.

It was barely eight.

She stumbled for her robe just as her door burst open. Julia's hair was wildly tousled, her feet bare and her eyes wide. "Look out the window. You won't believe it until you see it."

"I hear it," Gwen said as voices sounded in the hall. Doors opened and closed, feet pounded. "Sounds like everyone else does, too. What's Grandpa done?"

"Not Grandpa." Taking the matter into her own hands, Julia grabbed Gwen's arm and dragged her to the window. "It's Bran."

Stunned, Julia stared outside. There on the wide slope of lawn were ten burly men in kilts, leaping in a Scottish reel. "Ten lords a-leaping," she managed.

"Lairds," Julia corrected, grinning like an idiot. "Even better, there are eleven pipers piping, and twelve drummers drumming. I'd say that wraps it up, honey. Your true love didn't miss a trick."

"He..." She stared down at Branson. He stood in the midst of the melee, his hair flying in the wind. "He did all this for me."

"He's crazy," Julia stated. "He's in love. He's amazing."

"Yes. Yes." Laughing, Gwen pressed a hand to her mouth. True love, she thought, her true love had no sense at all. And wasn't that wonderful? "He's all of that. He loves me. He really does. It's not a mistake, it's not too fast, it's not a passing infatuation. It's perfect. He's perfect."

"Then what are you doing up here, when he's down there?"

"I'm going." She slipped on a pair of boots, and with her robe flapping behind her, she raced for the stairs. Her family was already ahead of her, bundling into coats or boots or just streaming out the door in their robes. She saw her grandparents by the door, with Anna calmly buttoning Daniel's overcoat.

"I don't need it."

"You do, it's a cold wind. I won't have you catching a chill. The pipers aren't going anywhere."

"And fine pipers they are." He caught sight of Gwen speeding down the stairs and sent her a smug grin. "Well, that's a lad, isn't it?"

"Yes." She caught his bearded face in her hands and kissed him long and hard. "But I'm not thanking you for at least a week." With that, she rushed outside into the cold and pushed her way through her family until she had a clear view.

"Be quiet," she demanded. "I can't hear." But she might have been talking to the wind for all the good it did her.

Then it didn't matter, they could talk and shout and laugh. She didn't hear them. She only heard the pipes and drums as Branson started over the snowy lawn toward her.

She didn't notice that her family actually became silent. She didn't notice that tears shimmered cold on her cheeks. She only saw Branson's face, and his heart was in his eyes.

"Merry Christmas, Gwendolyn."

"Branson—"

"I love you," he told her, lifting a hand to brush a tear from her lashes. "You're everything I want. I admire your strength, your honesty, your compassion and your logic. I need you in my life. I'm promising you here, in front of the people who matter to you most, that I'll never let you down."

"That's a lad!" Daniel boomed out, with tears in his voice. "I told you, by God, that's a lad!"

When Branson smiled, Gwen felt her mother take her hand, squeeze it. In support, in approval, with love. Then Serena let it go.

"It's not all the twelve days of Christmas," Branson told her. "But it's a start. Will you have me, Gwendolyn?"

Her heart brimmed over as she stepped forward, stood between him and her family, and took his hands. "I told you I wouldn't be pressured, I wouldn't be pushed."

"Oh, give the guy a break, Gwen."

Ignoring the order from her younger sister, Gwen kept her eyes on Branson's. "And I won't be. But I can't resist being loved, or loving you back. So I'll answer you in front of the people who matter to me most. Yes, I'll have you, Branson, and you'll have me."

"Well, kiss the girl," Daniel demanded.

Branson shot a look over Gwen's head, met Daniel's fiercely glinting eyes. "I think I can handle it from here," he said.

And he kissed the girl.

From the Private Memoirs
of
Daniel Duncan MacGregor

It's my pleasure to say that my choice of young Branson was better than even I anticipated. He's a clever Irishman. We're proud to have him as part of the family.

I watched his face when our Gwen started down the aisle toward him in her fairy princess gown and heirloom veil. There was love there for a lifetime, and more.

Anna and I, our hands linked, watched them take their vows. Life is a circle and love is what gilds it. In that church with the light streaming through the stained-glass windows in rainbows, my Gwen and her Branson began their own circle within those circles forged by all the generations before.

I take no credit for this—for to take it causes all manner of trouble. I'll just enjoy it.

So another spring is here. Our Gwen is beginning this new life. Our Laura is round and healthy with the babe she carries. Julia now, she keeps herself busy as six beavers. She's a sharp one, she is—takes after her grandfather.

She's my jewel, and make no mistake I've outlined my strategy there even while settling her cousins. She'll be a tough nut, but hah! There's no tougher nut than Daniel Duncan MacGregor.

I'm planning on enlisting a little help with this arrangement. Had my eye on this boy for years—and so has Julia though she'd suffer the tortures of hell before she'd admit it. Stubborn lass, God bless her.

The two of them are perfect for each other. A pair of hotheads who snarl and snap at each other at every opportunity. They'll make fine strong babies for me—for Anna, I mean. The poor woman pines for babies.

Anna's already packed the MacGregor wedding veil away. I didn't want to mention she'd be taking it out again before a year's passed.

I give my word on it.

Part Three

Julia

Chapter 21

There was no doubt in Julia's mind—but then, there rarely was. The wall would have to go. She walked from the tiny parlor into the tiny library that abutted it. Definitely. And when the wall was gone, she would have one generous, airy room, rather than two cramped ones. She nodded firmly and continued her tour, her eyes observing, assessing.

All the glass would have to be replaced with thermal, and the trim and molding would need to be stripped down to the original walnut. Whoever had painted it blue should have been hanged.

She said as much into the minirecorder she carried. Her notes were always logged in this manner, and her commentaries were invariably pithy. Julia MacGregor not only had strong feelings, she strongly believed in expressing them.

She already had completed and labeled two tapes

on the house on Beacon Hill—the house she had decided would be her home. She would make it uniquely hers. Every detail, down to the color of the grout in the first-floor powder room, would be decided upon and supervised by her.

The contractor and subs would be charmed or bullied—and she could do both—into providing her with exactly what she wanted. She had never been satisfied with anything less.

Julia would never have considered herself spoiled. She worked for what she wanted. She planned, she executed. And she could, if necessary, hang drywall, nail trim and grout windows. But she believed in hiring experts and professionals and paying them well.

She had been known to take advice, particularly when it agreed with her own point of view. And a project, once started, was never left undone.

She'd learned the value of planning, of working and of finishing, from her parents. Alan MacGregor had served two terms as president, with Shelby Campbell MacGregor beside him as a First Lady who did a great deal more than host parties and greet dignitaries.

The women in the MacGregor clan were not, and never had been, reflections of their husbands. A MacGregor woman was her own woman. So was Julia.

She headed up the gently curving stairs, a woman with rose-petal skin and curling, flame-colored hair. Her eyes were chocolate brown, focused sharply now to catch any minute detail or flaw she might have missed. Her mouth was wide and often mobile, her hands narrow and rarely still. Her curvy body was fueled with an inner energy that never seemed to be depleted.

Only the smitten would have called her beautiful, but even her detractors—and a strong woman who routinely voiced strong opinions had them—acknowledged her unique appeal.

One of the men she'd dated had called her "the Amazon queen." And though it hadn't been meant as a compliment at the time, the term suited. She was sturdy, self-sufficient and sexy.

And she was ruthless.

Tapping a finger on the subtle point of her chin, she studied the bedroom she'd been using for the past month. The delightful Adam fireplace needed to be unblocked. Its having been blocked off was another black mark against the former owners, in Julia's opinion.

She could imagine herself curled up in the wonderful teak sleigh bed she had in storage, pillows heaped around her, a pot of jasmine tea, a good book. And a fire crackling away in the hearth.

It was only late August, and summer still held Boston in a sweaty grip, but the image played for her. And would, she determined, be reality by Thanksgiving.

The house itself would shine by Christmas, and she would christen it with a huge and glittery New Year's Eve party.

Ring in the new, Julia thought, and grinned.

On cue, the doorbell rang. Mr. Murdoch, she thought, and right on time. She had used his company as her head contractor for nearly six years. This wasn't the first property Julia had purchased, or the first she had rehabbed, or the first she had lived in. Real estate was her passion. And her skill for wheeling deals came naturally, down through the blood.

Her grandfather had gone from pauper to millionaire on the qualities of a shrewd mind, a sharp eye and a gambler's heart. Of all his children and grandchildren, it was Julia who most closely followed in the big man's footprints.

She hurried downstairs, anxious to begin discussing plans and wrangling about fees with the crafty Scotsman. Daniel MacGregor himself had recommended Michael Murdoch and his company to her years before, and Julia blessed him for it. She felt she'd found a kindred spirit in those twinkling blue eyes and capable workingman's hands.

So she was smiling when she opened the door. And scowling a pulse beat later.

It wasn't Michael Murdoch, but his son. She considered Cullum Murdoch the only fly in the ointment of her excellent relationship with the contracting company.

"Where's your father?" she demanded.

"He's not feeling well." Cullum didn't waste smiles on women who irritated. So his cool green eyes, his full, sculpted mouth, remained sober. "I'm doing the run-through."

"He's sick?" The concern was instant and sincere, and had her reaching for Cullum's hand. "What's wrong with him? Has he seen a doctor?"

"It's nothing serious, late-summer cold." But he softened a bit. Her eyes were worried, her affection for his father was palpable. "He just needs to stay in bed and take it easy for a couple days."

"Oh." They stood where they were, on either side of the threshold, with the morning sun beating down. She released his hand and calculated. She didn't care to work with Cullum, but neither did she care to delay the project.

He read her, and dark brows lifted over amused green eyes. "I can stand it if you can, MacGregor."

Frowning, Julia studied him. Men who were as handsome as the devil rarely irritated her. And Cullum, with his sharp-boned, sculpted face, certainly qualified. There was the added appeal of the lion's mane of bronze-tipped brown hair, the quick and crooked grin—not that he ever aimed it at her—and the long, lanky body that fit so nicely in denim.

But irritate her he did, continually. Their personalities crashed and clashed like honed swords on a battlefield.

Annoying or not, she thought, he was good at his work. And it was only a run-through.

"All right, Murdoch, let's get started, then."

He stepped onto the wide squares of rose-veined tiles in the foyer, gave the staircase a sweeping glance, took a considering look at the ornate plasterwork on the vaulted ceiling.

"How's the foundation?"

"Solid as a rock."

"I'll check it out."

There, she thought, gritting her teeth. That was just it. The man constantly questioned her judgment, argued with her opinions, sneered at her tastes. She drew in a breath. "I've taken notes," she said, and took minicassettes from the pocket of her trim navy trousers.

"Yeah, the famous MacGregor tapes." Sarcasm edged his voice as he took them, stuffed them in the back pocket of his jeans.

"It's more efficient than scribbling notes on paper, and my plans and outlines can't be misconstrued."

"Yeah, you're in charge."

"It's my house," she snapped.

He shot her a bland look. "Who said it wasn't?"

He moved beyond her, into the small front parlor, and instantly thought that whoever had painted the molding should have been beaten mercilessly. "Cozy."

"Cramped," she corrected. "I want the right wall taken out. The room beyond is just as cramped, equaling two wasted spaces, in my opinion."

It was a good move, but she so clearly thought so, there was no need to confirm it—and there was an irresistible desire to challenge it. "Old, traditional houses like this don't like structural changes."

"The wall goes."

With unhurried, long-legged strides he strolled over, looked it up, looked it down. "Probably screw up this nice random-width pine floor."

"Then you'll just have to fix it." She walked through the still-empty room, her steps echoing hollowly. "I want the molding stripped down to natural wood, and there's some minor plasterwork you can see for yourself. The stone needs to be repointed on the fireplace, but the mantel is in excellent shape. And over in here..."

She strode out and into the next room, waiting for him to follow. "The patio door is too small. I want the opening widened, an atrium installed. Walnut, beveled glass, brass hardware."

He saw the results in his head, approved them, but shrugged. "That's going to mean cutting into the brick."

"I'm aware of that, Murdoch."

"It's going to cost you."

The sneer was in her eyes. "We'll discuss your estimate after you've worked it up. But to continue, naturally, all the walls will need to be repainted or repapered, and the fireplace in here..." She cocked her head, measuring the line and distance from the fireplace in the next room. "I'll want this mantel replaced with one to match the other. And the flue here's been blocked off. It needs to be opened. Thermal glass for all the windows, of course."

"Of course."

Ignoring the smirk, she brushed past him and continued. If it had been his father, she would have asked opinions, discussed strategies. They'd have been laughing over something by now, or been on their hands and knees examining the floor molding.

She would do none of those things with the son.

Her voice was as stiff as her spine, Cullum thought. And he wished to God she didn't smell so good. It was distracting, having that warrior-goddess fragrance assault him whenever he got within three feet of her.

He did his best to keep his distance.

He considered her a snotty, cold, bossy and arrogant woman. Anything but his type. The fact that he occasionally wondered what she would taste like was, in his opinion, just a reflex, and nothing more.

They moved through the first floor, room by room.

It was a great house, he mused, but then, he'd never known Julia MacGregor to buy a loser. She had an eye for buildings; he could respect that. And he could respect the fact that whatever she bought, she tended well.

But she never shut the hell up, he decided, and she treated him as if he were brain-dead, explaining and outlining every point and change.

Replacement tiles in the powder room. Yeah, yeah. New hardware for the pedestal sink. Did she think he couldn't see that the current faucet was rusted and clunky? He had eyes, didn't he?

They spent nearly an hour in the kitchen. Julia wanted a complete redesign there, all of it built around two points—the old brick hearth that she wanted in working order again, and the wall-spanning chestnut breakfront.

He was pleased to shut down a couple of her ideas as unworkable, and even more pleased to replace her plans with his own.

"You've got plenty of room." He stood in the center of the kitchen, on a shiny linoleum floor. "Why do you want to waste it?"

"That's not—"

"It's just plain stupid to have the stove and refrigerator that far apart. You want a flow, a traffic pattern. Aesthetics and convenience. It's pretty obvious you don't cook."

She angled her head. "And in your little world, women whip up hot meals nightly for their weary men."

"In my little world, people who cook eat better. You can keep your sink under the double windows there. The counter comes around here. You curve it, give it a nice fluid look.'' His gestures were brisk, economic, those of a man accustomed to being in charge—and being obeyed. ''Dishwasher here, stove there, fridge there. Keep the pantry under the back steps. Get rid of the ugly door on it. Now, if I were you—''

''You're not.''

''I'd run another length of counter out here. A serving and conversation bar. It'd break up the space, really use it. Then you take that summer porch, make it part of the room. Get rid of the wall.''

She winged a brow. ''I thought old, traditional houses didn't care for structural changes.''

Good one, he thought, but shrugged his shoulders. ''It's already too late for that. If you're going to figure out how to take out one, you can take out two. You ditch the screens, put in windows, then use that part of the L for a sitting area. I could run a bench under the windows.''

Oh, it was coming together beautifully in her mind. ''I saw this terrific old church pew last week.''

''Even better. You'll never use the porch the way it's set up now for anything but junk space. This way you'd bring those gardens inside—not that they don't need work—and add some great light.''

She wanted it, absolutely. ''Well, I'll consider it.''

''Fine, and you'll want to get rid of the floor covering.''

''It's brand-new.''

''Odds are it's covering up more random-width pine.''

''Nobody's that stupid.''

He took out a pocketknife, flicked the blade. Those green eyes flashed with challenge. ''Bet?''

She waffled between wanting him to be right and hating being wrong. ''All right, take up a corner. But if you're wrong, you take five percent off your estimate.''

''If I'm right, you do the kitchen my way.''

She nodded. ''Deal.''

He walked to the corner closest to the back door, and got down on his knees. It took him less than two minutes. ''You're going to be very happy.''

''Just subflooring, huh?'' Smug, she walked over, peered down. ''Oh.'' She scrambled down to her hands and knees, thrilled to see the pine boards. ''What idiots. Take off some more.''

''Likely it's scratched, scarred and stained.'' He worked off more linoleum. ''So they took the easy route and covered it up.''

It was like finding buried treasure. Julia had to stop herself from ripping at it with her bare hands.

They were hip-to-hip now, shoulder-to-shoulder. The curling cloud of her hair brushed his cheek. The scent of it drew him, and without thinking, he turned his head, inhaled.

She felt the flutter, the quick answer to it in the pit of her stomach. She straightened so quickly she nearly bashed his nose with her head. ''What are you doing?''

''Nothing.'' What the hell had gotten into him? was all he could think. Was he completely insane?

''You were sniffing me.''

''Get a grip. I was breathing. It's just something I do to get through the day.''

The fact that her pulse was dancing a jig infuriated her. Her mouth was dry, her skin hot. "Well, don't do it around me," she snapped, and got quickly to her feet. "Let's go through the second floor and get this over with."

"Fine." He closed the blade and shoved the knife back in his pocket, because it was tempting to jab it into his own heart as punishment for his momentary lapse. "And don't worry, MacGregor, I'll make sure I hold my breath."

"Idiot," she muttered under her own as she stalked from the room. But she wasn't sure which one of them she was referring to.

Daniel MacGregor imagined he was puffing on a cigar. Tipped back in the massive leather chair in his massive office in his massive home, he blew imaginary smoke rings at the ceiling while he listened to his good friend Michael Murdoch on the telephone.

"So the boy bought it."

"He did, indeed," Michael told him. "I hacked a bit, held my nose when I called him." Michael did so now, making his voice stuffy and wheezy. "You'll have to see to Julia today, I told him. I'm feeling poorly. He didn't care for it," Michael continued, his voice clear as church bells on Sunday. "But he's a good boy and takes pride in the company."

"He's a fine boy, your Cullum." Daniel grinned at the ceiling, shifted the telephone to his other ear. He'd known Michael Murdoch for fifteen years, respected him as a professional, liked him as a man. He'd grieved with him when Michael lost his wife a decade before. And plotted with him nearly as long.

"So, it's a big job," Daniel continued. "It'll take a few months, more or less, and keep them rubbing up against each other."

"I'll be sick for a week or two—gives me a chance to catch up on my reading. Then I'll be feeling a little off my feed for a week or two more. By that time, Cullum will be deep into the project. I'll be able to convince him he should follow it through. He'll want it by that point in any case."

"Don't understand for a minute why the boy hasn't made a move toward the girl already. They've known each other for years. Two strong, healthy, attractive people." He shook his head sadly, stroking his soft white beard. "I tell you, Michael, children today have to be led along by the hand or they get nothing important done."

"There's a spark between them, Daniel. You and I, we're just blowing on it a bit. It's time for my Cullum to settle down, find his happiness."

"Agreed." For punctuation, Daniel thumped his fist on the desk. "And Julia needs to do the same. Why, the girl's twenty-five years old. What's she waiting for?" Then he smiled, settled back again. "They'll make beautiful babies together for us, Michael."

Chapter 22

Blissfully unaware that her life was being arranged for her, Julia sat in the center of her bed, poring over books of samples. Wallpaper, paint, tile. She had mountains of catalogs listing hinges, doorknobs, bathroom and kitchen hardware. She scribbled down possibilities and recorded her final choices.

It had taken two weeks of meetings, of negotiations, and of snarling arguments, for her and Cullum to finalize the projected work, the deadlines and the estimated costs.

She'd had no choice but to accept him as head contractor on the job. When she slipped into the Murdoch offices and saw how tired and worn Michael Murdoch was, she'd stifled all complaints.

Until he regained his strength, he'd be riding his desk. She didn't want to be responsible for making him feel he had to drag himself to the site and supervise.

She shifted, sliding her legs from left to right for comfort. The morning had been spent at a settlement for a property she'd sold. She had yet to change out of the short summer-blue skirt and jacket she'd worn for the meeting.

Absently she tapped her fingers on a swatch of floral wallpaper. She had a weakness for colored stones, and a trio of them winked on her hand. Others gleamed at her ears, her wrist.

Because she'd pulled out the pins the minute she stepped into her room, her hair tumbled wildly over her shoulders. She hummed to herself, enjoying the background noise of saws and hammers traveling up from the first floor.

Men at work, she thought. Terrific music.

Cullum could only be grateful she didn't look up when he stepped into the doorway. She would have seen his tongue slide out of his mouth and hit his shoes.

My God, the woman had legs, yards of them, and that tiny little skirt wasn't covering up much. She didn't look the least bit like a businesswoman. More like a pagan goddess. It almost made a man forget she had a smart mouth and a snakebite temper.

When she idly rubbed a hand high on her thigh, he rolled his eyes to the ceiling, begging for mercy. He had to take two slow, steady breaths to pull himself in line.

"Got a minute, MacGregor?"

"Hmm?" The wild roses on dusky blue, or the sleek traditional stripes? Roses, she decided. Why be subtle?

"MacGregor? Jules?" He moved over, snapped his

fingers under her nose and had the pleasure of seeing her gaze shoot up in shock.

"What?" Surprise was what had her heart jolting, she told herself.

"Your wall's out. Thought you might want to see."

"Oh. Sure. In a minute." She hated to be taken unawares, not given time to engage all controls. "I'll come right down."

A man would be crazy to walk away from those legs when he could linger, Cullum decided. He sat on the bed, amused when her eyes narrowed. "Getting ahead of yourself, aren't you?"

"I was about to say the same," she said primly.

"You won't be needing wall coverings for some time yet."

"It pays to think ahead."

He leaned forward, studied the stripes she'd just rejected. "Boring." His gaze traveled up those legs. "That's about the only thing you're not."

"Let's see, compliment or insult?" She resisted tugging at her skirt. She wouldn't give him the satisfaction. "Insult," she decided. "Get lost."

"Why are you all dressed up?" He fingered her lapel, knowing she'd slap at his hand. She didn't disappoint him.

"I had a settlement. The Court Street property."

"Oh, yeah, nice place, but too downtown." He spread open her paint-sample booklet, considered the choices. "This is the kind of thing you want in this room. Deep green. It's rich and it's restful."

She'd been thinking along those lines. "Going into interior decorating, Murdoch?"

"You work on enough houses, you get ideas for what works." His eyes, as rich and deep and green as the paint he'd chosen, latched on to hers. "And when you put time and effort and creativity into rehabbing a house, then the owners screw it up with the colors and furnishings, it ticks you off."

Damn it, she agreed again. This was getting dangerous. "How's your father?"

"He's bouncing back." But a shadow of concern flickered in his eyes. "I've never seen him take so long to throw off a cold. He said he'd been to the doctor. He's got a prescription and orders to take it easy for another week or two."

"That's sensible." Understanding nothing better than she understood family love and concern, Julia laid a hand on Cullum's knee. "Oh, he'll be fine. He's as tough as they come."

"He keeps saying he's getting old. Damn it, he's only sixty."

"He's just feeling sorry for himself. I'm the same way when I'm sick." She gave his knee a comforting squeeze. "Don't worry."

"He asked about you, and the project." She was smiling at him, a rare event. Cullum discovered he wanted to draw it out a little longer. "He made noises about coming by, taking it off my hands, but he's just not up to it."

"Let's not bother him with it. I'm sure we can get through one rehab together without one of us bricking the other up behind a wall in the basement."

"We can try." He skimmed a finger up her calf, watched her eyes pop wide, and flashed a grin.

"Keep your hands to yourself, buster."

"You've got yours on my knee," he noted, patting it.

She snatched it back, fuming. "It serves me right for trying to be friendly. Get out of my bed."

"I'm not in it," he pointed out, "I'm on it. And to tell you the truth, up until now I hadn't thought about getting into it. You've presented me with a whole new world of possibilities."

"Murdoch, the day you get in my bed is the day they're building snowmen in hell."

He didn't know what pushed him to it, ego or desire. Perhaps a mixture of both. But he leaned toward her until their faces were close, their eyes locked, their mouths a breath apart. "Bet?"

Her blood was an ocean roar in her head, and her pride shuddered at the fact that for even one tiny instant she'd been excited. Tempted. "Unlike you, I don't wager on sex. And unlike you, I won't consider getting horizontal with someone I can barely tolerate when we're vertical."

Because he'd seen that quick flare of interest in her eyes, he was satisfied. With a shrug, he got off the bed. "I still like your legs, MacGregor. They're definitely top-of-the-line legs."

He walked out, leaving her vowing to cover up every inch of them anytime she was around him.

"And then he tried to bet me that I'd sleep with him."

Two days later, and Julia was still fuming over it. She paced her bedroom while her cousin Laura cuddled her three-month-old son on her shoulder.

"He was just trying to annoy you." Satisfied

young Daniel was fed, dry and sleeping, Laura settled him into the portable crib Julia had already set up near the window. "He knows how easy it is."

"I'm not easily irritated," Julia corrected. "Except by Cullum Murdoch."

"Exactly. Just ignore him, Julia. You've said yourself he does wonderful work. Take the ends, ignore the means."

"You're right, you're right." Julia closed her eyes, ordered herself to settle. The sound of work in progress was muffled by the closed bedroom door. She kept it closed now, at all times. "He doesn't even exist. There." She opened her eyes again, and smiled. "Gone. I sent him on the plague train to limbo."

"Good one." Then Laura bit her lip and looked down at her peacefully sleeping son. "Are you sure you can do this? I'll only be a couple hours. Three at the very most, but—"

"Of course I can. I'm looking forward to having him all to myself." Julia brushed her fingers over Daniel's soft black hair. "He's so beautiful, Laura, and already growing so big."

"I know. I hate missing even a minute with him. I know I have to settle the nanny business. It's just so hard. I didn't know it would be so hard."

"You're a terrific mommy, and Royce's a terrific daddy."

"Daniel makes it easy. He's the best baby." She sighed, shook herself. "Okay, okay, he'll be fine with his aunt Jules. I brought everything he'll need. He shouldn't be hungry, but there's breast milk in the bottle if he is. He'll probably sleep nearly as long as I'm gone. There's diapers, and his little bear, the number of the courthouse.'' It was an effort for Laura not to bite her nails. ''Two changes of clothes, Royce's and my beeper numbers. You know how he likes to be rocked when—''

''Laura.'' She had to laugh. ''I promise you, I will not sell him to Gypsies while you're gone.''

''I'm obsessing.'' Laura managed a smile. ''I'll stop. I do appreciate you taking care of him for me this morning.''

''My pleasure. I don't have any appointments, so Daniel and I will just admire each other until you get back.''

It took another ten minutes, but Julia finally managed to boot Laura out the door. Then, rubbing her hands together, she walked back to the crib. ''Alone at last, angel. I sure hope you don't sleep the morning away.''

Two hours later, she bitterly regretted those words. The angel was screaming like a banshee. She'd tried the bottle, the bear, the rocking, the walking, the singing. Nothing worked. His adorable little face remained red and furious as he exercised his lungs at full volume.

''What are you doing, beating him?''

With Daniel hugged to her chest, she whirled when the door opened, and snarled at Cullum. ''Yes, it's one of my favorite pastimes, especially when they are small, defenseless babies. Go away. Come on, sweetheart, hush now.''

''Is he wet?''

''No, he's not wet. Do I look like an idiot?'' With her free hand, she scooped the hair out of her eyes.

''He didn't want the bottle, he doesn't want to be rocked, and I've walked from here to Oklahoma, but it doesn't help.''

''Let's see.'' He rolled his eyes when Julia held Daniel away from him defensively. ''Come on, Jules, I haven't dropped a baby in at least two months. Here we go, big guy.'' He pried the screaming baby out of her exhausted arms. ''What's the matter, little fella?''

Julia blinked at the image. The lanky man, with tousled, gold-streaked hair, a tool belt slung at his narrow hips, a faded denim work shirt with the sleeves rolled up past the elbows of well-toned arms. And a baby cradled in them as naturally as air.

''Probably teething.''

''How do you know?''

''Because I've got three nieces, thanks to my sister, and every one of them has teeth. Your cousin bring anything for him to chew on?''

''She brought everything else. I'll look.''

While she did, Cullum offered Daniel his knuckle. The baby immediately began to gnaw. ''If your gums were this swollen,'' he told her, ''you'd be crying, too.''

''Here.'' Frazzled, Julia held out a blue teething ring. When Cullum slipped it into Daniel's mouth, the screaming stopped. Now there was just whimpering, and a tiny, tear-streaked face.

''That's some better, isn't it?'' Cullum murmured, and traced a fingertip over Daniel's cheek. His eyes were warm, deep green as he smiled down at the baby. ''God, he's cute.''

''You like babies?''

''What's not to like?'' He swung the baby up, making Julia's heart stop and Daniel gurgle with the beginnings of a laugh. "You've just got to take his mind off his gums," Cullum told her, jiggling giggles out of Daniel as he held him high overhead. "Want to go down with the guys, champ?"

"You can't take him downstairs. The dust, the noise."

Still grinning into Daniel's face, Cullum shook his head. "Women. Always worrying about a little dust. He'll like it. Babies like motion and sound. It stimulates." He perched the now busily chewing baby on his hip. "And then we'll go in the kitchen for lunch. A beer and a meatball sandwich."

She didn't mean to grin, it just happened. They were both watching her, the big-eyed baby, the cool-eyed man. "Well, maybe, just for a minute. But he can't run the power saw."

"Bummer." He planted a kiss on top of Daniel's head. "You coming, or do you trust me with him?"

"Surprisingly, I trust you with him, but I'm coming anyway." She snagged a burp cloth. "He spits up a lot," she explained.

"What's a little spit between real men?"

"Cullum, I..." She hesitated, didn't notice his amused surprise. She never called him by his first name. "I really appreciate it. I was about to tear out my hair."

"Nice hair," he said as his gaze swept over it. "It would have been a shame. Come on." He held out a hand. "Let's go see what the kid thinks of the job so far."

Her hand was in his before she could think about it, and then it seemed rude to take it back. "You're making good progress. Do you think you'll be able to start on the master bedroom next week?''

''That's the plan.'' The noise rose as they headed for the stairs.

''I'll get the furniture out over the weekend, and move into the bedroom down the hall.''

''We'll do it. Tile guy's nearly finished with the powder room down here. I know it wasn't a priority, but he was available. You liked his work before, so I wanted to get him before he started another job.''

''Great. I'll be sure to take a look at it.''

''You decide yet on the color and material for your kitchen counters?''

''Yes, just yesterday. I've got the tape upstairs.''

''I bet you do. What did you go with?''

''Slate-blue ceramic, four-inch tiles, navy grout.''

''Not bad.'' It would be stunning.

''Yo, Cullum.'' One of the carpenters came out of the expanded parlor. ''You want to take a look at this before we nail?''

''Yeah, be right there.''

''Here, let me take him.'' Their arms brushed as the baby passed between them. ''Go ahead, we'll watch at a safe distance.''

He gave Daniel a flick on the nose. ''Don't forget the brew and meatballs, pal,'' he said, and headed off.

''Well, that was unexpected, wasn't it?'' she murmured, shifting Daniel to rest him against her shoulder. ''Who'd have thought such an annoying man could be so sweet with a baby?''

Patting Daniel's back, she moved to the doorway. The wall was gone, the room wide and full of light. And full of men, noise and tools.

Nothing pleased her more than watching the stages of a job. Walking into a perfect home just wasn't enough. It was so much more satisfying to see a space and calculate the changes that could be made to enhance, to take action and to see, step by step, those changes taking place.

Drop cloths covered the floor, sawhorses held boards ready to be cut to size. The mason knelt at the hearth, perfecting the repointing of stone.

In the new opening, Cullum stood with two men. He had his hands tucked in his back pockets as they discussed the trim for the archway that joined the rooms.

He laughed, and the sound was all male.

All male, Julia thought with a quick thrill. That was the way to describe him. His hand had been hard and rough with calluses when it took hers. He'd smelled of sawdust and sweat. The muscles in his arms were lean and hard from use.

And the way the denim fit over his hips was…delicious.

"Oh, my." She hissed out a breath. What was she doing noticing how his jeans fit? And what did she care if there was a thin gold ring around his pupils before the dark and misty green took over? She wasn't the least bit interested in him as a man. He was simply a paid laborer.

Then he turned around, grinned that crooked grin at her, winked at the baby.

Her heart bumped hard once, then twice, against her ribs.

She was suddenly very grateful she hadn't taken him up on that bet.

Chapter 23

Julia's day had started with a breakfast speech for the Boston Businesswomen's Association. At one she'd been guest lecturer at a political science forum at Harvard. That evening she would be the dinner speaker at a real estate convention.

She didn't mind giving speeches. It was just talking, after all, and giving opinions. She'd always considered herself good at both. The eight years she spent as First Daughter had given her intense on-the-job training in how to handle people, crowds, media.

She agreed to such events several times a year, and tried to group them into one or two days.

Her schedule was tight, but by late afternoon she was combing the antique stores hunting for doorknobs.

She hadn't been satisfied with the available hardware. Her new plan was to go for variety. Every door in the house would have a different and unique look by the time she was finished.

She bagged oval brass, faceted glass, smooth wood, glossy enamel. There were hooks and knobs and wonderful shapes and textures. By the time she was finished, she had more than three dozen different door-closing implements in her box, and some were already labeled for location.

On her way home, she detoured by Murdoch and Sons. She knew how Michael Murdoch enjoyed talking salvage. She could entertain him, see for herself how he was feeling and dump the hardware, all in one short visit.

She drove through the industrial center, as at home there amid the low buildings and huge trucks as she was in Beacon Hill's tony neighborhood. She beeped her horn, sent out a friendly wave, when she passed people she knew. She pulled into Murdoch's, pleased to see that Michael's battered Chevy pickup was in the small lot.

She hefted her box, grunting only a little under its weight. She was still wearing her public-appearance suit, giving the men in the area the opportunity to send out the obligatory whistles.

She took it all with a careless grin and a wave. She knew most of the guys by name, had worked with many of them.

The outer office was small and comfortably untidy. Manning the ancient metal desk was a woman who wore a trio of pencils in her hair, a Murdoch and Sons T-shirt and a slightly harassed smile.

"Julia. Don't you look fresh and sunny."

"Hi, Meg. Busy day?"

Rolling her eyes, Meg answered the shrilling phone. "Murdoch and Sons, please hold." She let out a little sigh as she punched the hold button. "Business is good, which means I hear phones ringing in my sleep. What can we do for you?"

"I've got some things I want to show the boss." Julia jiggled the box. "Is he free?"

"For you? Are you kidding? Go right on back."

"Thanks. How's he doing?"

"Moving a little slow yet, but he'll get back on track. Seeing you will perk him up. I'll buzz him, tell him you're on your way."

"Great. I won't tire him out," Julia promised and, shifting the box again, started toward the short hallway that led to the offices.

It surprised her to find Michael's door closed. Open doors were part of the Murdoch style. Concerned, she managed to free a hand and knock. Concern was slipping toward worry when the door opened.

He was flushed and looked a little clammy. He'd had to move like the wind when Meg buzzed him. The footlong hot dog with the works that he'd smuggled in and been about to enjoy was now shoved into a file-cabinet drawer, along with his liter of Dr. Pepper. The handheld electronic game he'd borrowed from his granddaughter had gone in with it, and so had a generous slab of double-fudge-chocolate cake.

Such things, he knew, didn't jibe with his image as a sick old man.

"Julia." He didn't have to make his voice breathless and weak. Nerves did that for him. "So nice of you to come by to see me."

"Mr. Murdoch." Instantly concerned, she dumped

the box on his desk and took his hands. He looked feverish and shaky. "You should be home in bed."

"Oh, I'm fine. Fine." He added a quick, wheezing cough, which he thought was inspired. "I'm taking it easy, honey. Time was, a damn stupid chest cold wouldn't have gotten me down like this."

"I thought it was a head cold."

Oh, hell, he thought. "It's gone into my chest. Let's sit down." She took his arm to lead him to a chair. For a moment, she was certain she smelled onions, but she dismissed the thought.

Michael sighed heavily. "Tell me, how's my boy doing by you?"

She had a few complaints, chief among them the fact that Cullum still questioned every one of her choices and demands. But she smiled. "The project's coming right along. Of course, I'd rather have you than anyone, handsome."

He chuckled, squeezed her hand. A man couldn't ask for a more perfect daughter-in-law, he decided, if she'd been handpicked. And, of course, she had been. "Cullum's the best at what he does."

"Well, he was certainly taught by the best."

Michael grinned, waving away the compliment. "You're going to turn my head. Now, what have you brought me there in the box?"

"Treasures. Oh, I'm so jazzed about this, Mr. Murdoch. I've been hunting doorknobs."

His eyes lit. "Well, let's have a look."

For twenty minutes, they played with her new toys, discussed and speculated on age and history, debated the choices of doors they would grace. Julia gleefully shifted labels, added more.

"My bedroom door's a wonderful old oak Bible-style. One of the few original ones left in the place, after those peasants who owned it last got done. You saw how they painted the moldings."

Michael nodded sadly. "A crime, a sin."

"Did Cullum tell you they'd slapped linoleum down over the original pine floor in the kitchen?" She heated up just thinking about it. "It was in ragged shape, certainly, but it'll refinish. It'll be gorgeous." She waved a hand. "Anyway, don't you think this glass knob with the vertical carving would be perfect for the bedroom door?"

"Absolutely."

She flashed a smile. "I just love dealing with someone who agrees with me. Oh, Lord, look at the time. I've got to get home and change."

"You going out tonight?" A little probing never hurt, he thought. "Do you have a new beau?"

"No new beau, but I do have a dinner thing at seven-thirty."

"Why don't you leave your knobs here, and I'll give Cullum the box? He'll see to it for you."

"Terrific. I can't wait to see how they'll look." She leaned over to kiss his cheek. "And you take care of yourself, Mr. Murdoch. I want you dancing at my house-christening party."

"I'll be there."

He sat back as she went out, and grinned to himself. A little plot was working in his head. Cagily he rose slowly, pushed his door shut. Then he danced to the file cabinet and pulled out his early dinner. He'd eat while he talked to Daniel MacGregor and worked the kinks out of the latest plan.

* * *

"Damn fussy, impatient, irritating woman," Cullum muttered as he aligned the glass knob in the door. Oh, she'd been clever to go to his father with her demands, because if she'd come to him instead, he'd have given her a piece of reality.

What the hell was she thinking of, planning a party while the house was a construction zone?

Probably thought it would be a lark, having crowds of her fancy friends wandering around on drop cloths, eating canapés and commenting on half-plastered ceilings.

And she had to have her damn doorknobs on.

He didn't mind working overtime. He didn't mind doing punch-out jobs himself—when it was time for punch-out jobs—but he did mind being maneuvered into a corner.

He'd had no choice but to agree to take the box, go over to Julia's while she was out kicking up her heels and get the knobs on. Not with his father asking him to indulge one of their best clients, not when his father looked so tired and weak.

I can go over and take care of it myself, Cullum, if you're busy.

"Sure," Cullum said between his teeth. "Like I'd send him over here to work at nine o'clock at night so he could pass out cold on the floor."

It was nearly eleven now, and he was almost done. His temper had risen steadily as he moved from door to door. It didn't matter that he found her idea of unique antique knobs throughout the house inspired. Her methods tipped the scales.

She was, he thought again, a spoiled, arrogant, self-centered female. Hadn't he always thought so? He'd been stupid to think that maybe there was something else there. The way she'd held that baby, the way she laughed with the men or brought in boxes of doughnuts, gallons of coffee, to offer them. She learned their names, and little personal details, and always found a moment or two to compliment a man on his work.

Just politics, he thought now.

He heard the front door open and smiled grimly. So the party girl was home, he thought. He hoped she'd had a high old time, because she was about to hear just what Cullum Murdoch thought of her.

He'd reached the top of the stairs before he heard voices in the foyer. Julia's and a man's. It made him sneer. Brought one of her pretty boys home, he supposed and, indulging himself, moved quietly forward until he could see them.

"Tod, I'm really tired. I've had a long day."

"You wouldn't send me off without one drink."

She sighed, tried not to be annoyed. She'd dated Tod on and off—mostly off—for six months. And she was ashamed to admit that his main qualifications were that he looked terrific in black tie and could schmooze his way cheerfully through even the most boring of social affairs.

She supposed she owed him a drink for that alone.

"All right." She removed her wrap, revealing the sleek black evening dress she wore beneath. "What would you like?"

"What I'd really like..." He moved smoothly, slipping his arms around her waist, lowering his mouth to hers, before she could do more than register annoyance.

She didn't protest or respond. She'd already discovered, to her mild disappointment, that kissing Tod did absolutely nothing to bump up her blood pressure or her pulse rate. It was pleasant enough, but so was a good book.

"Tod, I'm tired."

"So, I'll wake you up a little." His hands stroked up her back, where two thin straps crossed over flesh. "I've been wanting to. I've been wanting you, Julia."

"I'm sorry. It's just not—"

The irritation came now, and a few muffled alarm bells. He tightened his grip, and his mouth grew hard and demanding. She lifted her arms to push him gently away, then felt his hands cup her bottom and squeeze. Her push wasn't gentle anymore.

"No."

"Julia." Still smiling, he reached out to toy with her slim shoulder strap. "Let's stop playing games here."

She set her teeth as his fingertip trailed down toward her breast. "Which part of no didn't you understand?"

He stopped smiling. "Look, you've been stringing me along for months. I've been patient, but now I'm tired of waiting."

Her eyes narrowed and sparked. "Oh, well, in that case, I should just lie back and let you have a go. How ridiculous of me to think that sex involves two interested people."

"You know damn well you're interested. You're

not going to tell me you wore that dress tonight to impress a bunch of Realtors."

That snapped it. She turned, walked to the door and opened it. "No, I'm not. I wore it because I liked it. And the last I heard, a woman is free to dress as she chooses. Now, I'd advise you to leave before I do what I really want to do, which is punch your caps out."

"You really are a cold and frigid bitch," he said as he walked past her.

She slammed the door, then shut her eyes as her breath began to heave. "What a jerk."

"And I thought he was such a nice guy."

Her eyes popped open, and the temper in them only sharpened with embarrassment as she saw Cullum come down the stairs. "What the hell are you doing in my house?"

"My job." When he realized his fist was still clenched—the fist he'd been ready to plow into Tod's poster-boy face—he loosened it. She'd handled herself like a champ, Cullum thought, and he admired her style even more now that he could see how shaken she was.

"It is a killer dress," he said, hoping to soothe her.

Her spine snapped straight. "Go to hell."

"Hey." Gently he touched a hand to her arm before she could stalk past him. Concern deepened his voice and the color of his eyes. "Sorry, wrong angle. You ought to sit down, Jules. You're shaking."

"I'm angry."

"Don't blame you. He *was* a jerk, but you handled it."

Humiliation warred with temper. "You got a real eyeful, didn't you, Murdoch?"

"Look, I'm sorry to have been your audience for that little play, but it's your own fault."

"Oh, is it?" Transferring her rage from Tod to Cullum was effortless. She jabbed a finger into his chest, hard enough to rock him back on his heels. "And I suppose any woman who makes herself look attractive is just *asking* for it. The minute she dabs on perfume, she's really saying, 'Take me, you wild man.'"

"I'm not talking about the damn dress, I'm talking about the damn doorknobs."

"Doorknobs." At her wit's end, she dragged her hands through her hair. "Have I lost my mind or have you?"

"You're the one who had to have the doorknobs on tonight." Now, his eyes sparked with temper. "You're the one who came by the shop whining to my father about some ridiculous party you're having. Do you think I want to work until nearly midnight?"

She pressed her fingers to her temples, unsurprised by the headache raging there, then held out her hands. "Wait. I did go by to see your father. I wanted to see how he was doing. I'd been antiquing. I took the knobs by so we could play with them together."

"And so you could wheedle him into pushing work forward to accommodate your party."

"What party?" She threw up her hands now. "I'm not having a party. How can I have a party when the house is in the middle of rehab? I don't know what..." She trailed off, then shut her eyes. "Oh, I get it. Look, I need some aspirin."

Without waiting to see if he'd follow, she headed back into the kitchen, giving Cullum a very distracting view of bare back and slim hips. It was a killer dress, all right, he thought resentfully. It was murdering him.

She found a bottle in the cupboard, poured a glass of water and downed three pills.

"Okay, there was a misunderstanding. I took the knobs by, and I did say something about not being able to wait to see how they looked on the doors. I didn't mean I *couldn't* wait. You know what I mean."

Frowning a bit, he nodded. "Okay."

"And I did mention a party. I'm planning on christening the house with one. But not until New Year's Eve. I wasn't specific, I just said I wanted him well enough to dance at my party. He must have mixed it up."

It wasn't like his father to confuse details. But then, Cullum admitted, his father hadn't been himself for a month. "Okay, I get it. Crossed wires, that's all."

"I'm sorry you were dragged out here tonight."

"Not that big a deal. I got some of the knobs on. You want to take a look?"

She worked up a smile. "Sure."

"How about that one?" He jerked his thumb toward the kitchen door, and had to smile when she made a little hum of pleasure.

"Oh, it's perfect. I knew the enameled knobs were made for this door." She hurried closer to admire the delicately painted bluebells against white enamel. "I love little details like this. It's what makes a home special."

"Yeah, I've got to admit it works." He was leaning

over her shoulder to study the knob himself. Then she straightened, and they were suddenly face-to-face and eye-to-eye. Close, close enough for her to see that fascinating gold ring around his misty green irises. Close enough for her blood to heat and stir.

Her heart bounced, hard and high. "I...appreciate you seeing to it."

Her scent was clogging his brain. "Like I said. No big deal." He wanted that mouth—and a great deal more than that. He tried to remind himself how disgusted he'd been with the jerk Tod. But that mouth looked so soft, so generous. So very tempting. "I'd better get going."

"Yeah." Her throat was heated and dry with lust. What the hell was wrong with her? The pressure built up in her chest as they stood there, not quite touching, but she couldn't seem to order herself to breathe. "I'll see you out."

"I know the way."

"Fine."

They moved abruptly, and somehow their lips met, their mouths tangled. Heat speared upward and spread like wildfire as teeth scraped, tongues touched. His hard, rangy body pressed her lush curves against the door, her body strained forward to better mesh with his.

His hands streaked up her sides, the heels pressing the sides of her breasts until her system screamed for full possession. Busily her fingers raked through his overlong gold-tipped hair.

"This is crazy," she said breathlessly.

"Insane." He fastened his mouth on her throat,

desperate for the taste of flesh. She smelled, he thought, like hot, smoldering sin.

"Cullum, we can't do this."

"I know."

She fisted a hand in his hair, dragging his head up until her mouth could fuse with his again.

They plundered, each of them equally greedy, until, all but gasping for air, they broke apart.

"This is not happening and it can't work." She had to brace herself against the door or simply slide bonelessly to the floor.

"No way can it work." He wanted, wildly wanted, to get to the body under that silk.

"This is just a temporary lapse."

"Right." He had to take a step back, but he couldn't take his eyes off her face. "I really want you, Jules."

"Oh, hell." She pressed a hand to her thundering heart. "We need to think about something else. Anything else." Why couldn't she breathe? "Listen, we don't even like each other, Cullum."

"It's tough caring about that at the moment, but yes, okay." Her face was flushed, her eyes smoking. And, he realized with shock and embarrassment, his knees were shaking. "If we do what we're both thinking about doing right now, we'll really hate ourselves and each other in the morning. Of course, I feel obliged to point out it's a while yet till morning."

She was grateful she could smile. "We'd better give this a wide pass. Chalk it up to stress and hormones and whatever." Watching him, she eased away from the door, giving him space to get by. "It'll probably go away."

"We can hope." Cullum started to open the door. God knew he needed air and space. "What if it doesn't, Julia?"

"I don't know."

He studied her for another moment, wondered if she could possibly be as baffled and aroused as he. "Me either," he decided, and got out fast.

Chapter 24

Julia found dozens of things to keep her occupied and out of Cullum's way for the next few weeks. Autumn had taken over New England, with its exceptional style. Trees roared with color, and as they passed their peak, the air took on a snap that hinted slyly of winter.

She looked at properties, put in bids. She dropped by her cousin's office, visited with Laura and her aunt and uncle, had lunch with friends. She shopped, scouring the stores for Christmas presents, and for baby gifts. Her cousin Gwen was three months pregnant. The three-foot stuffed Saint Bernard was the perfect excuse to drop by the house she and Gwen and Laura had once shared.

She found Gwen at home, poring over cookbooks.

''What are you doing?''

Gwen smiled helplessly, running a nervous hand

through her reddish-gold cap of hair. "I really think it's time I learned to cook. At least a couple of standard meals."

"Dr. Blade— Oops. Dr. Maguire." Julia plopped down at the kitchen table. "Why?"

"Well, I'm going to have three months' maternity leave. I'll be home. I should—" she gestured vaguely "—do home things."

"Does Branson care if you can whip up a meat loaf?"

"No, of course not. I do. It's the oddest thing." She ran a hand over her still-flat belly. "I suppose it's part of the whole nesting process. In any case, I'm a surgeon, I'm a scientist, certainly I can figure out the basic formula for, say, meat loaf, and deliver an edible product."

Resting her elbows on the table, she cupped her chin in her hands and grinned at the huge stuffed dog. "I like your new pet."

"Me, too. I was thinking my upcoming niece or nephew would take good care of him."

"That's so sweet, Julia. Did I tell you we're planning on doing an animal theme in the nursery?"

"No more than ten or fifteen times. No need to ask how you're feeling," she added. "You look great."

"I feel great. I've never been happier in my life—and I've had a very happy life."

"The hospital work isn't too much?"

"It's what I want. It fuels me, and satisfies me. You want some coffee? I'm off caffeine, but—"

"No, I don't want anything."

"How about you? How's the house going?"

"Coming right along. My bedroom's finished, and

it's fabulous. We've got a long way to go on the rest, but it's moving. They're working on the kitchen now."

Gwen angled her head, studying Julia's face. "What is it?"

"What's what?"

"What's under it? You've got something on your mind, I can see it."

"It's nothing." But she pushed away from the table to pace. "It's silly."

"Not if it's bothering you."

"It's not really bothering me. It's...surprising me." This was why she'd come, after all, Julia admitted, and dropped back down into the chair. "You know Cullum Murdoch."

"Yes, of course. He's the son of Grandpa's old friend. Construction. They did some work on this place when we first bought it."

"Right. Well, he's the head contractor on my job now. I don't get along with him. Personality clash, I suppose."

"Then why is he working on your house?"

"Long story, and not the point." Julia brushed it away with her fingers. "A couple of weeks ago we were alone in the house, and it was late, and..."

"Oh." Gwen bit the inside of her lip. "I see."

"No, you don't." Julia huffed out a breath. "It was just a sudden animal attraction—and we didn't follow through on it. We agreed it would be a mistake."

"Because you don't get along."

"That, and we've got this professional relationship. I adore his father. That's just one more thing. If Cullum and I ended up in bed to, well, sort of flush this out of our systems, let's say, I don't know how I'd face Mr. Murdoch."

"As I remember Mr. Murdoch, he's a sensible man who loves his son. I can't imagine he'd be shocked that the two of you find each other attractive."

"Finding someone attractive isn't a license to tear up the sheets with him." Julia blew out a breath. "Gwen, I really want to tear up the sheets with Cullum."

"Is he a decent man?"

"Decent? Well, yes, I suppose."

"Does he have humor, intelligence, kindness?"

"He's—" She remembered the way he'd held little Daniel. "Yes. It's just that we butt heads. He's very opinionated and stubborn."

"Oh." Gwen didn't bother to suppress the laugh, just let it roll. "And of course you're so flexible and open-minded."

"Compared to him, I am," Julia said defensively, then laughed at herself. "Okay, that's probably the root of the problem. We both know our own minds and have no problem pushing our opinions on others. He can be right occasionally. It's just that I'm right more." She leaned forward. "He's got these incredible hands. Wide and rough and really strong. I think about them a lot."

"And you wish they were attached to the arms of a more amenable man."

She started to agree, then debated with herself. "I'm not sure. I would have said so a month ago. Now I'm starting to find even the abrasiveness appealing. Sexy. I think I need to get away for a few days."

"Well, that couldn't hurt. But I've never known anyone more sure of their own mind and heart than you. Or more willing to risk going after what she wants. If you end up wanting Cullum, I'd tell you to be careful, to protect yourself, but to trust yourself."

"Good advice." Julia skimmed her hair back from her face. "It may be a good time for me to visit my parents in Washington for a few days. A little distance couldn't hurt. And there's some property down there I want to check on, anyway."

"Be sure to give them my love. And—" she smiled wickedly "—be sure to keep me up-to-date on the Murdoch project."

It was a good way to think of it, Julia decided as she pulled up in front of her house. The Murdoch project. She was an expert on projects, figuring the angles, the profit and loss, the effort and time.

That was exactly what she was going to do, she thought. She would figure the angles, calculate what she could gain or lose, and how much effect Cullum Murdoch would have on her life.

And she was going to do it from a nice, safe distance.

She walked inside, gave an absent wave to some of the workmen, and headed upstairs to pack.

It would be great to surprise her parents, to just drop in for a few days. She really hadn't spent any time alone with them in nearly a year. For the most part, they got together with most or all of the family. And that was more a riot than a visit.

Tapping her foot, she contemplated her wardrobe. She adored the walk-in closet, the space and organization. To her, it was much more practical in this incarnation than it had been as a dressing room. She selected casual clothes, blazers, slacks, one basic dinner dress, and was carrying them toward the bed to the open suitcase when Cullum walked in.

He lifted his brow. "Going somewhere?"

"As a matter of fact, yes. And I don't believe I heard you knock."

"You forgot to close the door this time."

"Oh." She laid the clothes on the bed and walked back into the closet.

He'd never known a single female to own so many clothes. And the shoes—didn't she have the standard two feet? But he'd already told her his opinion on this a couple of times and he felt it was likely to be a waste of time to repeat it.

"Where are you going?"

It was her turn to lift a brow. "Out of town."

"For how long?"

She brushed by him to take her choice of sweaters and blouses to the bed. "Excuse me, but why would you think that's any of your business?"

"Because we're in the middle of a major rehab. I don't want you coming back and whining that something didn't turn out the way you wanted."

"I don't whine." How could she possibly be attracted to someone so irritating? she wondered, and moved to her Duncan Phyfe bureau for lingerie.

"Where can you be reached?"

"I'll call in regularly."

"Look, MacGregor—" He had to stop himself, pull back a step. He didn't know why the sight of her packing a few clothes sent him into a panic. He'd been wanting to get rid of her for weeks. "The kitchen cabinets are coming in next week. If you're not here to approve the delivery—"

"I'll be back by then." Without a hint of embarrassment, she folded frothy-looking bras and panties into a silk lingerie bag. "If you must know, I'm just going to D.C. for a few days."

"Something wrong with your parents?"

She softened. There was no denying the quick and sincere concern in his voice. "No, they're fine. They don't even know I'm coming."

"Then why can't it wait until the kitchen's wrapped? It's the biggest part of the project. If you start wanting us to tear out work—"

"You have my tapes. I've made it perfectly clear what I want done, and if you'll recall, most of the kitchen remodeling is of your design."

"Which is why I don't want to take the heat if you change your mind."

"I do not change my mind once I've made up my mind." She slapped the silk bag into the suitcase. "Get off my back, Murdoch. I come and go as I please."

He felt the snap in the air, all too familiar now. Slowly, he turned, shut the door.

"What are you doing?"

"Insuring some privacy." He studied her, objectively, he told himself. She was flushed with temper. Why that look suited her so well, why it made his blood swim, he didn't know. It just was. She had her hand clenched at her side, as if ready to do battle. Pretty colored rings glittered on it. Her hair was loose, tumbling over the shoulders of a dark green jacket that molded her curves.

She always wore soft clothes, he mused. The kind that drove a man crazy, wanting to get under them.

And there it was, he admitted. He still wanted to get under them.

"Is this impromptu trip a way of running from that thing that went on a couple weeks ago?"

Her head angled, her voice went regally cool. "I don't know what thing you could be referring to."

"The thing where we nearly ended up naked on your kitchen floor?"

"That was a lapse," she snapped, hating herself for wishing they had, just so that the tension in her gut would be gone. "We agreed."

"We did. But was it?"

"We agreed," she repeated stubbornly, then surprised herself by backing up when he stepped forward. "Stay away from me."

For the first time in weeks, he felt an easy smile curve his lips. "Why? Nervous?"

"I don't want you to touch me."

"Who said I was going to touch you? I'm just asking a question. One thing I've never been able to fault you for is honesty. You always tell it like it is, so I'm asking. Was it a lapse for you?"

"I don't know." She nearly shouted it, then whirled around to begin hurling clothes into the suitcase. "It should have been. I'm not running away from anything. I just want to have some distance, to see my parents, to get the hell away from you before we do something stupid."

"Okay, that's honest. So I'll be just as honest. I

don't mind getting away from you for a while, either. Seeing you every day is difficult."

Her hands calmed, carefully smoothed out a wrinkled blouse. "Is it?"

"More difficult than I figured it would be. I keep imagining what it might be like if we had another lapse."

Because she'd never been a coward or a liar, she turned back to face him. He had such a strong face, she thought. All angles and planes set off by that firm mouth and compelling eyes. "I suppose I've wondered the same thing." Her lips curved upward. "What's wrong with us?"

"Damned if I know." This time, when he stepped forward, she stayed where she was. "Do you still not want me to touch you?"

She let out an uneven breath. "It's the middle of the day, what could it hurt?"

"Let's find out." His hands slid up that cloud-soft jacket, then under it until they moved firmly up her back to draw her against him. "Eyes open this time, Jules."

Though he hadn't meant it literally, they watched each other as their mouths met. She saw his eyes darken, saw herself trapped in that deepening green. Experimentally she changed the angle of the kiss. Their lips touching, testing now, hesitating, and with every second that passed, her heart picked up its rhythm.

He ached, and the taste of her had the ache centering in his gut and radiating out to his fingers. He toyed with her mouth, taking his time, though the blood was roaring in his head. Gradually, gradually, he saw her eyes cloud, her lashes flutter. And he swallowed the catchy sigh that slipped from her lips.

"I need to touch you." Even as he said it, his hands skimmed over her breasts, cupped them, possessed. He knew he'd never felt anything more erotic than the way her nipples pressed hard against his palms through the thin silk.

A strangled moan, a flood of need. Her head fell back in a limp surrender that staggered them both. "You have to... Oh, Cullum... You've got such hands."

They were on her flesh now, her blouse open, the front hook of her bra flicked apart. With her heart pounding against his palm, he forgot the men working downstairs, the job needing to be done, the consequences of what he so desperately wanted to do.

"Now." He savaged her throat, her mouth. "Right now."

"Yes— No." Panic, excitement, desire, all twisted inside her. "Wait. What are we doing?" Shuddering, she pulled back, dragged the open blouse together. "We can't, here, like this. We just can't."

He did his best to imagine a bucket of cold water splashed in his face, an icy waterfall raining over his head, anything to help him cool off. The best he could do was shove his hands in his pockets before they started ripping at her clothes.

"Okay," he said as calmly as possible. "But, Jules, you'll have to admit that was a little more than a lapse."

"I've got to stay away from you." She clutched her blouse tighter. Beneath it, her breasts were still tingling from his hands. "We need to take a break, then we need to decide, if this is going to happen—"

"I think we've just answered that part of the question," Cullum said dryly.

"All right, this is going to happen, so we have to figure out how to handle it. We'll go to our respective corners—so to speak—for a few days. You can outline what your thoughts on this are, and I'll do the same. When I come back, we can..."

"Negotiate terms?" he finished for her.

"In a way. We certainly have to have some groundwork here, so we know how we'll deal with...after."

It was sensible, and it annoyed the hell out of him. "Okay, MacGregor, you work up your proposal and I'll work up mine. We'll have a meeting on it when you get back."

"There's no need to get testy."

He stared at her. There she was, he thought, her hair rumpled, her blouse undone, her mouth swollen from his, and she didn't think he should get testy because she was turning it into a business deal.

"Have a good trip, MacGregor."

"Cullum." She sighed once when he stopped with his hand on the door and shot her a fiery look. "I have a professional and a personal relationship with your father, and with you. It's important to me not to compromise it."

He could think of nothing he wanted to say to that, and only nodded briefly and walked out.

Alone, she sat on the edge of the bed and waited

for her system to level. Unless she was very much mistaken, her Murdoch project had taken a sharp detour, and might very well already be hopelessly compromised.

Chapter 25

Julia loved the elegant row house in Georgetown. She had started life there, then, after an eight-year residence at another Washington address, had spent the last of her teenage years in the lofty-ceilinged and airy rooms.

She had no complaints about the time when she'd been able to play in the Rose Garden, or entertain her cousins in the private theater. Her parents, against all odds, had made that Pennsylvania Avenue mansion a home for their children. She'd been given the opportunity to travel all over the world and been taught a sense of responsibility for her neighbors, whether they lived next door or across an ocean.

She could remember even now the warm rush of pride she'd felt when she saw her father man the desk in the Oval Office, or when she watched her mother rise to a thunder of applause before she gave one of a thousand speeches on human rights.

She'd tolerated the omnipresence of the Secret Service, something that had become particularly smothering during her teenage years. She'd accepted the restrictions, the impossibility of just dashing off to shop with friends or share pizza and foolishness at some local restaurant. Her parents had done their best to provide areas of normalcy for Julia and her brother. But Julia had always known she came from greatness. And such miracles had a price.

She remembered the day they had moved back into the home of her early childhood, how her mother had hugged them all, then grinned and told them that they were all going out for pizza and a movie.

It had been one of the sweetest nights of Julia's life.

Now she stood on the sidewalk as her cab drove off. The house still drew her, still comforted. She knew she bought and sold houses to give herself that comfort time and time again, and then to pass it on to others.

Love needed a home to shelter it, and she had been so fortunate in hers.

She hefted her bag and walked up the few brick steps, then rolled the bag behind her down the narrow walk. The fall flowers were fading, she mused. Their autumn brightness dulling as winter blew close. In a bit more than a month, the house would gleam with colored lights, a wreath would hang on the tall front door, and a fresh pine tree, laden with ornaments made by her family, would shine through the graceful front window.

Memories such as those were welcoming.

She knocked, using the brass crest of the Mac-

Gregors to thump on the door. The crowned lion eyed her fiercely and made her think of her grandfather.

When the door opened, Julia beamed at the small, tidy woman who stood there. "Boxy, don't you ever change?"

"Miss Julia!" Elizabeth Boxlieter threw her short arms around Julia and squeezed. Boxy had served a multitude of functions for the MacGregors over a fifteen-year period. Administrative assistant to Mrs. MacGregor had been her title during the White House era. But what she did was manage. Everything.

Boxy drew back, and even though pleasure sparkled in her eyes, she wagged a scolding finger. "You didn't let anyone know you were coming, didn't give us a minute's notice. What if we'd been away?"

"Then I'd have let myself in and felt very sorry for myself." With a laugh, Julia ducked down to kiss Boxy's cheek. "I wanted to surprise all of you. Mom and Dad are home, aren't they?"

"As it happens." Boxy shut the front door. "Your father is just back from Camp David. I swear, they won't leave the man alone, always asking him to negotiate this, advise on that."

"Well, someone has to keep the free world safe, don't they?"

"He did more than his share. The man should be able to go off fishing for a month."

"Dad doesn't fish."

"What difference does that make? He's up in his office on an overseas call, and your mother is back in her workroom."

"I'll interrupt Mom," Julia decided, "then we'll interrupt Dad. Don't carry that suitcase up, Boxy," she said as she started down the hall. "I'll take it myself in a few minutes."

Boxy huffed. As if she'd leave luggage cluttering up the foyer. And, taking the suitcase, she went upstairs.

Shelby MacGregor's workroom was a converted summer kitchen that offered space for her potter's wheel and kiln, her worktable and supplies. Throughout her husband's administration she had continued as a working artist, as much to satisfy her need to create as to make a statement on the human right to pursue a career.

Now, the former First Lady was perched on a stool at her wheel, throwing a pot. Her hands were slicked with clay to the wrists, her forearms speckled. Her dark red hair was bundled messily on top of her head, and her smoke-gray eyes were dark with concentration.

Music played in the background, a somewhat violent concerto. As Julia watched, the clay formed under her mother's clever hands, changing from a shapeless mass, elongating, slimming, becoming an elegant vessel. Julia leaned on the doorjamb and waited.

"Not bad," Shelby muttered, rolling her head and working the kinks out of her neck as she stopped the wheel.

"It'll be beautiful. They're always beautiful."

"Julia!" Shelby popped up, and was halfway to her daughter before she stopped. "Oh, I'm a mess," she said with a laugh, holding out her coated hands. "Here, you kiss me."

Julia obliged, pressed her lips to her mother's cheeks in turn.

"This is a surprise."

"A good one, I hope."

"The best. Let me wash up so I can hug you. Have you seen your father?" Shelby asked as she hurried to a sink to scrub the clay from her hands and arms.

"No, Boxy said he was on the phone, so I came back to interrupt you first."

"Well, he needs a break, so we'll double-team him." She dried off quickly, then turned around to throw her arms around Julia. "Oh, I've missed you. You'll have to tell me everything that's new and wonderful. How are your cousins, little Daniel, how's the house going? How long can you stay? Are you hungry? Answer any or all of the above questions in the order of your choice."

Laughing, Julia walked arm in arm with her mother up the back stairs. "Let's see, the cousins are wonderful. Laura looks like a Madonna with young Daniel, and Gwen's glowing like an angel. I ate something remotely like food on the plane, and I can only stay a couple of days. The house…it's going very well."

Shelby noted the hesitation, decided to probe its cause shortly. She turned toward her husband's office, gave what passed for a knock and opened the door.

Alan MacGregor sat behind his desk. His hair had gone a rich silver, and the sunlight that poured through the window glinted off it. As always, Julia thought him the handsomest man in the world, and she watched as those lines of care around his dark eyes turned to lines of joy.

The phone still at his ear, he got to his feet, held out his hand. "I'll consider it. Yes, seriously consider it.'' He wrapped his arm around his daughter, brought her close to his side. "I'm sorry, Senator, I'll have to get back to you. Something's come up here. Yes, I will.'' He hung up and, turning, gathered Julia close. "Something irresistible,'' he murmured, kissing the top of her head.

Within an hour, Julia was stretched out in front of the fire in the family parlor, sipping an excellent white wine and more relaxed than she'd been for weeks. Her instincts in coming home had been right on target, she decided.

"This is wonderful.'' She rested her head against the arm of her father's chair, all but purring when he stroked her hair. "Is Boxy going insane canceling your evening obligations?''

"Only one dinner party,'' Shelby told her. "A really tedious one. I'm delighted to be able to stay home.'' She crossed her bare feet at the ankles. The quick glance she sent Alan was a signal. Picking it up, Alan ruffled Julia's hair.

"Are you used to living on your own yet?''

"I miss them,'' she admitted. "Laura, Gwen and I were a trio for so long. I still see them all the time.''

"But it's not the same,'' Alan finished for her.

"No, it's not. In some ways it's better. They're so happy, it's a kick to see it.''

"Are you happy?''

"Yes.'' She turned her head so that she could smile up at him. "Yes, I am. I love where I am and what I'm doing, how I'm doing it. Right now I'm having tremendous fun watching the house come together.''

There, Shelby thought, was her opening. "I can't

wait to see it.'' She smiled at her husband as the conversational relay baton was passed smoothly. ''How far along are you?''

''My bedroom's finished. It was a priority for me. Of course, I had to butt heads with Murdoch over getting the subs in to paint and paper, but I am the one writing the check.''

''Absolutely.'' Not Mr. Murdoch, Shelby noted, but Murdoch. That would be the son. ''Having some trouble with your head contractor?''

''A bit. It's Cullum Murdoch I'm working with on this. His father's not quite well.''

''Michael?'' Concerned, Alan straightened in his chair. ''What's wrong?''

''He caught a nasty summer cold, and it took him some time to shake it. He's on the mend, but Cullum's already hip-deep in the job, so...'' She trailed off with a shrug. ''He does excellent work. It's just that we...clash styles, I suppose. He wants it done his way, I want it done mine. Simple as that.''

Julia drained her wine a took a deep breath. ''I'm thinking about becoming involved with him.''

''Oh.'' It was a quick little stab, just under the heart. Instinctively Shelby rubbed a hand over the ache. ''But if you don't get along...?''

''That's one level.'' Letting out a little sigh, Julia stretched out her legs. ''On another level we appear to get along like gangbusters.''

''The physical level isn't enough,'' Shelby interjected, then fought to stem her panic as Alan sent her a warm, amused look.

''It appears your mother is thinking about another lovely young woman who tried to convince herself she couldn't get along with a certain young man on a particular level." His dark eyes glinted when he grinned. "So I seduced her."

"Alan." Caught between laughter and concern, Shelby shook her head. "This is our little girl here, and I don't think either one of us wants her seduced by a Murdoch."

"Sounds more like the MacGregor than the MacGregor," Alan murmured to his daughter, and watched the warrior's light he loved flash in his wife's eyes. "I'd say that depended on the Murdoch," he continued. "And on Julia. You're a smart woman, Julia. You know right and wrong and what's right for you."

"What seemed right, for the moment, was to get some distance, and to talk to both of you. Don't worry about me, Mom." She laid a hand on Shelby's knee. "It wouldn't be seduction. If I get involved with Murdoch, it'll be with eyes wide open."

The three of them talked for a while longer, and then, when Julia left to unpack and change, Shelby turned to her husband.

"Alan, this is serious."

"Hmm." He rose to refill his wife's glass.

"Don't use that diplomatic *hmm* on me." She scowled up at him over the rim of her glass. "I'm not naive enough to believe Julia hasn't been involved with a man before. But none of them has ever mattered enough to worry her, or to have her come to us to talk about it."

Sitting on the arm of her chair, Alan skimmed a finger along his wife's bangs. "Are you worried that she's in love, or in lust?"

"Both." She sighed. Her little girl, she thought. Her baby. She hadn't had enough time to prepare. "I just think it might be wise if we knew a little more about him."

"My father's known the Murdochs for years." Alan's mouth quirked as he brought his glass up to sip. "I imagine he's going to be very pleased with the situation."

It only took Shelby an instant. She clamped a hand over Alan's. "You don't think he arranged this somehow?"

"No." Alan leaned down, kissed his wife's scowling mouth until it softened, then added, "I'm absolutely sure he did."

Chapter 26

Cullum brooded into his beer while the jukebox tinkled out a song of love gone sour. Didn't it always? he wondered. Nothing lasted forever—if it did, he'd be out of business. Dry rot set in, or age, or simple monotony. Buildings weren't all that much different from people, he mused. And some were high-maintenance.

Julia MacGregor was definitely high-maintenance.

It was a good thing he'd had a couple of days to kick back, cool off and come to his senses. Tangling with her was bound to cost a man, and personally, he was very careful when it came to investments of any kind.

The woman wanted to negotiate sex, for God's sake. Draft out contingencies and clauses, with the bed as the bargaining table. Well, the hell with that, he decided, lifting the bottle to his lips. He figured, if a man and a woman were single, healthy and wanted each other, negotiations were over.

So she could just find somebody else to do business with.

Probably would, too, he thought as his lips curled into a snarl. A woman who looked like that, she wouldn't have any trouble finding a "business" partner.

And what did he mean, she looked like *that?* he wondered, not even hearing his own sigh. She wasn't even really pretty, if you thought it through point by point. But somehow, when the package was put together, it slugged a man right between the eyes.

She'd know that fact, she'd use it to her advantage. Well, it wasn't going to work on him. The impulse had passed all right, and he was back on track.

One of the men sidled up to the bar to order a drink and slapped Cullum companionably on the back. "How's it going, boss?"

Cullum's response was a grunt. He didn't know why he'd let the crew talk him into going for a beer after work. He wasn't in the mood to socialize. But then, he hadn't been in the mood to go home, either. The fact was, he didn't seem to be in any mood except foul.

"Sure hope Miz MacGregor comes back soon." The trim carpenter pushed up the brim of the baseball cap he wore and grinned. "The boys miss seeing her walk through—especially when she's wearing one of those little skirts. I'm telling you, that woman stands on some classy stilts." Unaware of the red haze beginning to cloud his boss's vision, the carpenter leaned on the bar to sip his cold draft. "Smells good enough to eat, too."

Because quite suddenly he wanted to smash the bottle over the edge of the bar and jab the jagged end toward this man's face, Cullum set the beer down very carefully. "You keep your mind on your work, Jamison, and off the client's legs."

"Well, hell, Cullum..." Jamison began, then cleared his throat when he caught the smoldering violence in Cullum's eyes. "Sure, boss, just making conversation."

Saying nothing, Cullum tossed some bills on the bar and rose. He walked out before he could do any damage to his crew.

Jamison blew out a breath, then chuckled and called over to his friend. "Hey, Jo, looks like the boss's got his eye on Miz McG." Jo immediately moved over and sat himself down on the recently vacated seat to discuss the new information.

It would have infuriated Cullum to know that his crew spent over an hour grinning and gossiping about him and Julia. It would have mortified him if he knew those grins and gossip were being spread like chain lighting among the subcontractors. By noon the next day, there wasn't a man or woman working on the MacGregor site who wasn't wondering what was going on with the boss and the client.

The betting pool was inevitable.

Cullum walked in as twenty dollars passed from one of the men to another. But Murdoch and Sons didn't hire the slow-witted.

"Thanks for the loan, Mike." The man pocketed

the bill with an easy smile. "Get it back to you on payday. Hey, boss, we're about ready to put the chair rail up here."

"Then let's get to it."

The dining room would be the most formal room in the house. The wainscoting, the intricately carved chair rail, the trio of tall, slim windows and the beautiful coffered ceiling deserved the best. He hoped Julia wouldn't put lady furniture in it. The room wanted big, heavy pieces—chairs with high backs, a table with some age and weight to it.

She had the little sitting room upstairs and the back parlor for the fancy and the delicate. This room wanted strength.

"Probably put pansies on the wall," he muttered, and, after he'd checked the first run of the rail, moved into the kitchen.

Work there was progressing nicely. Eyes focused on details, Cullum didn't notice the sly looks and speculative grins sent his way. The linoleum had been stripped off, the pine beneath protected with drop cloths. Refinishing it would be one of the last steps. In preparation for cabinet installation, the walls had been painted. He had to approve the toasty yellow Julia had chosen. It was a warm, interesting shade, and would go well with the wood. The wall had been torn down, bringing the side porch into the room. Even now, the windows were being installed.

It was going to be a good room, he decided, talking details with his men as he considered the space. His design was coming to life. Such things always gave Cullum a flash of satisfaction. But this time it was deeper, brighter. He told himself that if he felt more proprietary this time, it was only because he found the house so special.

It had nothing to do with the owner.

Still, he could picture himself coming into the completed kitchen early in the morning. There'd be pots of herbs under the south window. Good sun there, and he liked having his own fresh herbs when he cooked. He'd make coffee at the counter he was building himself. Grind the beans fresh. Then the room would smell of rosemary, coffee, and the flowers on the old oak table in the sitting area.

He'd drink the first cup standing up, then take the second over to the wrought-iron table that belonged in the corner, just there. For family meals.

Sunlight would be slipping into the room when Julia walked in, rumpled and sexy from sleep. She'd smile at him, come over to lean over his shoulder and rub her cheek against his. And steal his coffee.

He was so caught up in the scene that when Julia walked in, rumpled and sexy from travel, he gaped at her. "What? Where?"

"Who, why?" she finished, and laughed at him. "That must have been quite a side trip, Murdoch." She tucked her hands in the pockets of her cashmere blazer and surveyed the room. "Wow, progress. I'll have to take off for a couple of days regularly. It really hits you then. This is fabulous. I knew this paint would work. And, oh, the windows are going to be wonderful. Give you full points on that. I've just seen the side terrace doors. They're perfect. Just perfect."

He could only be grateful she was talking so much. At the moment, he needed more than a minute to find his balance. He'd decided against her, hadn't he? So why was he viciously fighting the urge to grab her right this second and kiss her until her bones rattled?

He was staring at her as if she'd walked through the wall, Julia thought, and began to feel her pulse bump and jitter. She'd considered the matter of their relationship carefully while she was in Georgetown. All the requirements and details, all the demands and rules, had been carefully outlined in her mind.

And now she couldn't think of any of them.

"I guess I'll..." Stutter, if you keep looking at me that way, she thought. "Ah, take my stuff upstairs, then poke around and see what's up. The, um, the cabinets come in yet?"

"Day after tomorrow."

"Fine, good. Can't wait to see them. I'll just..." She waved a hand vaguely. "Go now."

She turned, hurried out, then muffled a gasp when he took her arm and walked beside her. "I'll help you take your things up. We need to finalize some details on the guest suite."

Not now, she decided. Definitely not now, when she couldn't put two rational thoughts together. "I don't want to interrupt your work. And I have some calls to make, and—"

"Won't take long." His brow winged up when he saw the pile of luggage at the base of the steps. "You were only gone three days."

"I knew I was going to shop, so I took extra bags." She grabbed one to keep her hands busy. "I'm more than half done with Christmas."

"Good for you." Cullum started to heft the other two bags, shook his head at the weight and put his back into it. "Where do you want them, Santa?"

"Just up in my room. I have to organize everything before I wrap. How's your father?"

"He's a lot better, I think." Puzzled, Cullum looked down as half a dozen laborers edged into the foyer to watch him walk upstairs with Julia. "What? You guys finish the house while I wasn't looking?"

That sent them scurrying. Cullum shrugged off the hoots of laughter that followed him up the stairs. "They've got to remember to keep windows open while they glue. Turns them into idiots."

"Here, just dump them on the bed," Julia told him. And that way, the bed would be too crowded to be any sort of temptation to either of them. "I'm really anxious to see the—"

The sentence ended against his mouth. He had her hauled against him, her hair fisted in his hand and her lips captured in a hard greedy kiss before she could take one full breath.

Then breathing didn't seem so very important. The bag she'd carried fell out of her hand, hitting the floor with a thud.

"We have to talk about this," she managed.

"Shut up, Jules."

"Okay, all right." With a broken moan, she ran her hands up his back, hooking them over his shoulders and straining to get closer. Something jabbed her hip, something poked hard into her thigh. "Ouch, damn."

"Tool belt," he muttered, and eased his grip before he lacerated her. "Sorry."

"It's all right." With an unsteady hand, she rubbed the slight pinch. "We have incredibly poor timing. Look, I don't know how much you've thought about this, but I've thought about it quite a bit. We need to discuss it."

"I want you. That's my input into the discussion."

With a shaky laugh, she sidestepped until the chest at the foot of her bed was between them. "I have a little more to say than that."

"What a surprise. We knock off here at four-thirty. I'll come back at six. If you want, I'll bring dinner."

"Dinner." Sensible, she decided. "Maybe we should go out."

His green gaze stayed locked and heated on hers. "Some other time, Jules. I don't feel much like going through the mating dance of menus and waiters and small talk tonight."

She nodded slowly. "So we'll eat in, but we will talk."

Now he smiled, a slow, sensual curving of lips that sent small delicious chills up her spine. "Wanna bet?"

"I'm serious, Murdoch."

"So am I, MacGregor. Six o'clock," he repeated before he turned to the door.

"Six-thirty," she said. It was arbitrary, she knew, but she needed to have some say in the matter.

Understanding her perfectly, he shook his head. "Fine then." Then he lifted a brow. "Are you coming?"

"Where?"

"The guest suite, remember?"

"Oh." Flustered, she brushed at her tousled hair. "I thought you'd just said that for the crew."

"I say what I mean. Let's go look it over. The rough-in's been inspected and approved."

She did her best to shift from potential lover to client. It irked her that he seemed much more graceful at the segue than she. "Okay. Then I'd like to go over the rest of the new work, if you have the time."

He held the door open for her. "My time's your time. At least, until four-thirty."

Her eyes narrowed on his face as she walked by him. "Why does that sound like a threat, Murdoch?"

He smiled blandly. "I couldn't say. What it is, MacGregor, is fact."

At four-forty-five, she watched the last truck—Cullum's naturally—pull out. Less than two hours, she thought, but this time she'd be ready. This time he wouldn't get her mind hazed over with sensation before she could speak it. They'd discuss the situation rationally, negotiate terms that both of them could live with.

When the affair ended, as it undoubtedly would, both of them would walk away with minimum fuss and pain. They were, she'd already decided, much too much alike to mesh well. And the basic lust they were experiencing was entirely too strong and hot to burn for long.

She didn't want to be hurt at the end of it, and she didn't want to hurt him. So they would set down rules, follow them. And enjoy each other while it lasted.

Julia turned away from the window, wondering why she suddenly felt so depressed. Maybe it was because she'd been so close to Laura and Gwen, and both of them had tumbled into love so fast. With hardly a moment to think or plan or worry about rules.

But this wasn't love. It was chemistry. And she remembered enough of that particular science to know that volatile experiments could blow up without careful planning and execution.

And she wasn't going to end up getting singed.

Still, there was no reason in the world not to drive him insane in the meantime. Nearly two hours, she mused. More than enough time to complete the indulgent female ritual of preparing for a lover.

By the time she was finished, tough guy Cullum Murdoch would be putty in her hands.

Chapter 27

She was going to melt like butter. He was going to see to it.

Though it was tempting to use his key to irritate her, Cullum knocked on the door at six-thirty. He'd changed into a navy sweater and fresh jeans—no way was she going to think he'd fussed over tonight. If she knew he was the least bit nervous, the least bit anxious, it would give her too much of an advantage.

He liked the fact that Julia used her advantages, even respected her for it. But he wasn't willing to let her get a step ahead, or over him.

He shifted the bag he carried from arm to arm, and was reconsidering using his key when she opened the door.

She didn't look like she'd fussed much, either, which gave her no right to set his pulse rate soaring. She'd left her hair down, curling wildly, the way he liked it best. It tumbled over the shoulders of a sleek black cat suit that displayed her curves with mouth-watering accuracy. She'd draped some sort of silver belt fashioned out of big links loosely at her waist. Her feet were bare.

She looked like some kind of high-class bohemian, with her chocolate-colored eyes thickly lashed and her generous mouth soft and naked.

"You're prompt." Her unpainted lips curved slowly. "I like that in a man."

"You're built." He smiled with the same lazy coolness. "I like that in a woman."

"Aren't we lucky? Come on in." She closed the door behind him and ordered herself to ignore the jitters in her stomach. "So, what did you bring for dinner?"

"Extra crispy." Her eyes lit with a quick, appreciative humor that had him grinning in response. "And a nice white Bordeaux that'll enhance, rather than overwhelm, those famous secret herbs and spices."

"Who'd have thought we'd have similar taste in food? Let's take it upstairs." She inclined her head before he could get any ideas about rushing her. "My room's the only one in the house with the ambience for dining at the moment. Unless you'd rather sit on a couple of drywall-compound buckets and eat on a sawhorse?"

"Your room's fine."

"Go ahead up, I'll see if I can dig up a couple of wineglasses."

"Everything we need's in here." He patted the

bag. "Plastic and paper. No use dirtying up dishes while your kitchen's torn up."

"Excellent point." And a considerate one, she noted as she turned to start up the steps. "The work's progressing smoothly."

"Just takes planning. And a little luck."

"I'm looking at a building downtown. It should make into six very nice two-bedroom apartments. With a little luck, and a lot of planning." She paused at the door to her room to glance back at him. "Do you think you and your father would be interested?"

"If you don't need to get started on it until after the first of the year."

"I haven't even bought it yet, so it'll be at least that long."

She'd built a fire, both for warmth and for atmosphere. It crackled away behind an ornate brass screen. The mantel was crowded with candlesticks and candleholders of varying sizes and materials. She hadn't yet lit the tapers and votives.

She had, however, lit a fat column of waxy white in the center of the little table in the sitting area.

"Very nice." The room smelled seductive, and so did she. Cullum set the red-and-white bag on the table, wondering if that was her plan—to seduce him before he could gain the upper hand.

It was going to be an interesting night.

He took out the wine and a corkscrew, watching her as he opened the bottle. "Since we're being sociable I'll tell you that you're doing a hell of a job putting this house together. You move fast, but you don't rush. You put some thought into the pieces you pick up. You're making it classy, but it's still friendly. Not everyone could pull that off."

She tried not to gape. It was a compliment designed to flatter a woman like her, one that touched on mind and style and heart. "Thanks, that means a lot to me. I grew up in a classy, friendly home."

"You grew up in the White House," he reminded her, and offered her a plastic wineglass filled with straw-colored wine.

"True enough, but I was thinking about our house in Georgetown. Still, my parents did what they could to make the White House a home."

"Must have felt like a fishbowl."

"Sometimes. Often it was surprisingly cozy and intimate. If I live there again, I'd work to give my family the same."

His brows lifted. "Thinking of marrying some future president?"

"No, I'm thinking of being some future president."

She waited for him to choke on his wine, to laugh and to make a sarcastic comment. Instead, his eyes narrowed in speculation, and he nodded. "If you do half as well as your father, you'd be a good one."

"You surprise me again."

"Why? Do my knuckles drag the ground?"

"I've thought they did a few times." She sat and opened the bag to sniff. "I'm ready if you are." This time he did laugh. "To eat," she specified mildly. "And to talk about the rest."

"I don't mind a little dinner conversation."

They divvied up chicken and french fries on paper plates. Cullum winced as she waterfalled salt onto both. "I know," she said with a chuckle. "It's disgusting. Gwen just closes her eyes when we eat together." She took a big, healthy bite of a drumstick and sighed with pleasure. "But it's so good. Things that are bad for each other always seem to be. Cullum, could we be very bad for each other?"

"Could be. Life's a gamble."

"Agreed. I like to gamble, but I always figure the odds and options—and I always know just how much I can afford to lose and stay comfortable before I play. So, we're attracted to each other for some possibly insane and contrary reason."

He picked up his wine, enjoying her as much as he enjoyed the smooth, dry taste. "Agreed."

"Speaking for myself, I don't take a lover just because I'm attracted. There has to be a little more foundation. Mutual respect, understanding, affection. I also prefer to go into a relationship with the agreement that if things don't work out, both parties will accept and step back. And the relationship has to be monogamous for the length of term. If either party finds that unsatisfactory, the relationship ends. No harm, no foul."

Amused, Cullum grinned. "So if I decide I want a little variety—or you do—the contract is void."

"Exactly. And no hard feelings. That cuts down on the temptation to lie and cheat. I won't tolerate either in any area of my life, and certainly not in bed."

"I don't lie." It was annoyance that flickered in his eyes this time. "And I don't cheat."

"I didn't say you did," she returned evenly. "But people often do—and the excuse for it invariably comes down to sparing someone's feelings. I don't need, or want, my feelings spared."

"Fine. The first time I want to try my luck with some hot babe, I'll let you know." Deliberately he wiped his fingers on a paper napkin. "And the first time you decide to try yours with some slick-faced guy in a tux... Well, I'll have to hurt him."

The fact that her pulse took a little bump of pleasure infuriated her. "That's exactly the sort of attitude that doesn't work."

"Works for me. I get the gist here, Jules. You want respect. I respect you—your mind and your integrity. I understand you well enough. You're used to getting your own way, and you like to run the show. You're pretty good at it. And I like you well enough, some of the time. There's your foundation. Now let me add some of the trim."

He topped off their glasses again, sat back with his. "If you want to make deals and contracts, try it on someone like that Tod you booted out the other night. This isn't business, and neither of us is going to be able to plan our way through the stages of it. We want each other. Maybe after tonight we won't want each other anymore, and that'll be that."

"And if one does, and one doesn't?"

"That'll be damn bad luck for somebody." He rose and, taking her hand, pulled her to her feet. "Let's find out."

She wasn't finished yet, not nearly, but he had already wrestled the controls out of her hands. His mouth was firm, possessive, and gave hers no choice but to open to his on a moan of the purest pleasure.

She'd wanted to light the candles, to drive him slowly mad until he agreed to everything. But the need sprang free inside her, primal and raw.

Seduction on either side would have to wait.

Her hands streaked under his sweater, gripping the hard ridge of muscle up his back. His strength tantalized her, fascinated her. She hiked the sweater up, dragging it over his head, tossing it carelessly aside. And was desperate for more.

"I really love your body," she managed.

He tugged the shoulders of the snug suit down, latched his mouth on her throat. "Same goes." He grabbed the hook of her belt and sent it rattling to the floor.

His hands roamed over the slick material, tormenting them both, then onto flesh, a rough scrape of callus against pampered skin. Their mouths met again, hotly, wetly, with a tangle of tongues and a scrape of teeth and echoing groans of need.

Her breath caught when he swept her up. For a moment, she felt utterly helpless, overpowered, conquered. Panicked excitement prickled along her skin. Then he was laying her on the thick duvet, and his eyes were on hers as he peeled away the suit.

The quick shudder surprised her. She'd prepared herself for him, she'd known the evening would end in just this way. But she hadn't known, couldn't have known, that a long, searing look from those intense green eyes could sever the knots of her control so quickly.

With a sound of greed, she reared up, arms and legs snaking around him, mouth fusing with his.

She was as erotic as any temptress, as dangerous as any siren. The blood raced through his veins, with the flavor of her spiking it like a drug. He was rough, couldn't help himself. She'd already snapped his tenuous connection with the civilized.

His fingers dug into her hips, would leave bruises. His mouth crushed down on hers until she whimpered in dazed delight. Then, dragging her head back by her hair, he savaged her throat.

Her skin was already damp from the heat when he pushed her back, when his mouth and hands possessed her breasts. The air was too thick to breathe, and each gulp of it made her head reel. There were flames inside her, heating her system beyond bearing. As desperate as he to touch, to taste, to take, she rolled with him over the bed.

Their legs tangled as she dragged at his jeans. Every second was delicious torture, every movement a wild thrill.

He felt his own muscles quivering as his slick skin slid over hers. There had never been anything or anyone he craved as he craved her. Every inch of her, every curve, every tremble, every moan. The need for her was like edgy fingers gripping at his throat, his heart, his loins.

He drove himself into her, blindly, fiercely, felt her clamp around him like a hot fist. Triumph, heady and sweet, streaked through him when she cried out. Then those long, limber legs wrapped around him.

Her hands fisted on the bedcover as the first violent orgasm ripped through her. The pressure inside her tore free, then built again, forcing her to sob in air. Mindlessly she scraped her nails down his back, arched against him, and met the next crest head-on.

He fought back the mists that blurred his vision. He wanted to see her, had to see her, as their bodies plunged toward the edge. Her face was flushed and damp, her eyes were closed, her lips trembling, her hair a wild tangle of fire over the rumpled bedclothes.

Something struggled for freedom inside him, something more complex and more demanding than lust. He fought it back, let himself ride on the towering wave of sensation.

But it was her name that broke from his lips as he emptied himself into her.

They didn't speak. Julia wondered if her vocal cords had been singed by the heat they generated together. She'd never felt like this before, so sated and weak, so sinuously female. She was content to drop off into sleep just like this, sprawled naked on the bed, with Cullum's body pinning hers heavily to the mattress.

When he shifted a little, she sighed, and wondered if it was the only sound she'd be capable of making for the next decade or so.

She looked…smug, Cullum thought as he managed to lift his head to study her face. As his mind cleared, he'd worried that he'd hurt her. He knew his hands were big and rough, and though he doubted he'd be considered a gentle lover, he'd never been quite so unrestrained. He was afraid he'd come perilously close to brutal.

But judging by that contented-cat expression on her face, it didn't appear apologies were in order. He was grateful. He hated apologizing.

Then her eyes fluttered open and met his. Her lips curved wider. "Mmm…" she said.

"At the very least." It surprised him that he

wanted to—needed to—trace a fingertip along her jawline. Her skin was soft there, despite the arrogance of the shape. Giving in to the urge, he lowered his head and brushed his lips just under her chin.

The gesture made her heart flutter. She told herself it was a foolish reaction, even a dangerous one. Her heart had to maintain a safe distance. Despite the warmth of his body, she shivered.

"Cold?" He wanted to bundle her up, to keep her warm. To keep her. And that wayward thought tied an uneasy knot in his stomach.

The shiver had had nothing to do with the cold, but she latched on to the excuse. "A bit." She couldn't stop herself from lifting a hand, running it through the tousled length of his hair. "I guess we could use another log on the fire."

"I'll get it." He leaned down, intending to kiss her lightly, casually. And lingered over it until they were both clinging.

Desire built again, too quickly for either of them to build a defense. Together, they reached out, draped the duvet over themselves, and yielded to it.

Chapter 28

November, Julia decided, was the most interesting month of the year. It was so transitional, with the air both smoky and bracing. Hints of winter blew on the wind, with all the adventures and surprises that accompanied the holiday season.

She was almost sorry to see it end. She'd never spent a more fascinating or exciting month.

She believed she and Cullum were being very discreet. They kept a professional distance during working hours. For the most part, Julia acknowledged, remembering a brief and torrid encounter in the remodeled pantry. And that, she had to admit, had been her doing. There had just been something about the way he stood in that tidy, homey area, his tool belt slung on his hips, his skin smelling of sawdust, that fried her circuits enough to have her pushing him up against the door and attacking him.

Not that he'd put up much of a fight.

The basic truth was, they had a hard time keeping their hands off each other. Struggling to do so for the best part of eight hours a day, five days a week, added quite a bit of desperation to their after-hours meetings.

Her bedroom and the pantry weren't the only rooms they'd enjoyed. She thought of how they'd ended up rolling around on the drop cloths in the half-finished library, laughing like loons and fighting with buttons and zippers.

They didn't seem even close to getting enough of each other.

"You certainly look...content," Laura commented. Both she and Gwen had set aside the first Saturday afternoon in December to help Julia decorate her tree. Though each had their own home now, none of them had forgotten the years they'd lived together, or the bond they had formed.

"Why shouldn't I be?" Julia searched for the perfect spot to hang the carved wooden Santa riding his sleigh over a crescent moon. "The house is nearly finished, and it's coming together exactly as I wanted."

With her hands on her hips now, she turned to study the completed living room. The space streamed with sunlight that gilded the highly polished pine floor. A fire crackled in the stone hearth. The wood trim was dark and glossy, curved softly over doorways and windows. The plasterwork was stunning.

Gone were the two dark little rooms. And in their place was a huge, airy space where she'd arranged favorite pieces of furniture. The curved-backed settee with brocade seats, the long, deep sofa, perfect for midday napping. Two of her brother's original watercolors of Boston hung on the wall over an occasional table where one of her mother's pieces, a wide, shallow dish in swimming pastels, rested.

An antique doll's cradle held magazines. Two lofty ficus trees flanked the archway that joined the rooms.

Every piece, every detail, was very personally hers.

"It's a terrific room," Gwen told her.

"I knew it would be, but it's better than I imagined. I'm glad Cullum talked me into a wide archway instead of straight open space. It adds character."

Gwen and Laura exchanged a look behind her back, pointing at each other, shaking their heads, rolling their eyes. Laura finally gave an exaggerated shrug of agreement.

"So..." Laura chose a tiny silver bell for a branch. "I guess he'll be finished in a couple of weeks."

"Should be. According to his flowchart, we're coming down to punch-out work."

"Is that what you two do—study flowcharts in bed?"

"Sometimes, but—" Blinking, Julia turned back. "What?"

"Julia, for heaven's sake. It's obvious the two of you are involved." Gwen walked over to pour more hot chocolate out of a china pot shaped like a grinning elephant.

"It is?"

"Every time we drop by, we have to go home and defuse." With a laugh, Laura hung a gauzy angel. "The air around here sizzles. Okay, we're nosy." She turned around. "But we're also concerned. We always talked about this sort of thing, but with Cullum you've been uncharacteristically mute."

"I don't know what to say. I suppose we realized a lot of the antagonism between us was just sexual tension. When we started working closely together..." Julia shrugged her shoulders. "It just happened."

Her smile broke through as she looked at her two cousins. "It's wonderful. He's wonderful. I had no idea we'd have such fun together—and not just in bed. We drove out to the Cape last weekend, had a picnic on the beach. It was freezing." She laughed. "It was great. And the man actually likes to go antiquing. Can you imagine? He finds terrific stuff, and bargains like a champ. Look."

She dashed over to the recessed shelves and snagged something off one. "He got this for me a couple of weeks ago. The dealer practically gave it to him by the time Murdoch was done with him."

Gwen's brows drew together as she studied the metal knob and mechanism attached to a square of old wood. "What is it?"

"It's an old telegraph key." Julia turned it around to show it off, unaware that her heart was in her eyes. "I love things like this. I hadn't expected him to notice. And he makes incredible pasta. Who'd have thought someone like him would cook? He's helping me pick out the things for the playroom I'm putting together for little Daniel and all the other nieces and nephews that are going to come along. We're looking at old pinball machines. He's handy with mechanics and stuff, so he thought it might be fun to rebuild one. And I—"

Her breath began to hitch, and she had to press a hand to her heart. "Oh, God. Oh, no." Her legs trembling, she sank into a chair and stared at her cousins in horror. "What have I done?"

"Fallen head over heels, from the look and sound of it." Gwen poured another cup of chocolate and brought it to Julia. "Take your time, catch your breath."

"This wasn't the plan, this wasn't the idea. This wasn't the agreement," she finished, as her voice upped an octave in pitch.

"Let me be the first to tell you, you can't plan it."

"But I don't even like him." She closed her eyes as Gwen smiled at her. "Well, I didn't. I thought I didn't."

"If it helps, I think you're perfect for each other."

"It doesn't help." Julia took the cup in both hands and drank deeply. "It doesn't help at all. What am I going to do? He'd be furious—or hysterical—if he knew."

Laura sat on the arm of the chair. "You ask me, a man who cooks you pasta, buys you weird gifts and wants to rehab a pinball machine for you is as over his head as you are."

"No, he's not. Do you think? No." Disgusted with herself, she sprang up. "Oh, how did this happen to me? Ten minutes ago I was on top of the world. He's going to be here in a couple hours. He's going to rewire this art deco lamp we found last night."

"He's rewiring lamps," Gwen said with a sigh. "That's so sweet."

"It's not sweet, it's impossible. I don't want to be in love with him."

"Why?" Laura cocked her head.

"Because it's... Because he's..."

"I see the witness is having trouble answering the question," Laura said soberly. "Let me rephrase— Oh, shoot," she added as the sounds of a fussing baby sounded through the intercom. "Court will take a brief recess. Be right back."

"Julia..." Gwen began as Laura raced upstairs. "I'd like to say something."

"Go ahead."

"You've never looked happier than you did when you were talking about Cullum and all the time you've been spending together. And I've been around here enough to notice the way he looks at you. The way he watches you. I don't think you're any more in love with him than he is with you."

"If that's true..." Julia took three deep and careful breaths. "It could work. Don't you think?"

"I've never known you to back off from something you wanted. I know it's scary. Sometimes what I feel for Branson, and now the baby..." she murmured touching a hand to her stomach. "It's so huge, it still scares me. But I wouldn't want it any other way."

"So, I need to convince him that he's madly in love with me."

"I'd say it's more you have to persuade him to admit it, the way you just have."

"Out loud." She nearly laughed again as Laura brought Daniel back into the room. "I can't imagine Murdoch saying it out loud." She gnawed at her lip as she considered. "Unless I trick it out of him."

"Same old Julia," Laura commented. She sat in

the bentwood rocker, unbuttoned her blouse to nurse the baby.

"I don't mean trick, exactly. More like...drag it out of him."

She was ready for him. Julia opened the door for Cullum with a warm smile, then, sliding her arms around his neck, presented him with a long, deep kiss.

"Nice to see you, too." He backed her into the house, kicked the door closed to keep out the cold and the thin fall of snow. "What mood is this you're in, MacGregor?"

"Happy." She nibbled down along his jaw. "Affectionate. What mood is this you're in, Murdoch?"

"Appreciative."

"You haven't seen anything yet." She eased back to smile up at him. "I cooked dinner."

"Isn't that dangerous?"

"I happen to be a very competent cook." Nearly, she amended silently. "How do you feel about stuffed pork chops and mashed potatoes?"

"Very friendly."

"Good." She linked her arm through his and, with stars in her eyes, walked with him to the kitchen.

She had the table set with colorful dishes and candles. Music played low through the hidden speakers and a bottle of champagne was chilling in an antique bucket.

Puzzled, he shook his head. "Are we celebrating something?"

"Nope. Just a home-cooked meal, MacGregor-style. Why don't you open the bottle now? Dinner will be about twenty more minutes."

"Smells terrific." He applied himself to the bottle and wondered what the hell she was up to. If this wasn't a stage set by a woman who was after something, he'd be very surprised. "Do you want me to tear out a wall I've just rebuilt? Change your mind about the tile in the guest room suite?"

"No. I just felt like cooking. Must be the holidays coming up. Oh, I should have showed you. We got the tree up today."

"I saw it through the window when I drove up. Looks great."

"We can have dessert in the living room later and enjoy it."

Wary now, he poured the wine into two slim flutes. "You made dessert."

"Cream puffs. Old family recipe." She took her glass from him and smiled. "I had a great time making them." Three times, she thought, and suppressed a sigh. The first two attempts were buried in the garbage. "So how was your day?"

"Productive. I've nearly finished the wooden train set I'm building for my nieces."

"I'd love to see it. I could help you paint it. I'm no Shelby or D. C. MacGregor, but I'm not too bad."

"Sure." He searched her face. "That'd be great."

"Well, I'm going to check on the chops and toss the salad."

"I'll give you a hand."

"No, this is my production. Just sit down and relax."

When she put on an apron, he decided sitting down was a fine idea. What the hell had gotten into her? he wondered. She was bright, solicitous, all but subservient, and she was wearing an apron.

This was not his Julia.

His Julia? He took a deep gulp of wine as the ramifications of that exploded in his head. Since when had he been thinking of her as his?

Since...forever, he realized. Since always. He'd wanted her for years, covered up the want with sarcasm and annoyance. But it had been there, buried deep and growing roots. Now that they were lovers, it was impossible to deny that he was in love with her.

And even if he managed to get his tongue around those words and tell her, he'd be out the door before the sentence was complete.

Well, damn it, he thought as she continued to bustle around the kitchen and chatter, he was in love with her. He'd see to it that she fell in love with him. And she'd be the one to say it first.

Setting his glass aside, he rose and moved behind her. His arms slid around her waist, his lips brushed the nape of her neck. "You smell even better than dinner."

Her knees melted away. "Do I?"

"And I'm becoming more interested in nibbling on you." He reached over, turned the stove and burners down to warm.

"I'm becoming more interested in being nibbled on."

She was smiling as he turned her around. But the smile faded and nerves kicked in as he stared and stared as if absorbing her. "What is it?"

"Sometimes," he said slowly, as this new realization of love flooded him, "you're so beautiful. This is one of those times."

He'd never told her she was beautiful, never cupped her face gently in his hands and kissed her with such slow, such deep, concentration. Every emotion inside her swam to the surface, shimmered in her heart, in her eyes. "Cullum."

"Why are we always in such a hurry?" he murmured against her mouth. Why hadn't he savored this, drawn this out to forever?

"I don't know." But she knew she didn't want him to stop kissing her just like this, touching her just this way.

"Let's not be this time." He picked her up. "And see what happens."

Chapter 29

Something was wrong with her, Cullum decided. She wasn't acting like herself, and hadn't been for days. The woman was smiling all the time. She was asking his opinion and advice on everything from lamp shades to andirons. And she wasn't making a single sarcastic or dissenting remark.

She'd baked him a cake.

He'd known he was sunk when he actually forced himself to eat two pieces. Whatever she used to frost it had tasted distressingly like carpenter's glue. He was beginning to wonder if some alien life-form had taken over Julia's body.

He was playing along, Cullum mused as he pulled up in front of the shop after closing time. What else could he do? How could a man argue with a woman who agreed with everything he said?

He missed arguing with her.

He saw that his father's pickup was still parked beside the entrance. With everyone else gone for the day, they'd have a chance to catch up on the status of jobs under way, discuss holiday schedules. Then Cullum decided he'd catch a quick shower before heading to Julia's for another home-cooked meal.

He rubbed his uneasy stomach. God help him.

As soon as he charmed her into confessing she was in love with him, he'd tell her they were getting married. Timing was everything. He'd have the advantage, get a ring on her finger and sweep her along before she had the chance to figure out he'd planned it.

The minute they were married, he'd find a tactful way of banishing her from the kitchen for the next fifty years.

Meanwhile, risking a little food poisoning wasn't such a big price to pay. Not when Julia was the prize. And she was a prize, he thought as he climbed out of the truck into a frigid wind. It might have taken him close to five years to figure out she was the only woman in the world for him, but he knew it now.

Nothing, not even the threat of Julia's Cajun chicken surprise, was going to stop him from making her his.

Inspiration struck when he unlocked the shop door. He'd call her, Cullum decided. Tell her he'd made reservations for dinner—a pre-Christmas celebration, as she'd be leaving shortly for Hyannis to spend the holiday with her family.

He could get away with changing plans on her at

the last minute, thanks to the mood she'd been in lately.

Cheered, he stepped inside. He'd just tell his father he had to make a couple of calls before they got down to business.

As he started down the short hall, Cullum heard his father's laugh boom out. It made him grin. He'd been worried about the old man for months. But just lately, Michael Murdoch seemed to have bounced back. The sparkle was back in his eyes, the lift back in his step. He was still taking it slow, with periods of rest, but he was coming around.

He started to step into the doorway of his father's office, just to let Michael know he was there. Then he heard what his father was saying, chortling with glee, and stopped dead.

"I tell you, Daniel, Cullum'll be proposing to her before the end of the year. No plan ever worked better."

On the floor beside the desk, Michael continued his series of one-handed push-ups, while Daniel's voice pounded out of the speakerphone.

"What's taking the pair of them so long?" Daniel demanded. "They've been in each other's pockets for more than three months."

"Well, Lord knows the pair of them are slower than limping turtles, but we're coming down to the wire." Fit as six fiddles, Michael switched arms to do another twenty reps. "My sources tell me she's been cooking for him."

"Julia? Cooking? God have mercy, Michael. Don't tell me the boy's been eating it."

Barely winded, Michael laughed again. "Indeed he has been, and as I had a sample of a cake she baked for him, I can tell you any man who swallows more than a mouthful of what she makes in her kitchen is a man sunk to his ears in love."

"Ah, what a pair they are. Made for each other, though they'd not thank either of us for pointing it out to them. We'll give them a hell of a wedding, Michael."

"That we will, Daniel, and it'll be a great relief to me to have recovered my full health."

"Just be sure you don't recover it too soon. If the two of them balk, you may have to have a relapse. Julia will be here for Christmas. If she isn't wearing his ring on her finger, I'll give a wee bit of a nudge from this end."

"And I'll keep an eye on this end."

"Merry Christmas to you, Michael."

"A merry Christmas to you, Daniel."

Michael bounced up lightly to the balls of his feet to disconnect. The grin that stretched over his face froze, the healthy flush that colored his face drained. His son stood in the doorway, his eyes dagger-bright, his mouth curled into a snarl.

"Cullum." He all but squeaked it, and didn't have to feign weak limbs. "I, ah, didn't hear you come in. How long have you been standing there?"

"More than long enough." Fury and humiliation tangled inside him until he couldn't separate one from the other. "You weren't sick a day."

"Sick? Of course I was sick," Michael said, desperately calculating. "Chest cold." He managed a wheeze, sank down into the chair behind his desk. "I'm feeling considerably better. Considerably. The doctor said exercise was—"

"Just save it," Cullum snapped, and walked slowly to the desk. "You're as strong and healthy as a team of Clydesdales. You lied to me." He slapped his palms on the desk and leaned in. "I was worried half to death about you. The men took up a collection to send you a fruit basket."

"It was considerate of them. I was very grateful. Fruit—"

"I said save it!"

Now Michael's eyes narrowed, and he rose to stick his face close to his son's. "You'll mind your tone with me, Cullum Murdoch. I'm still your father."

"Which is all that's saving you from having me haul you up bodily and throw you through the window. You and Daniel MacGregor cooked up this little plot to push me and Julia together. The two of you figured if I was in charge of the rehab and we bumped up against each other often enough, we'd realize we were meant for each other and fall in line."

Michael set his jaw. "That sums it up well enough. And it worked, didn't it, so what's the problem?"

"What's the—" He had to step back, had to turn away. Never in his life had he considered punching his own father. "I'd like to knock your heads together."

"You've had your eye on Julia MacGregor for years, Cullum, and don't bother to deny it."

"It was my choice and my eye," Cullum muttered.

"And she's had hers right back on you. All Daniel and I did was give you a push in the right direction."

"Your direction. Do you think I'm going to thank you for it?"

"Well, and so you should." Placating the boy would never work, Michael decided. Temper against temper would be cleaner. "A blind fool on a galloping horse could see the two of you are in love with each other. She makes you happy, and you do the same for her. And whether you know it or not—being as stubborn a man as I've known in my life—the pair of you have already built a home together."

"It's her house."

"The hell it is. It's yours just as much. Your heart's in it."

He couldn't argue with that. But neither, he decided, was it the point. "Julia and I had an agreement before we started seeing each other." It didn't matter to Cullum that he hadn't agreed to the terms she outlined, or that he'd considered them ridiculous. He was going to use them now. "The relationship isn't permanent. It isn't permanent," he repeated through his clenched teeth when his father snorted. "And if you think I'm going to propose to her, think again."

"You're in love with her, aren't you?"

Cullum opened his mouth to deny it, jammed his hands into his pockets and simmered in silence.

"There, you've just told me you are, even if you can't get your tongue around it yet. Lamebrain." Sighing, Michael sat again. "She's a bright and lovely woman, a match for you in strength and will.

She has brains and humor and the foundation of a fine family."

"Then you marry her."

Michael only smiled. "If I were twenty years younger, boy, I'd have snapped her up from under your nose long before this. And if you don't get your feet moving, someone else might just do it."

"She's not seeing anyone else."

"Of course not," Michael said mildly. "Why would she, when she's in love with you?"

Defeated, Cullum pulled his hands free so that he could press his fingers to his eyes. "This is getting me nowhere. You and MacGregor decide to be a couple of puppet masters, and Jules and I are supposed to dance. Let me tell you something," he continued, dropping his hands. "If she found out what the two of you have done, she'd boot me out of her life to spite you."

"But you're not going to tell her, are you?" Michael asked with a winning smile.

"No, I'm not going to tell her. But from this point on, the two of you stay out of it." He jabbed a finger at his father. "Completely out of it. Julia and I will fumble around on our own. If and when we decide to get married, it'll be because we decided, not because my father and her grandfather think it's the thing to do."

"Of course it'll be your decision." Michael's smile never wavered. Oh, the boy was on the ropes, he thought, and didn't even know it. "It's the biggest decision a man makes in his life. Your happiness is what matters to me more than anything in the world, Cullum."

Cullum felt himself weakening. "Look, I know you meant well, but—"

"Meant the very best," Michael said, and opened the middle drawer of his desk. "I'd like you to take this. If you decide Julia's the woman you want to build your home and family with, I hope you'll give this to her." He opened the small white satin box. "It was your mother's." Sentiment and memories swamped him as he offered Cullum the box. "I couldn't afford a diamond when I asked her to spend her life with me. It's a topaz. She always said it was like a little piece of sunlight, and wouldn't have it replaced later on, when the money was there."

"Dad—"

"I'm not pushing you. I always meant you to have it when it was time. Your mother wanted it passed on. She'd have loved your Julia, Cullum."

"Yeah." Helpless, Cullum took the box, slipped it into his pocket. "She would have."

What had gotten into him? Julia dragged out her suitcase. She needed to pack for the trip to Hyannis. And she needed something to take her mind off Cullum and his odd behavior.

He'd insisted on taking her out every night for a week. Dinner, dancing, theaters, parties. She knew very well he preferred quiet evenings at home, but suddenly he was a social animal. It was driving her crazy trying to gauge his changing moods and adjust hers to them.

With a little sigh, she folded sweaters into her bag. She didn't know how long she could keep up this agreeable-woman routine. The only real benefit so far was that she'd been able to unchain herself from the kitchen. Cooking was definitely not her forte. It was just her bad luck that Cullum loved her cooking.

Obviously the man had a cast-iron stomach, she thought. She could barely force her own preparations through her lips, but Cullum always cleared his plate.

That had been a bad miscalculation on her part. Now he was going to expect her to cook with some regularity. She hated fighting her way through a recipe almost as much as she loved Cullum.

Love, she realized, was making a fool of her.

And he was being so gentle, so tender. This new tone to their lovemaking weakened her limbs and turned her mind to mush. It made her ache for the words. Every time he took her into his arms, she was sure this would be the moment. Now he would tell her he loved her.

But he never did.

She wasn't going to say it first, she thought, and tossed clothes into her bag. She couldn't. She had already made dozens of compromises, given him so much control. She needed to stand firm on this one point.

And where the hell was he? She scowled at the clock, tossed in more clothes. He knew she was leaving today, that this was their last chance to see each other until after Christmas. She had to be on her way within the hour if she was going to make it to her grandparents' before dark.

What was she doing? she asked herself. She was dawdling like a lovesick idiot, bending her own plans to suit his. One more time.

It was going to stop. With a decisive nod, she fastened her suitcase. Being in love did not mean being a doormat. She was leaving, on schedule, and she was sticking to her plans. And if Cullum Murdoch didn't like it, he could lump it.

She carried her suitcase out to the car, then began the laborious task of hauling shopping bags loaded with gifts. Her mood wasn't filled with holiday cheer when Cullum pulled his truck in behind her car.

Neither was his. A problem on a job downtown had taken most of his morning. And he would have to go back and finish it up himself tonight, regardless of the fact that it was Christmas Eve.

The traffic had been insane, even for Boston, and he'd gotten a ticket for running a red—though the damn thing had been yellow—because he was in such a hurry to get to Julia's.

And here she was leaving.

He did his best to rein in his temper, reminding himself that it was Christmas, that this was the woman he loved—that he would tell her so as soon as she had the good sense to tell him.

"I'm running behind," he told her, taking one of the bags from her to stuff it in with the others crowding her back seat.

"So am I."

"Traffic's a mess. You might make better time if you wait another hour."

"Thanks for the bulletin," she said sweetly. "But I'll manage. Of course, if you'd gotten here on time, I'd already be on my way."

"I got hung up." He struggled to keep his voice mild, but couldn't bank the temper simmering in his eyes. "Do you have any more bags?"

"Yes." She turned, walked back into the house, seething. And, seething, he followed her. "These are the last three."

"Overdid it a little, don't you think?"

"I enjoy giving gifts." She snatched the lone box from under the tree and slapped it into his hand. "Here's yours."

Watching her, he slipped it into his pocket so that he could take the bags. "What's your problem, MacGregor?"

"If you don't know, I'm certainly not going to tell you." She turned and sailed out of the house in front of him.

"Look, I didn't drive across town in miserable traffic and get a ticket just to come here and get frosted."

"It's certainly not my fault if you drove irresponsibly and got a ticket, but that explains your bad mood."

"My bad mood? You were snarling at me before I got out of the truck."

Her chin shot out. "I don't have time to argue with you. You've already made me late."

"Fine. Dandy." He dragged a long, slim box with

a crushed bow out of his coat pocket. "Here's your present. See you later."

He strode back to the truck, cursed, then strode back, gave her a hard yank into his arms and crushed his mouth violently to hers. "Merry Christmas!" he snarled, and turned away.

"Same to you!" she shouted, then slammed into her car. She waited for him to drive off before she indulged in a storm of angry tears.

Chapter 30

She was done with him. Finished. Her mistake, Julia decided, had been in deluding herself that she'd fallen in love with him, and that love meant she could adjust herself to his needs and wants.

Because of that, she'd spent the past couple of weeks tiptoeing on eggshells and collecting recipes.

It was mortifying.

Thank God she'd come to her senses. She was an independent woman, one who made her own decisions, lived her own life and outlined her own goals. When she spoke with Cullum again, she would calmly and clearly explain that their relationship no longer suited her, and that would be that.

She'd never been more miserable in her life.

She'd done her best to put on a cheerful face for her family. If it had cracked from time to time, she'd had plenty of excuses handy. She had a little headache, she'd been wool-gathering, she had a new deal on her mind.

Not that she believed she'd fooled anyone for a moment. But she'd gotten through it, and now she was home again, alone in her house. The lights on her Christmas tree were too bright, too colorful, and hurt her eyes. Still, she refused to turn them off. Cullum Murdoch was not going to spoil her holidays.

She had the final details of her party to keep her occupied. The minute she had everything under control, she would contact him. Certainly she would do so before the end of the year.

Ring out the old, ring in the new, she told herself, and looked at the phone yet again.

Why hadn't he called her?

Without realizing it, she lifted a hand to touch the antique necklace she wore. Cullum's Christmas gift to her was a lovely lariat-style necklace fashioned of tiny pearls and garnets and citrines. It had given her a jolt to see it, to remember that she'd seen it before, in one of the shops she patronized.

If she hadn't been in Christmas-gift-buying mode, she would have snatched it up for herself. Still, she hadn't given it more than a brief, avaricious glance. But he'd noticed, and remembered, and bought it for her.

It made her want to weep again.

Pushing away the creeping depression, she sat down at her rolltop desk to go over her list for the party. The caterer was hired, the menu approved. The flowers and music had been chosen.

There was literally nothing left for her to do, Julia

realized, and felt her eyes well up. Furious with herself, she pushed away from the desk. She had to get out of the house. Go somewhere, anywhere.

Cullum argued with himself as he drove toward Julia's. He was behaving like a whipped puppy going back for another kick. He hated himself for it. She could have called him when she got back to Boston. He'd given her two days to call, hadn't he?

She was the one who'd gone out of town, so she was the one who should have called.

He intended to point that out to her, in words of one syllable. Then he was going to tell her there were going to be some changes made. They would put things back the way they had been a month ago, or she could just forget it.

When he pulled in front of her house and saw that her car was gone, he could have chewed a fistful of sixpenny nails. Even the anger he'd been able to work up was nothing compared to the need.

Just to see her, to talk to her, to touch her.

"Typical," he muttered, scowling at the cheery lights of her tree through the graceful window. "She can make me suffer without even being here."

Deflated, he reached into his pocket, took out the old brushed-gold pocket watch she'd given him for Christmas. How the hell could she know him well enough to choose such a perfect gift, and not know when he was hurting?

What was he going to do about it?

He closed his eyes, let his head rest against the seat. He couldn't live without her. He'd thought he could, he'd worked for days to convince himself he could. But coming here now, seeing the house they'd worked on together, empty of her, he knew it wasn't possible.

He didn't want a life empty of Julia.

He was whipped after all.

"So what do you think? Everything looks great, doesn't it." Julia fussed with her lipstick, barely giving her grandmother the opportunity to speak. "I'm so happy you and Grandpa are here early. Nothing to do, really, but I'm a little nervous, if you can believe it. It's my first party in the house."

"Julia—"

"And I really want it to be perfect. How do I look? Do I look all right?"

Anna studied her granddaughter calmly. Julia had chosen a scoop-necked dress in hunter green velvet, the long sleeves snug, the skirt short. Her hair was pinned up, curls escaping strategically. And her eyes, Anna thought, were overbright.

"You look lovely, sweetheart. Why don't we sit down?"

"I can't, really. I've got to go check on the caterer. People will be here soon, and—"

"Julia." In her gentle, unarguable way, Anna took Julia's hand. "Sit down and tell me what hurts."

"I don't know." Julia's breath hitched before she could control it. "I don't know what to do, what to feel. Everything is mixed up, messed up. I'm in love with Cullum Murdoch and I can't make it go away."

"There now." Anna led her to the sitting area of

the bedroom. "Why do you want to make it go away?"

"He doesn't love me. He doesn't even like me anymore. I ruined it, and I don't know how. I tried to—I stopped arguing with him, even when he was wrong, and I cooked, and everything got weird and we argued. He went away. I went away. I don't know. He hasn't even called me since I got home."

"Have you called him?"

"No. I'm not calling him until he calls me. He was the one who was late and surly. Damn it." She swiped her fingers under her eyes. "I'm ruining my mascara."

"You'll fix it. Now, you're telling me you had a fight with Cullum and you haven't made it up yet."

"Not exactly." Julia sniffled. "We're always fighting, we like it." Feeling foolish, she let out a huge sigh. "Then I realized I was in love with him. I didn't mean to be, but I was, so I thought if I tried to be a little less...me, I suppose. If I was more agreeable, if I cooked him a few hot meals, he'd fall in love with me and tell me so I could tell him back. And this sounds so lame I can't believe it's coming out of my mouth."

"Neither can I. But being in love often scatters some of the brain cells. Being less you was a mistake."

"Probably. I just wanted him so much, wanted him to love me. I thought we could start working on the rest after we got to that point. But he doesn't love me. I don't want him to. He's arrogant and argumentative and bossy."

Patient, Anna opened her evening bag and drew out a tissue to mop at Julia's now streaming eyes. "Of course he is. You'd walk all over him otherwise, and you'd despise a man who'd let you walk over him. You want one who stands up to you, who stands with you."

"I thought I could make it all happen. But you can't make feelings happen any more than you can stop them. They just are."

"Then you've learned a fine lesson. Are you going to tell Cullum yours?"

"So he can sneer at me?"

"Do you really think he would?"

"Maybe not, but he might feel sorry for me. That would be worse." She shook her head and rose. "I'll be all right, really. I guess I needed to get that out. I'm sorry I blubbered."

"Darling, from the day you were born, I've never known you to blubber."

"And I won't start now." Determined, Julia moved back to the mirror to repair her makeup. "I want this party to be special. It's the beginning of my new home, a New Year, a new life."

"Where are my girls?" Daniel asked at the top of his lungs as he came into the room bearing a tray with three brimming flutes of champagne. "There they are, and more beautiful than they've a right to be. We're drinking to them."

He set the tray down, and then his wide smile faded when he saw Julia's tear-streaked face. "What's wrong, little girl? What's the matter here?"

"Nothing. I was feeling a little blue." Julia carefully dried her face. "Men. Why can't they all be you, Grandpa?"

"What's the boy done?" he demanded. "Why, if he's done something to make you cry, he'll answer to me."

Julia started to chuckle, but then a wayward thought, a wild and wayward thought, circled in her head and took root. "What boy?"

"That Murdoch boy, of course." Female tears always terrified him. Daniel paced the room, arms waving. "He's a fine boy, make no mistake, but I won't have him causing you a moment's unhappiness. What's he done, and I'll fix it."

Slowly, Julia turned from the mirror. "How much have you fixed already?"

"Making my little girl cry when she should be on top of the world, kicking up her heels. I'll have a word with Cullum Murdoch, see if I don't. And when I finish..." He trailed off, finally catching the gleam in Julia's eye. "What did you say?"

"How did you know I was crying over Cullum?"

"Well, you said so." Hadn't she? A little desperate, Daniel looked to his wife for support, but met a stony stare. "We'll think no more of it," he said quickly. "Let's have that toast."

"How could you be at the bottom of this?" Julia wondered. "You weren't here—you didn't arrange for me to buy the house, or for him to work on it."

"No indeed." Grasping the straw, Daniel picked up a glass and handed it to her. His eyes were a bright and innocent blue. "Let's have a drink to your fine new house. The boy's work does him credit."

"But Mr. Murdoch was supposed to be contractor," Julia murmured. "You're awfully tight with Michael Murdoch, aren't you, Grandpa?"

"Known him for years. Fine family, strong stock."

Julia sucked in her breath, ready to rage. Still spry in his nineties, Daniel skipped back as the knocker beat against the front door.

"Guests arriving. Don't you worry, I'll greet them. Anna, help the girl put her face back together. I'll take care of everything."

He deserted the field while he still had his head.

"I don't know how he did it," Julia began, "but he did."

"I agree with you." Anna defeated the indulgent smile that wanted to curve on her lips. "But there's just no stopping him."

It didn't matter, Julia told herself. Whatever her grandfather had tried to arrange hadn't worked. She and Cullum had taken care of that. The house was finished, and so were they.

Music swept through the rooms, along with laughter and voices. Family and friends were scattered through the house, exactly as she'd planned, exactly as she'd wanted them. Fires crackled, lights sparkled.

"You've made a beautiful home here." Shelby slipped an arm around Julia's shoulder. "It's perfect for you."

"Yes, it is. I'm putting it on the market next week."

"What?"

"It's not a place I want to live alone." Her gaze

swept the spacious living area, the fine details, the gleam of wood. "There's too much Cullum in here."

"Honey, don't do anything rash."

"It's not rash. It's necessary. I'll be all right." She leaned her head against her mother's. "I always am. I think I might come down to D.C. for a while. I might relocate."

"You know your father and I would love having you close by, but—"

"Don't worry about me. I'm going to figure it all out before I do anything. Now, who's the woman who's clinging to D.C.?"

"Your brother met her in Maine. She's a poet. She quotes Elizabeth Barrett Browning incessantly. I'd always been fond of Browning before."

With a laugh, Julia sipped her champagne. "She's that irritating?"

"Oh, far more," Shelby said with feeling. "Believe me. If I thought for a minute he was serious about her, I'd..." Shelby trailed off, and her heart lightened considerably. "You have another guest, Julia."

"Oh? Who?" She turned and saw Cullum step into the room.

He'd worn a suit, and the damn tie was strangling him. But it had seemed only right that he dress the part. You couldn't very well come to a fancy New Year's Eve party in flannel and denim.

And fancy it was—silks and velvets, glittering jewelry, glossy finger food and wine in heavy crystal. She'd put it together, he decided, exactly as it should be. He'd have done the same.

Then he saw her and his heart twisted and he knew she could have just as easily made do with pizza and beer.

She pinned a smile on her face and, assuming the mask of hostess, walked over to greet him. "I'm so glad you made it. What can I get you?"

Listen to her, talking to him as if he were a mild acquaintance instead of her lover. "Got a beer?"

"Sure." She signaled to a waiter. "Mr. Murdoch would like a beer. You probably know almost everyone, but I'd be happy to introduce you around."

"I can take care of myself."

"Undoubtedly. And how was your Christmas?"

"It was fine. Yours?"

"Wonderful. We had a nice light snowfall on Christmas Eve."

"We had sleet."

"Ah."

He took the beer the waiter brought him, muttered his thanks and sipped. And noted that Julia was wearing the necklace he'd given her against the creamy flesh exposed by the low-cut dress. "Looks good on you."

"What? Oh." She could have cursed herself for giving in to the sentimental urge to wear his gift. "Yes, it's made for this dress. It's lovely, Cullum. Thank you so much for thinking of it. I hope you liked your watch."

It was weighing down his pocket even then. "It keeps good time. Thanks."

"You're very welcome. Well, be sure to try to buffet, as well as the canapés that are circling around. If you'll excuse me."

His hand clamped hard on her wrist. "Where the hell do you get off, talking to me like this?"

"I have no idea what you mean."

"Don't take that snooty tone with me, MacGregor, it doesn't suit you."

"You'd better let go of me, Murdoch."

"The hell I will. I want some answers. I've been waiting for you to come up with them, and since you didn't bother, I'm here to see that I get them."

"You want answers." The heat of temper was beginning to blur her vision. "*You've* been waiting for answers. Okay, try this one." Her hand shot out and tipped his glass of beer onto his suit.

She regretted it instantly. It had been petty and foolish. It had been public. She knew several conversations that had been going on around her came to a dead stop. She also knew, by the way Cullum's eyes kindled, that she couldn't back down.

"Now that you have your answer, you can leave."

She intended to turn, walk away with dignity, to laugh off the incident. Later, she could crawl into a hole, but for now she had to maintain her poise.

She shrieked when Cullum boosted her up and tossed her over his shoulder. She cursed him without restraint as he carted her upstairs.

Below, Daniel hooked an arm sentimentally around Michael Murdoch's shoulders. He sighed, blinked a tear from his eyes. "Aye, they'll give us fine babies, Michael."

"Let's drink to it."

With a hoot of laughter, Daniel watched his granddaughter disappear up the stairs. "I'll buy the first round."

Cullum marched straight to Julia's bedroom, ignoring the punches and kicks, ignoring the wet jacket and the yeasty smell of spilled beer. Inside, he kicked the door shut, turned the lock, then tossed her unceremoniously onto the bed.

She continued to spit at him as he dragged off his soiled suit coat. In all the years he'd known her and fought with her, he hadn't known her to be quite that inventive with the language. When she started to scramble off the bed, he merely put a hand on her head and shoved her back.

"Stay put, and be quiet."

"You think you can order me around, after that hideous and revolting scene?"

"You started it." And at least it gave him an excuse to pull off his tie. "I don't know what's gotten into you. One day you're up, the next you're down. One minute you can't do enough for me, the next you talk like you barely know me. You haven't even bothered to get in touch with me in a week."

"I haven't bothered? *I* haven't? Is your finger broken, that you can't dial a damn phone." Then, to his horror and her humiliation, she buried her face in her hands and sobbed.

"Don't do that. I mean it, cut it out right now." At his wit's end, he dragged both hands through his hair. "Okay, I'm sorry. I'm really sorry."

"For what?" she asked, still weeping.

"For anything you want that'll make you stop crying."

"You don't even know." Wanting it over, she swiped at tears even as they fell. "You don't even know. Oh, go away. I don't want you here when I'm making a fool of myself."

"I've seen you make a fool of yourself before. I don't mind, usually. Come on, Jules." He leaned down, intending to pat her head or her shoulder. And found his mouth homing in on hers. Before he knew what he was doing, he was sitting and pulling her onto his knees and holding her close. "God, I missed you. I missed you."

Her hands were in his hair. "Did you?"

"Yeah, I did." He rested his brow on hers. "Are you done?"

"Mostly. I guess I'm sorry I spilled your beer."

He wondered what there was about the pair of them that she could make him smile at such a moment. "You guess?"

"Well, you made me mad. So it was as much your fault as mine." She answered his smile with a watery one of her own. "But I'll have your suit cleaned for you."

"Want me to take the pants off now?" He saw, with fresh surprise, her lip quiver and her eyes fill. "I was only joking."

"I know. It's all right. I don't know what's wrong with me." She brushed her fingers under her eyes again and climbed off the bed to go to the mirror. "Public scenes and tears weren't part of the deal," she said briskly, and began, once again, to repair her makeup. "We have a mutually agreeable physical relationship, and a friendship of sorts. No point in spoiling it by getting sloppy."

He tucked his hands into his pockets, watching her swipe color onto her cheeks. "What do you mean by sloppy?"

"Overemotional, I guess. Must be the holidays. I've been a little unsettled recently."

"Tell me about it," he muttered, and her eyes narrowed.

"Which means?"

"Look, it's New Year's Eve. I don't want to end the year fighting with you."

"Why not? We do it so well."

"Then why'd you stop for so long? The last few weeks—except for the day you left for Hyannis—I couldn't get a rise out of you with a forklift. All of a sudden you're agreeing with everything I say, cooking me dinner, practically bringing me my pipe and slippers."

"And you object to that?" Insulted, she whirled around. "I went to a lot of trouble to be nice to you, and now you throw it back in my face. Well, you don't have to worry, because I won't bother to be nice to you anymore."

"Thank God."

"And I won't be around, anyway," she finished in a rush, "because I'm selling the house and moving to D.C."

"The hell you are."

"You can't stop me. I don't want to live here. I don't know why I let you talk me into doing so many of the changes you suggested. I don't know why I let you do things your way."

"Because it was the right way, and that's the way you wanted it, and I'll be damned if you're selling this house."

"You can buy it yourself if it means so much to you."

"Fine, name your price. But if you think for one minute you're moving out—"

"I'm not staying. I can't."

"You're not going."

They were all but nose-to-nose now, panicked and furious. Their voices rose to shouts, but it still took several minutes before either of them heard the other say three particular words, since they said them simultaneously—

"I love you, and I'm not staying here and being unhappy."

"I love you, and you're not going anywhere without me."

She blinked. Cullum stepped back.

"What did you say?" he demanded.

"I didn't say anything. What did you say?"

"You said you loved me."

She tried to swallow, but her heart was stuck hard in her throat. "That's what I thought you said. Did you mean it?"

"What if I did?" He spun away to pace. "Damn woman's always talking so much you don't know what you're saying back when you say it. What if I do love you?" he shot out in exasperation. "What are you going to do about it?"

Why, he was perfect, Julia thought. Absolutely perfect for her. "Ask you to marry me."

He stopped pacing to stare at her. At first glance, she looked remarkably cool and unruffled. But he knew her, knew where to look, and her eyes were dark and wet. "What?"

"You heard me, Murdoch. Do you want to or not?"

He walked to her again, and in a moment, in the silence, they both began to grin. "I've got a ring in my pocket."

"You do not."

"Bet?"

She angled her head. "Let me see it."

"It was my mother's." He took out the box, flipped open the lid. "It's not a diamond, but you like colored stones better anyway."

"Oh, Cullum." She lifted her gaze to his. "You really do love me."

"I said I did. If you'd said it first, weeks ago like I wanted you to, we'd have saved a lot of time."

"You were supposed to say it first. Why the hell do you think I cooked dinner for you so many times?"

"Jules, believe me, nobody who wasn't crazy in love with you could have eaten any of those meals."

She tried to be insulted but ended up laughing. "If you ask me to marry you, I'll never make another pot roast."

"You already asked me, but under the circumstances, that's a deal." But when he reached in his pocket and took out his watch, she shifted impatiently.

"What are you doing? Can't you do this right?"

"I am doing it right. It's eleven-forty-five. Fifteen minutes till midnight. I'll just fix that." He turned the stem until the second hand hovered at twelve, then took her hand.

"That's cheating." She beamed at him. "I do love you, Cullum."

"You're what I've wanted without even knowing it." He touched one of her stray curls. "We made this house together."

"No." She closed her hand over his. "We made this home together. I couldn't live here without you."

"I want to end the year and begin it, right here with you." He brought their linked fingers to his lips. "We'll make a hell of a team."

"I'm counting on it."

"Marry me, Julia."

"I thought you'd never ask," she said, and kissed him.

From the Private Memoirs of Daniel Duncan MacGregor

I've a head for business, a skill for the art of the deal. My life has been a rich one. I've worked hard, and I've gambled. I've won and I've lost. Business—the making of money—is a pleasure to me.

But family is God's reward.

Strip every penny from my pocket, and leave me my family and I will die a wealthy man.

When I started these memoirs I had hopes and plans, schemes some might say—and what the devil do I care what people say?—for my family.

Well, I've done what I set out to do. Laura is a happily married woman, a beautiful mother. She and Royce are making a good life for themselves, and for my precious young namesake, Daniel MacGregor Cameron. Oh, there's a lad, a bright, sturdy lad. Good blood. Strong stock.

Nothing pleases me more than seeing how Royce dotes on the boy—or how Caine delights in being a grandfather. And he and Royce are as thick as thieves. It's a fine friendship they've made out of their love for Laura.

Of course, I had no doubt of it.

Gwen and her Branson are expecting a child any day now. She frets a bit, I know, about taking time off from her duties at the hospital. But Anna is the first to tell her that she can have both her career and a family, and do a magnificent job with both.

Branson fusses over her—wouldn't leave her side to tour for his book. I'd have been tempted to take a strap to him if he had. And did it make any difference? Hah! It was a bestseller the minute it came out of the pipe. He's a good storyteller that lad. Kept me up half the night reading about his murdering woman doctor and his cagey detective playing cat and mouse, falling in love. Who'd have thought she'd end up killing herself at the end rather than taking the life of the one man who'd touched her dark and troubled heart?

Ah, well, love matters most after all.

Now my Julia and her Cullum are making their life in the home they built together on Beacon Hill. They still scrap like terriers—and I'd worry if they didn't. There's such passion between these two—a perfect match and I don't mind saying so. I expect to hear there's a baby on the way soon.

And if I don't, I'll want to know the reason why.

She made a magnificent bride, tall, stately, elegant—and there was a moment, when she stepped beside Cullum, took his hand and their eyes met. They grinned at each other, wide and happy, with laughter all but bubbling out. A moment, I could feel my heart swell with joy—and with pride for having brought it about.

Now the MacGregor veil is packed away and waiting. But I've no intention of letting it lie in its box for long.

It's time my grandsons started doing their duty. I've given them time to ripen a bit. A man needs some years and some experience under his belt before he takes a wife and starts a family.

But let's face it, I'm not going to live forever. So far I've been subtle with Mac—him being the oldest of my boys. But does he take the hint? Hah. Well, we'll just have to give him a few heftier nudges.

I've done well by my first three girls, but I'm not one to sit on my laurels for long. I'll see the rest of them wedded, and the circle completed before my time is up.

That's a promise, on the word of Daniel MacGregor.

* * * * *